Taking Earth
House of Xannon Book 4

Copyright © 2015 Melinda VanLone.

Published by: WrittenHouse Publishing, Rockville, MD

This is a work of fiction. Names, characters, businesses, places, events and incidents are either the products of the author's imagination or used in a fictitious manner. Any resemblance to actual persons, living or dead, or actual events is purely coincidental.

ISBN-10: 0-9887455-7-7
ISBN-13:978-0-9887455-7-5

Cover Illustration: Carrie Osborne

Cover design and book layout: Book Cover Corner, www.bookcovercorner.com

VanLone, Melinda.

Taking Earth / Melinda VanLone

Visit the author website: melindavan.com

TAKING EARTH
HOUSE OF XANNON BOOK 4

Melinda VanLone

WrittenHouse Publishing

Tallahassee, Florida

For Dad,

who made a lot of sacrifices
for the sake of family.

1

LETTA ROBERTS SLUMPED in a chair at the back of PJs coffee shop and tried not to notice the noise. News given by worried reporters blared from two flat panel monitors, doing its best to be heard over the people in the shop who'd made a sport of analyzing the content. The baristas operated machinery that whirred and hissed, while they shouted to be heard above the chaos. "Skinny mocha double shot with a twist!"

Letta hunched over a steaming cup of the best coffee in Philadelphia, no skinny, no mocha, no double shot, and definitely no twist, and contemplated her situation. She didn't look at the TV. The news didn't matter. How people reacted to it did. A person might seem pretty normal face-to-face, but people as a group were skittish animals capable of just about anything.

Even in this tiny coffee shop on a side street in Center City, the people milled about as though they were all upstanding citizens going about their evening. They were excited by breaking news blurted from anything with a speaker, maybe, but otherwise normal citizens. But there were three standing in line that she knew were part of the flash riot just last week. Two more were out on bail for assault.

She scanned the crowd, recognizing several more who acted like her friends because they thought her to be part of the underground, and because she'd provided drugs in her runner capacity. Two of them grinned at her, tilting their heads in a silent salute. She offered a bored wave, and they moved on. *They'd turn on me in a heartbeat if the right circumstances hit them in the ass.*

She'd been embedded in the neighborhood for a year now. At the drug corners she looked like a pusher. At the coffee shop she looked like a student. At work she looked like an upstart, bitchy young detective trying to push back at a male dominated profession. At home she looked like what she really was—a semi-broke, single, utterly alone black woman trying to make a name for herself in the big bad city.

That's the thing about Philly. On the surface it looks one way, but underneath, it's a whole other ball game. Just like me.

Letta played with the dangling stone beads on her bracelet and tried to get her facts straight before her partner showed up for a report. The details were so squishy they didn't make a full picture. Yet. She went over them again, trying to nail it down before she had to say it all out loud.

They all think Carl's the one, the top. I know he ain't. Know it like I know my own skin. He looks like the king of the hood, to them. If anything, he's a pawn. Someone's giving him orders. Someone sparked that fear in his eyes. She thought back to the moment she'd become certain that the guy she'd been sent to nail wasn't who they thought he was. She'd managed to get him dirty dancing in a corner of the seedy local haunt, willing to sacrifice her body to get the intel. Anything that would prove her hunch was right. Somewhere between the shots of tequila and her hand on his crotch, he'd whispered things.

"Life ain't a game. Some think it is, but it ain't." Carl had burped as he rubbed Letta's ass. "Can't always think of the next move. Sometimes ya gotta live in the here. The now. Right now, baby. Right fucking now. You just all kinds of now, ain't you?"

Letta shifted to give his crotch a tight rub. "You want it right here?" She teased him with more pressure. "Games can be fun, Carl. Especially if you're the one calling the shots. You can make people dance to your tune. You got that look about you."

Carl barked a laugh. "Ain't nobody dancing to any tune I'm spinnin'. Nah, I'm just one piece of the game. There's always a hand moving the pieces, ya know? Always. But I got this, right now. Tomorrow might never come. Tonight, baby, 'sall we got."

Letta looked up at him, willing a flirtatious smile onto her face even though being this close seriously upset her stomach. The man reeked of smoke and liquor and teeth that needed to meet a brush. She met his inebriated gaze, and the words she'd been meaning to say died on her lips. She saw a deep-seated fear that burned right through her soul. She'd seen this sort of thing a few times, but usually in abused women. Even kids didn't get this haunted look. It reeked of desperation, despair, and a certain knowledge that the end was close at hand. Death knocked on Carl's door. At least he seemed to think so.

She wondered who made this kingpin so afraid. His rep of all powerful drug pusher, with plenty of beat downs and bodies on his sheet, was legend in this section of Philly. Somehow he always managed to stay one step ahead of jail. Bad police work, lost paperwork, bad busts, and destroyed evidence. He always managed to skirt the edge. Usually he stayed invisible. It'd taken months of playing young gangster/hooker to get this close to him. And now, without a doubt, she realized that Carl wasn't the one she searched for. The shit on his sheet wasn't his. If it wasn't his, whose was it?

"Ya know, I used to think I was a king. Right hand to the rook. Playmaker. That's what he called me. But now...now I know." Carl tugged on her ass, pulling her so tight her hand was stuck between them like cheese between bread.

Letta pushed her breasts into his chest as she got close enough to his ear to whisper. "If you ain't the king, what are you?" She nibbled his ear.

Carl shoved her away so violently she rammed into a table behind her. He wiped his mouth as he glared at her.

"I'm the fucking pawn, bitch. I got no use for you." Carl shoved past her, out the door of the bar so fast she couldn't track him in the dim light. By the time she got to the street, he'd melted into the shadows.

After replaying the conversation in her mind a thousand times, she was no closer to answers. All she had was more questions. *Right hand to the rook. What the hell's that supposed to mean? Rook as in chess?* She didn't know a damn thing about chess. The only thing she knew was the king was important, and the pawns got sacrificed. Carl thought he'd be sacrificed. By whom? *Rook. Which ain't a real name. What good is a street name gonna do me? Brass won't want it. They want something they can trace.*

Letta swirled the liquid in her cup and contemplated the connections. *Rook rules the Mansion district. He's using Carl and the 5-0s to move product, and the darker stuff. No way Carl is doing the darker stuff. It's too slick and smooth for him. He's a bull, charging through things. The guy in charge is sophisticated, intelligent, and subtle. Whoever he is, that's the real deal. He's got the gangs doing the ground work, with Carl the middle manager, while he sits back and...*

She shook her head. Rook, whoever he turned out to be, was pure evil in human form. A man...no, snake...who snatched young girls off the street and sold them to the highest bidder.

She'd seen the website. A place called The Exchange. Girls on display behind bars, like stores for the deviant.

It's more than that. There's something he's after. A type. The girls that go missing seem random, but they ain't. Something connects them. I just can't see what. Yet. And where the hell is he keeping them?

That's why Letta had a job. That's why she'd spent months undercover with one of the worst gangs in the country, and that's why she waited in this coffee shop. The man operated a trafficking ring so bold he'd take from the rich to sell to the richer. She'd sold the brass on that. Once the latest girl hit front page news, she'd even got some resources. But five weeks later, all she had was a street name, and a lot of speculation. So now she sat in PJs, waiting to get chewed out for not being able to answer one simple question: Who was Rook?

Someone shouted for the barista to turn up the volume on the already blaring TV, making it impossible to avoid the live report. Letta looked up at it, noted the Love sign in the background and the intense reporter in the foreground, then returned to studying the crowd.

"Reports are coming in now from Dallas concerning some effects of the rain. It's the same as encountered across the West Coast. Claims of strange phenomena are mounting, and people are understandably nervous. All work has been suspended across the entire state as authorities try to assess the situation.

"The DFW Metroplex, as well as Houston and Austin, is now under martial law. Everyone has been told to stay off the streets as reports flood in of things ranging from random fires springing out of nowhere, to raindrops the size of basketballs, to looting. One thing is certain, the storm is headed to the East at a slow but steady pace, ignoring current weather patterns which should have led the storm north into Canada. Experts are predicting it will reach Philadelphia

within the next three hours. It also appears to be spreading, rather than diminishing, as it goes.

"*The northern edge, as you can see from this map, has already intruded well across the Canadian border, while the southern edge covers most of Mexico and all of the US as it makes its way into Pennsylvania and up and down the coast. The mayor has placed Philadelphia on high alert, enabling every law enforcement effort at his disposal. The National Guard has been activated and is currently setting up patrols along major streets. All emergency personnel are on permanent standby, and police have begun to set up barricades and checkpoints to limit travel. Four hours from now, Septa service, both rail and bus, will be suspended. Emergency crews will remain active.*

"*Citizens are advised to be home and indoors well before the storm arrives. Try to keep dry, folks, as it's uncertain whether it's the rain itself causing issues, or some unknown, dangerous, atmospheric issue.*"

Try to keep dry? That's the best they could come up with? Letta snorted at the absurdity. *How about "Keep your shit together, people!"* Seemed a lot more practical. These storms never ended up being as bad as weather people predicted. Didn't matter anyway. What mattered was how the herd reacted to it.

Letta twisted the bracelet around on her arm to put the clasp at the back of her wrist, then tapped the side of her paper cup, making the liquid splash over onto the table. As she pushed the puddle around with her finger, a dumpling of a woman slid onto the seat opposite her, clutching some sort of brownish liquid that defiled coffee. She'd made some effort to blend in by wearing jeans and a denim jacket instead of her usual uniform. She looked like a school mom on a field trip. She raised the cup to her nose and sniffed, a blissful smile on her face.

Letta grimaced at it. "Hey, Shelley. What the hell is that sludge?"

"Chai latte on ice." Shelley took a long, slow drink. "It's great. Wanna taste?"

"No." Letta took another sip of her coffee and waited. If she was going to be fired, she sure as hell wasn't going to make it easy on her partner.

"Nice bracelet."

"Thanks."

"Seriously. Where'd you get it?" Shelley leaned forward to fondle one of the beads.

"All over. I made it, from stones I picked up as a kid."

"Make me one." Shelley glanced around the shop, then up at the TV. She huffed. "That damn storm. Wish it was over already. Anticipation of a thing is worse, don't ya think?"

"I think it's a load of crap." Letta shrugged and took a sip of the now cold coffee.

"It's serious, Letta. People could get hurt. We need all hands, including yours." Shelley leaned forward, her eyes intense. "Listen, I know you tried hard to crack this ring, but brass don't give a rat's ass about hints and rumors. They need facts, and right now they're up to their eyeballs prepping for the storm. They want you to back off, come in, work the desk."

Letta stared. Not fired, exactly. Demoted. If she went in now, she would never be able to work undercover with this crew again. Or any other crew in the city. Word like that traveled faster than fire.

"I ain't workin' no desk. Some shit is going down, and I'm gonna be there to stop it. How can they…" She sucked in a breath and balled her hands into fists on the table. Anger always made her slang come out. It made her sound ignorant, but she didn't care. She tried to lower her voice, but it came out as a hiss. "I'm almost there, dammit! I'm so close I'm practically up his ass, and now I gotta back off? No fucking way."

Shelley's upper lip twitched. "Look, I know you think you need to prove something, but you don't. Not to me, not to anybody. You got further than anybody has in a long time, but now is just not the time. If you go back out, you go without backup. That's just stupid. Even for you."

"Fuck you." Letta pushed at the coffee cup, and it tipped over, spilling coffee all over the table.

Shelley ignored the spill, though she did pick up her own cup and shift it away from the coffee puddle. "Told him you'd say that."

Letta crossed her arms and gripped them for good measure. The tiny vein in her forehead throbbed like a worm inching across her skin. Never a good sign. She closed her eyes and counted. *One. Two. Three.*

Four.

Five.

When she opened them, Shelley's patient stare helped calm her the rest of the way. It's what made them such good partners. She might be quick to anger, but Shelley never, ever lost her temper.

"I gotta do this, Shelley. If I quit now, I'll never be able to get back in. All that work, for nothing. Something big is going down. It's not just a girl snatched here or there. It's evil, pure fucking evil. Hell, any one of them girls coulda been something." She stabbed at the cup, sloshing coffee over the sides. "They coulda been…"

"You? Your sister?" Shelley's eyes wore a look of understanding that just pissed Letta off even more. "You can't make this personal, Letta. This isn't about you."

Letta swallowed the lump in her throat and ignored the stinging in her eyes. "Ain't nobody cared about these girls until the last one. This'd be front page news, if it weren't for that storm.

And that storm is what's pushing this up a level. I can feel it. I'm *this* close. I got this. I can find this guy. I can do it." She glared at Shelley, willing her to believe. To trust. "I got solid leads now. Good intel. We got a name. I know what to listen for. Rook. And anything to do with chess."

"What, he hangs out in the park with the old guys?" Shelly snorted. "Brass says Carl is still the one to bring in. And you let him get away."

"Carl's just the doorman. The pawn."

"Stop with the chess names already. This isn't a game, Letta."

Letta glared at her partner. "It is to Rook. He's playing a game, and everyone around him are pieces of it. It's all about moves and counter moves. He works in the shadows. Never does the work himself."

She leaned in close, forcing Shelley to make eye contact. "The number of girls missing has been increasing, and they usually come from the bad neighborhoods, right? Well, he's running out of girls. So he's branching out. Don't you get it? He's stepping up his game. These last three girls? Center City. Solid middle class. Smart. The last one's a poster child for white America. With lawyer parents who could afford detectives to make noise. Get it? He's escalating." She sat back and swigged coffee, wishing it was hot enough to burn. Maybe it'd take the edge off her emotions.

Shelley frowned. "He's not a serial. No bodies."

"Just 'cause you ain't seen 'em, don't mean they ain't there." Letta took a deep breath and blew it out hard to get rid of the slang talk. She tried again, with a calmer tone and better words. "Here's what I have. One, Carl let the name slip in a way that tells me it's real. Rook. Now I know what to listen for, I'll find out more. Plus, I know what Carl looks like now. My face was inches from him. I found him once, I'll find him again."

Shelley nodded, patiently waiting.

Letta held up two fingers. "Two. For the last week Donna Ray's been preaching from the church steps, stirring up the 'hood. Not just the borders, but the next 'hood over too. Church was so full on Sunday they couldn't close the doors. She's telling them all to meet during the storm."

Shelley shook her head. "So? That's what church is for. Gathering."

Letta snorted. "It's not just what she says, it's the way she says it. You haven't heard the woman. She's like a snake charmer, and we're the snakes. I couldn't walk away. I drifted to the church before I could stop myself. It was like my feet had a mind of their own. Like someone made me go."

"And I know how you feel about churches." Shelley laughed. "No way you'd go on purpose. So she's charismatic. What's that got to do with the prostitution ring?"

"It ain't prostitution." Letta slammed her fist into the table, making the cups jump and people nearby stare. She swore under her breath.

Shelley raised an eyebrow, waiting for her to reign in her temper.

Letta clenched her jaw so tight it hurt. "He's not just selling sex. He's selling *products*. Sure some are kept in a home nearby for the rent money, but most are sold on the black market. You saw the website. Submissive slaves, organs for transplants, virgins for rituals. It's not a prostitution ring. It's a damn 'get your victim here' ring."

"Yeah, I got a glimpse of some sick stuff, for about sixty seconds before it shut down." Shelley shook her head. "Tech couldn't get an IP or anything. No trace. Can't say if it's real or not if it's not there to investigate."

"Whatever. It's there. These girls are young, Shelley.

They're babies."

Shelley pursed her lips. "I know. I've seen the missing reports. I know what they look like, and I agree. It sucks. It's a bad, bad thing. But we need more. Right now all you got is reports of random missing girls that could just be runaways, a street name, and a hunch. Where's the evidence? Where's he stashing them? Where is this so-called Exchange? Right now we couldn't convict this Rook of a parking violation."

Letta took a deep breath. "You ain't looking at the big picture. Three. Social blew up the last two days with times, hints at a date. Talk of the storm. The hashtag is raindance. Check it."

"That could just be excitement over violent weather. Normal stuff." Shelley pulled out her cell phone and made a note of the hashtag.

Grateful that at least her partner was listening, Letta pushed harder. "It ain't. It echoes things Donna Ray's been saying. Meet up during the rain. Gather blessings. See angels. Stupid shit, but under it a command. If they don't show, they're in big trouble. Like death will rain down on you and your family trouble. And now that I know the name Rook, it all makes sense. Last night Donna Ray flat out said, 'Be at the park, or the Rook will put you in check.' Check, get it? As in mate? As in, game over? He's telling them they better show up at the park during the storm."

"You're reaching, Letta."

Letta rubbed at her eyes, surreptitiously wiping away a traitorous tear. If her partner wouldn't see, then she'd just go do it on her own. Each one of the girls held captive in The Exchange had a family who would wonder, forever, what happened. Letta couldn't just let him have more. Wouldn't.

Shelley studied Letta's contorted face, eyes softening a

little. Her tone was gentle when she finally asked the damning question. "Why?"

Letta leaned back and sighed. "I don't know." It hurt to admit it, but she had no choice.

Shelley nodded and took a sip. She swirled it around her mouth as if savoring some exotic delight, then swallowed. Slow, deliberate.

Letta blew out an impatient huff. "Stop trying to calm me down." She punched Shelley in the arm for emphasis.

"Why? It's working." Shelley grinned. "Here's the deal. I told them you wouldn't want to leave, that your news is solid, yada yada. That this is vital, that things were *escalating*." She emphasized the word. "Like you said, if one guy is behind all this, and I'm not saying that's so, and he's stepped into new neighborhoods, it's a real problem. One that might visit their own families. I told brass his own daughter could be next. He's not so sure, but being the persuasive woman that I am, I convinced them it might be good to have someone in the Mansion during the storm, just to be sure panic over there doesn't spill into other parts of the city. The edges might get blurred, with everything going on. Even if nothing happens with Rook, you'd be good to have in the area. You know, as boots on the ground."

"And…"

Shelley shrugged. "They agreed. You can stay there, keep digging behind the scenes, but they don't want to push the Rook thing until after the storm. It's just too much, Letta. They want you to report every hour, give a heads-up sit-rep. And be ready to pull out if they send word."

At first, Letta felt a shot of relief at the words. She remained on the case. But the way Shelley ended the sentence, with her voice lilting a bit, hinted at more to come. "What's the but?"

"You need more than that? I just handed you a juicy steak, and you want sauce?"

"I can hear the 'but' loud and clear, Shelley. Don't skate around. Tell me straight."

Shelley's lip twitched again. "Fine. Remember you asked. Between you, me, and the crowd here, I'd say if you don't come up with an ID for Rook pretty damn quick they'll pull you off detail, permanently. You know the guys. They think you're way too green. Too young. They don't think a woman can cut it. They think, best case, you're right and this guy will have you for dinner. You look just like the girls who've been snatched. You're a prime target. And you don't have backup in there."

Shelley paused, swirled her tea.

"And?" Letta prompted, impatient.

"And they think worst case you might be telling stories to puff yourself up higher, seem more important." She held up a placating hand. "I don't. And there's a few on your side. But the higher ups, they don't have patience when a story like this hits the fan. They need answers yesterday, and you didn't deliver. You're a failed experiment. So now they want to send in the big boys, but they can't, until after the storm. They're too busy to deal with you right now, but when the storm passes they'll have plenty of time to haul you in and pin you to a desk or maybe a traffic beat. This district." Shelley snorted. "They haven't heard that women in America are liberated."

Frustrated, Letta threw herself back into the chair, which nearly tipped over with the force. Not fired. Not exactly. But might as well be. Hell, it'd be worse. Everything she'd been working for ripped away, without the possibility of getting it back.

"So what you're sayin' is you bought me a few hours to prove myself? You think if I bring Rook in, I'll earn my place?"

Shelley nodded. "That's what I'm saying. You do what they can't. Find Rook. Find this Exchange before they get a chance to pull you away. You do that, you make that big of a splash, and you're on the permanent task force. But here's the thing." Shelley leaned in, her eyes filled with an understanding and sympathy that irritated Letta. "Even if you don't make it, even if they don't treat you right here, the next place will. You're young, Letta, and this isn't the only city in the world. You can have a career, but you need to prove it to the establishment."

"You mean the lazy ass men."

Shelley grinned. "Exactly. And hell, if it doesn't work out here, you could always move to a smaller city or town and work your way up that way. That's how I got here, you know."

"This is *my* place. *My* people. I don't fit anywhere else." Letta contemplated the coffee puddle on the table. "How much time I got?"

"Twenty-four hours. Maybe forty-eight. They won't do anything until after the storm, which is due here in…" Shelley glanced up at the TV for the countdown clock at the bottom right of the screen. "Three hours, give or take. Might take as few as twelve hours after to clean up the worst of the mess. Not counting downed trees and power outages. Who knows? You might get lucky, and there'll be a blackout of Center City. That'd buy you some more time. Maybe."

Shelley drained her cup, then stood. "Good luck, kiddo. I have faith in you, even if they don't. Watch your back. If you get into trouble, call."

"I thought you said I was on my own."

Shelley punched her in the shoulder, reminding Letta of how she got so successful in a man's world. She'd probably left a bruise.

"You gotta report every hour once the storm hits. That's the deal. Besides, you know if you call, I'll come running. So to speak. Just try to keep me out of the Mansion. I'm way too fluffy and pale for that crap."

Letta nodded. "Thanks."

Shelley turned and pushed her way through the crowd without a backward glance. Letta watched her go until she'd been swallowed by the crowd.

She had twenty-four hours to figure out who Rook really was and bring him down, during the strangest storm the world had ever seen. *How the hell am I gonna make this happen?*

2

LETTA SWIPED AT the coffee puddle with a napkin, which spread it out into an even bigger mess, then gave up trying to clean it. She tossed the wet napkin and cup in the trash and pushed through the crowd and out into the street where street lights had already kicked on but did little to lighten anything.

The atmosphere outside pressed in on her. Clouds had already started to roll in, bringing with them an electric smell and a sense of expectation. The entire city waited with bated breath for something to happen.

As with most storms, she suspected this one was blown way out of proportion. All the news stations repeated the same information…odd cloud formation, eruption from a clear sky outside of Spokane, fast-moving, with bizarre things happening in its wake. Nobody explained what the bizarre things were, exactly, though she'd heard talk from her crew of voodoo or witch power. The news, however, tended to lean toward scientific explanations. The more religious claimed it to be either Armageddon and the Lord Has Truly Come, or the Devil Has Risen.

She'd laughed when she heard that one. *Sure, the devil lived in*

Washington, and now he's going on vacation in Philly. Right.

Smarter to worry about things right in front of her. Like Rook. The devil, magic, witchy powers…they didn't exist. Somewhere nearby Rook lived, breathed, and played his game with innocent girls as the pawns. She'd find him, dammit. Find him, and find those girls. She'd force the misogynistic assholes at the station to see her, really see her. A smart, capable black woman who deserved to be detective. Who deserved to lead a team. Someone capable of helping make this city what it should be.

She could almost hear her mother's voice in her ear. *Big dreams, baby girl, big dreams. But dreams don't pay the rent.* She'd say it every time she walked out the door to work a street corner. Not that she'd ever admit to her profession.

Letta took the steps down into the subway and waited for the next train. Announcements proclaimed that the entire system would close at ten p.m. due to the upcoming weather emergency.

When the hell did this become an emergency? It's just a little rain, for fuck's sake. This city, always overreacting. When the train came, she stalked onto it and threw herself down onto an empty seat, the perfect picture of sullen adolescence.

The Mansion was only three stops away. Not a lot of time to plan, but then she'd always been more of a fly-by-the-seat sort of girl.

She knew what she had to do. *Find Rook. Find where he's stashing the girls. Call it in. Simple.* She lost herself in a daydream featuring her as the hero, swarming the Exchange with guns blazing, saving the girls, and sending Rook to his grave. For what he'd been doing, the man deserved worse than hell.

Knowing what to do and doing it were two different things. Plus, she'd never actually killed anyone. Wasn't sure if she had what it took to take a life. But if she were faced with a choice, his life or some innocent girls, she'd find a way to pull the trigger.

What do I really know about Rook? Nothing. He slithers in the shadows, like a snake. The man moved carefully, using so many layers of protection it rendered him invisible. The only one who'd popped up with intimate knowledge of Rook was Carl, and he didn't get out much either. Usually he stayed in a car, delivered drugs and instructions as he drove by. Kept his shades on and his head down. He snooped around for fresh meat, but once he'd made contact he never spoke to the person again, using the 5-0s as go-betweens. She'd had her one moment. She'd known the contact was blown before the door swatted him in the ass.

How do I catch a ghost? Where you hiding Rook? She thought about it. The man had to know someone. He had to live somewhere. Sure, he knew Carl, but who else. *Sistas? Nah.* She thought of the leaders in the small all-girl gang. They wore suspicion like a fine leather coat, shiny and tight. All of them turned lethal if provoked, though most of the time they looked like average street rats. They didn't fight in your face—they'd fight behind your back. They didn't just aim to settle a disagreement— they ended you. And probably your dog. Maybe your family too. They didn't forgive, and they didn't forget. But one thing was certain—not one of them had a contact even as high as Carl. They dealt with the 5-0s, period.

Letta glanced up as the doors opened. Two more stops to go. *Damn.*

She searched her mind for some way through the tangled mess of rumor and innuendo. Something as yet unexplored. A friend of a friend. Someone who knew someone who knew Rook.

The train doors slid open. One more stop.

Letta glanced around at the other riders on the train. All kinds on this train. Most commuters, heading home most likely, ahead of the storm. Some kids, probably out because schools closed early today. Across from her sat a boy, about twelve or thirteen, and his kid sister. The girl kicked her feet back and forth and chatted away about something. Her braids were tied with bright blue ribbons, her face stretched wide in infectious excitement. Letta smiled, reminded of her sister, Jenna. She'd been about that age when… She thrust the thought away. *No time for wallowing now.* Still, something about the girl nagged at her. She tried to follow the thought, but it fled as the train stopped and the doors slid open.

Letta surged through the door with the rest of the crowd, made her way to the street level, and set off for the worst district in Philly, without a plan.

She reached the edge of the Mansion district as the shadows grew long and hostile. No denying the hellhole it'd become. Ironically named for a large dwelling once called Strawberry Mansion, which housed an elite family back before the whole area went to hell. The Strawberrys sold and raced for greener pastures, and the neighborhood claimed the building as tribute. The house itself had fallen down long since, replaced with warehouses and a small church, but the name held.

Letta glanced at the sky filled with red-tinged clouds that seemed to vibrate with the setting sun. *Never seen clouds that color.* It cast an eerie light over the abandoned buildings and row homes that bordered the park formed by the awkward intersection of streets. On one side, two abandoned warehouses stood guard with an old church sandwiched in between. On the other, row homes with a couple of liquor stores and an abandoned pizza place, now used as a hangout for the Sistas. At the top of the triangle huddled a combination "convenience" and grocery store, a sleazy bar, and one thrift store that only the locals would step into.

As she walked, Letta automatically assumed the persona she'd cultivated. Edgy, tough, ready for a fight. Basically her regular personality, buried deep down when she'd tried to better herself by becoming a cop. It also made the gun she carried seem like a regular accessory rather than something a cop would carry. She'd made sure it was street, not cop. Most of the Sistas didn't carry guns, preferring knives and other weapons. It gave her cred with the guys, plus she felt a lot safer.

May in Philly wasn't exactly warm, so the sequined hoodie she wore seemed appropriate, plus it went great with her jeans and biker boots. She'd already made sure she wore plenty of eye shadow and bright red lips. Being one of the Sistas meant keeping up a certain appearance.

Letta crossed the street and entered the park at an easy pace. She scanned the area to see which of the crew handled the corners today. The usual suspects, all under fifteen years old, none high enough on the list to get even handler attention, much less Carl's. As shadows moved under the dilapidated trees, she took a quick count. *A lot more than usual. Double, even. Shit is definitely going down.* With the storm fuss and the rumors on social media, the best plan might be to wait and be here when it developed. *Weak. But what choice I got? None. Time to make somethin' out of nothin'.*

Letta drifted back across the street and waited off to the side of the church, near the larger of the two warehouses. It'd been boarded up and abandoned a long time. Long enough for nearly every surface to be coated in graffiti and the entrance to be littered with abandoned drug bits and pieces. She'd never been in it, didn't know anyone who had. Something about the whole building shouted "go away." She'd never seen any homeless or kids hang out there either. It had all the looks of a perfect crew hideout, but she knew the crew never went in there either. As far as she knew, nobody did. *Someday I'll have to find out why.*

A door creaked behind her, and she turned to see a large group of black women bustle out of the church. They all wore bright spring colors, hats, and attitudes. Organ music wafted out from inside the church with a general flurry of "Amen" and "Praise Jesus" and "Yes, Lord." She tried hard not to roll her eyes.

Letta watched the women waddle down the steps of the church. A smaller group hung back from the others, clustered around one woman in the center. Donna Ray Morgan, one of the steady churchgoers and Oprah to the community. Rumor had it she lived off a pension from her long-dead husband. But she lived a lot better than most in the neighborhood, so it must have been one hell of a payout.

Letta studied the group with interest. Whatever Donna said to her gaggle of friends, they nodded furiously. She had them hanging on her every word, as though she controlled every thought they possessed. *She'd make a great politician. That woman could sell a diet plan to a starving man.* Letta hung back, trying to stay far enough away to not get caught in the woman's charismatic snare, but close enough to maybe hear what they said.

Behind the women, a young girl dragged her feet, clearly not wanting to be a part of the group, but not daring to take off either. Letta recognized her as Donna Ray's only child, Kia. Kia liked to play in the park and seemed to know just about everyone in the neighborhood. She usually wore an infectious smile and an odd worldly innocence, as though she'd seen horrible things but hadn't let them bother her. The girl clearly had the exuberance of her mama, but hopefully not the zeal. She wore her hair in braids with dozens of brightly colored barrettes in butterfly shapes.

Shit. Kia. Of course. Letta mentally slapped herself. Now

she knew why the girl in the subway had sparked a flicker of recognition. Kia looked a lot like her. *Get to know someone who knows someone who knows Rook.* That elusive person shuffled on the sidewalk right in front of her. Kia was Donna Ray's daughter. Donna Ray was probably acting on orders from Carl, who'd received his orders from Rook. She might even be in direct contact with Rook. *It's a start.*

Getting close to either Donna Ray or Kia might yield a wealth of information.

As Donna Ray stepped down the last few steps, Letta caught part of the conversation.

"Remember. Be in the park just after the storm ends. That's when the game starts. You be there, with your product, and you're protected. Your own pieces are off the board."

Game. Pieces. Rook. Letta stepped out from beside the stairs and joined the group as they walked down the sidewalk. She hung back and hunched her shoulders. The women ignored her, just as they ignored the park, the drug corners, the drugs, and the fact that their own children were the ones dealing. Most of them put food on the table thanks to those efforts, so they weren't about to stop it.

She managed to catch a few more snippets of conversation.

"Rook got it right This storm is the Lord's way of showering blessings."

"God has sent us the means to slay our enemies and lift up our friends."

"The Lord does provide."

"Donna Ray, don't you think…"

Letta sped up a bit to get closer to the group. Lightning flashed across the sky, and thunder clapped so loud she startled and nearly shrieked.

"It won't hurt you. Not today." The words scared her nearly as much as the lightning had. She glanced down in the direction of the high-pitched voice and into Kia's eyes. She hadn't even noticed the girl following, she'd been so focused on the women's conversation.

"What?" She couldn't think of anything smarter to say. *Smooth, Letta, real smooth.*

"Change ain't always a bad thing." The girl smiled and held out her hand. "This change gotta be good, 'cause it's natural. I'm Kia. I seen you before in the park."

Ignoring the ping of guilt at using a small child, Letta took her hand. Kia squeezed, and the warm pressure brought a smile to Letta's face. Something about the girl just made people want to smile back.

"I've seen you too. My name's Letta." She glanced at the group moving away from them.

Kia giggled. "I like you."

"You don't even know me," Letta protested.

"Don't gotta know you. I can just tell. You got a nice color 'round you. Why you here?" Kia gestured at the group moving slowly but steadily toward the warehouse. "You come to hear Mama preach?"

"They're closing Septa." Letta kept her words soft and hoped that Kia took her words for a full answer to her question. The truth was entirely too complex to explain.

Kia tilted her head and eyed her with a look that said she knew Letta hid something. "A nice man told me never walk the park alone. I promised. So here I am, keeping my promise. You don't like them much, do you?" Kia pointed at the backs of the women in front of them.

"I don't know them."

"You don't do church?"

Letta smiled. "Nah."

"Me neither. But Mama made me today. She don't want me home alone no more."

"Why?" Letta looked down at her and saw a hint of a cloud skitter across the dark brown eyes.

"I got snatched once. Bad man. He did...things. Magic things. But I got saved, and them that saved me made me promise not to be here again alone."

"Whoever they were, they're right. This ain't the place to be walking alone, no matter how old you are." Letta glanced back at the park. No sign of any activity other than the usual lurkers.

Kia noticed her look and squeezed her hand. "Bet he wouldn'ta snatched you. You be one of the Sistas. Maybe I should join, then I won't get snatched again."

"No, you shouldn't. They ain't no good." Letta shook her head. That group would wring every bit of innocence right out of her. Kia was a special spirit. It made Letta want to scoop her up and carry her away from this place.

"But they be strong. I seen the stuff they do. Don't want to be bad, but it'd be nice to be strong. But Mama says Jesus won't like me no more, if I join them."

Letta coughed a bitter laugh. "Not sure Jesus gives a shit."

Kia stayed silent at the words, as though processing the thought. Somehow the silence made Letta want to explain herself.

"It's just I haven't noticed Jesus offering to save anyone around here lately. It's hard to have faith in someone when they don't give you a reason, ya know?"

Kia nodded, a wise look on her young face.

Letta's lips twitched. Kia was an old soul and pure sunshine. Why would anyone want to harm such a creature? They had to have been real bastards. And wasn't she a complete bitch for lying to the girl? She tried steering the conversation into better territory. "What you mean by magic things? What happened to you?"

Kia shrugged. "Alls I know is there was drawings on the walls, and blood. We was trapped by invisible rope and couldn't yell. This tall man chanted, and his face got covered with scales and the walls vibrated. Then I done went to sleep. Next thing, two white people woke me up. The best part was the way we got home. They made this space in the air, like a wet spot painted on the sky, and then we stepped through it, and I felt so cold! And spinny, like. Dizzy. And then we stepped out, and I was in front of my house. Wish I could do that again." Kia gestured wildly with her hands and did a spin to indicate the method of travel.

"Me too. It sure would be faster than the Septa." Letta grinned. *This girl sure has an active imagination.*

"You don't believe me." The words, so matter of fact, didn't even sound hurt.

Letta shook her head. "I never heard of something like that before, Kia. That's all. I gotta operate in the real world, and here in the real world Septa ain't workin' and I got ten blocks to go before the rain starts." Letta glanced back at the park, as if looking for a ride. She couldn't even explain to herself why lying to Kia mattered so much. Usually lying came naturally, as part of the job, but somehow…it hurt to lie to Kia. But the truth might turn Kia against her, and she desperately needed to keep talking to her. *They have the information I need. They can lead me to Rook, and to the girls.* A tiny glimmer of doubt flitted through her mind. If she was wrong…

"You could stay with us. Our place is two blocks down that way." Kia pointed off to the right. "Past the bad warehouse. I walk by it every day. I remember, though Mama don't like to talk about it.

Magic is hard to forget."

Letta pondered the idea. It sure would be nice to not be alone tonight. Not to mention get closer to Donna Ray and her little posse. But a little girl had no business asking a stranger to stay the night.

"Mama won't mind. She's having a prayer meetin' tonight. One more won't hurt." Kia glanced up and whispered, "You don't hafta pray. We can play in my room instead."

The group reached the intersection, and half split off to the left while the other half continued on to the right. Letta paused, uncertain.

"Mama," Kia shouted. Donna Ray turned back. Her floppy red hat slipped down over one eye, giving her a rakish look that nearly made Letta giggle. Donna Ray gripped the tattered Bible so tight her knuckles had gone white. "Can Letta stay over tonight? She ain't got no family."

The woman scrutinized the two of them for a moment. Letta pushed her hood back so the woman could see her face. She narrowed her eyes, and for a second Letta thought she'd tell her to get away from her little girl. Then a glint of recognition softened her expression. Her fingers twitched on the Bible in her hand.

"I've seen you in the neighborhood. You run with the Sistahood. You moved here 'bout six months ago? You been staying in the shelter?"

Letta shrugged. She'd never told anyone where she lived, though if they followed her home they wouldn't find anything remarkable. Certainly not a place they'd figure a cop would inhabit.

"It's not a night to be alone, child. Come on with us. Hurry up now, both of ya." The woman turned back and continued on with her friends.

"Told ya." Kia let go of her hand and skipped ahead, gesturing for Letta to follow.

3

CROSSES AND PLASTIC Jesus and Mary figurines adorned Kia's house, making it stand out among the broken-down, overgrown row homes that otherwise lined the dilapidated block. Tall weeds enshrined Mary in thorns. Jesus teetered on the steps. Every surface sported a cross, including the steps.

"She trying to keep out the devil?" Letta grinned at the display.

Kia shrugged. The group of women paused to say goodbyes and left shouting, "Amen."

Kia's mother made her way up the steps slowly, pausing at the top to glance back. "What'd you say your name was?"

"Letta." Letta stood on the sidewalk just before the steps as the woman examined her from top to bottom. "Letta Roberts."

"If you die today, Letta Roberts, do you know where you're going? Do you know who your Savior is?" Donna Ray glared at her, eyes searching for something.

As Donna Ray's gaze met her own, Letta felt herself drawn toward the woman like a fly to a spider. Her brain tingled, and a voice in her head whispered, *You will join us.* It sounded soft, inviting, and insidious.

Letta took a half step toward the woman then stumbled to

a halt. *I didn't mean to do that.* She fought against the buzzing in her head.

Again the voice. *You are mine.*

Donna Ray tilted her chin up. "Do you know who your Savior is?" she demanded.

Letta opened her mouth to answer, then bit her tongue to stop herself from speaking. If she said yes, the woman would probably leave her alone. But it'd be a lie. She didn't really believe that, any more than she believed in Santa Claus. *So why did I want to say yes?*

"Oh Mama, don't be bothering her with that. Let her have dinner first. Didn't Jesus say we should be nice to people, no matter what?" Kia took Letta's hand and smiled up at her mother. The tingling in Letta's head vanished, along with the voice and the urge to proclaim Jesus as Lord.

"That he did, sissy, that he did. And that's what we'll do." Kia's mother nodded at her. "Don't you stay out too long, now. I want yo' behind in this house before the rain. I'll fix a snack for you."

The woman opened the door and shut it behind her without a backward glance.

Letta shook her head. *What the hell was that?*

"You like to be outside?"

Letta glanced down at Kia, who beamed at her. "Sometimes."

"Today's a good day to be outside." Kia announced it as though it were fact, despite the weather. "Today, things change."

"Bet not a lot changes around here."

"That's why today's exciting." Kia bounced on the balls of her feet. "Everything looks prettier today."

Letta glanced up at the darkening sky full of angry looking red clouds. Pretty wasn't a word she'd use to describe them. She wouldn't use it to describe the neighborhood either. She glanced around at the street now shrouded in darkness except for a couple of streetlights. Most had been knocked out, so only two lit the way through the debris-filled neighborhood. It was probably one of the better streets in the Mansion, which wasn't saying much. Both sides of the street lined with row homes, litter in the gutters, and graffiti on anything that didn't move. But nobody loitered on the corner, and no gunshots disturbed the quiet. Yet.

"She leave you out here alone a lot?"

"Ain't never really alone out here. They watch." Kia nudged her chin toward the opposite side of the street, where Letta saw the curtain held back just enough to let a tiny beam of light shine out. "This be part of the 5-0, and most of 'em got family on this block. Plus the Sistas make sure nobody messes with too much here."

She picked up one of the smaller plastic figures and sat down on the lowest step. Letta joined her. Together, they watched the sky for a bit. The clouds had deepened to a blood red on the edges, black in the center, and a glow that didn't look like it came from the sun. The air felt ripe with expectation.

"You scared?" Kia shuffled her feet along the walk in front of her, moving pebbles around.

Letta shrugged.

"Me neither. Don't know what the fuss is. 'Bout time everybody had a little magic."

Letta nodded. Of course the girl believed the talk shows and the news. She wanted to believe in something special. Who could blame her, living here? The real world didn't wave a magic wand and fix your problems. You had to fix them yourself.

"You don't believe. But you will. You'll see. When you get your magic, you'll learn all about what makes you special."

"What do you mean?"

Kia shrugged. "It'll be different for everybody, won't it? People's got different talents and abilities, like playin' the piano. They been saying that about the people in Texas anyway. You ever been to Texas?"

Letta laughed. "I ain't ever really been outside Philly."

"Me neither."

Silence hung in the air along with the promise of rain.

Letta shook her head. The girl believed the rain would bring something special. Magical. It'd probably just flood the metro. Nothing magical about that. All the same, she looked up to study the clouds again. They boiled like a pot on a stove, ready to simmer over.

"That a pretty bracelet." Kia pointed at a stone dangling off Letta's arm. She held her wrist out for the girl to inspect.

"Ain't nothin' special. Rocks I picked up around the neighborhood."

"Don't matter where they come from." Kia rubbed one of the large stones with her fingers.

The air, heavy with impending rain, pressed down on Letta's skull. Goosebumps marched up and down her arms. Letta shivered, trying hard to ignore the fact that it all felt like a horror movie come to life. She fully expected Freddie or Jason to leap out from behind the plastic Jesus at any moment. Or maybe Jesus would come to life.

"Kia. I heard your mama's friends talking about Rook and the park. You know anything about that?"

"They don't like me listening." Kia glanced over at Letta from underneath her eyelashes. "But I hear anyways. They having a party at the park. You know, to welcome the magic. They's gonna play games and get blessings, but really they gonna get magic. But Mama told me to stay home. No school, no playin' in the park.

Stay out the way, she said."

"Suppose Rook will be there too?" Pushy to ask out right, but what the hell. No risk, no reward.

"Gotta be. Mama say somethin' this big gotta have a leader. But she don't want me to play the games. It's not fair."

Letta nodded as she digested the morsel of information. *Rook likes to play games? What game is he playing, and who is he playing it with?* She thought about what Donna Ray had told the church ladies. *Bring the package? What package?*

She shook her head. *Why during the storm? Maybe Rook believes they'll get magic? But even if that was true, why would he care? What the fuck is going on?*

Letta glanced up at the clouds again. Definitely thicker, heavier, darker than they'd been before. Blood red. The sun had to be on its last legs too. It'd be dark soon, and the storm would unleash. What had the news said? Three hours? That'd been almost two hours ago. With the air so heavy, it was hard to believe it would take another hour for the rain to fall. No telling how long it would last, though they probably had predictions already.

"Did your mama say what time the games start?" Letta kept her voice low in case Donna Ray was listening at the door behind them. She didn't see any shadow there or at the window, but that didn't mean nobody watched.

Kia popped up off the step and picked up a small ball nestled near one of the Jesus statues. "Sometime after it gets dark and the rain gets going."

That's no help at all.

Kia tossed the ball to Letta. She caught it and tossed it back, smiling at the girl. All she could do right now was wait for the rain to start, then make her way to the park. Rook would hopefully be there. *Hope he stands out in a crowd.* She'd no idea what he looked like. But he'd probably be near Donna Ray. She'd stick to the woman and hope something panned out. *I should text Shelley, keep her in the loop. Probably gonna need backup if he plans on snatching girls right there in the park.* She started to pull her phone out of her back pocket but hesitated. Kia bounced the ball off the side of the house. It lit up every time she made contact, and in the dimming light it made her look eerie. If she pulled out the phone, Kia would want to see. It'd have to wait.

The front door creaked open behind them, and they both turned to find Donna Ray standing there holding it open, a spoon in one hand. "You two get on in here and eat. Prayers start up in thirty minutes. You're welcome to join us, Letta."

They both stood up and followed Donna Ray into a row home so narrow, Letta could touch both walls if she stood in the center and stretched her arms out wide. An eclectic array of furniture filled the space. None of it matched, all of it looked as though it'd been plucked from street corners. A love seat, three armchairs, a small coffee table with three legs and a book pile for the fourth, and old Tiffany-style lamps adorned the front part of the room. Near the back squatted a dining room table too large for the space. She'd have to suck in her stomach to get past the chairs and into the galley kitchen beyond. No thief would ever sneak his way through Donna Ray's house.

Stairs right at the front door led up to the second floor, where she assumed the bedrooms were.

It all felt strangely homey. Her own place sported a couch that served as dining table, bed, and seating, and a TV perched on the kitchen counter.

Donna Ray gestured toward the table. She'd covered it with a lace table cloth on which rested paper plates filled with finger foods of varying types. Sandwiches, chips, cocktail wieners, crackers, vegetables, dips. Kia ran up to the table, scooped up a paper plate, and started piling her favorites. Letta shrugged and joined her. Food, the universal way to build connections and cement relationships.

When they both had their plates full, Kia led the way to the living room and perched on the love seat. Letta joined her. As they munched, Donna Ray took a seat in one of the armchairs opposite them, a beer in her hand. She took a long pull of it, keeping her eye on Letta the entire time. She'd been studied less by prison inmates or rabid dogs. She obviously hadn't earned Donna's trust yet.

"What's yo' story, girl?" Donna Ray burped, which she didn't bother to excuse. "Where's yo' folks?"

Glad I still look like I need parents. It wouldn't last forever. She was twenty-nine, but looked seventeen. How long could she keep that up? Make-up helped but sooner or later age was bound to catch up. "Mama's doing a bit at Stanton." Letta shrugged, as if to imply that the rest was unimportant.

Donna Ray nodded, took another sip. "What she do?"

"Solicit. She be out in a year, they say. Wouldn't be in now but she hustled the wrong guy, over at Cherry Hill." It wasn't the truth, but it wasn't far off either.

"She should turn toward the Lord. The Lord will save her and put her on the path to salvation. She won't need those men. You have her come talk to me, when she gets out."

Letta nodded, but kept her mouth shut. The more details she gave, the more likely she'd get caught.

"What you doing with your life, Letta Roberts?" Donna Ray

narrowed her eyes and leaned forward.

A buzzing tingle started up at the back of Letta's head. She resisted the urge to rub her neck. Instead, she maintained eye contact with Donna Ray, trying to read the woman's intentions. Donna Ray's eyes widened slightly and almost seemed to bulge, as though she were straining at something. Her nostrils flared like a horse's sniffing at a fresh scent on the air.

You're mine now. You'll be in the park. You'll go with Rook.

The buzz of a million bees filled Letta's head, obliterating all thought, shattering all notions of control. Donna Ray's eyes, the whites almost glowing while the pupils edged toward an unnatural black, dominated everything. The voice whispered a singsong chant that filled her soul with need and longing. Letta wanted to please this woman. She wanted to be in the park and follow the voice wherever it led. God himself reached down from heaven and touched her heart, gave her purpose. Such a clear purpose. Such a blessing, to be touched like this. Letta stared into those eyes, while some part of her, a distant, faint part, protested. Her lips parted to draw in a breath. Her body felt heavy, deeply relaxed as if on the edge of sleep.

Follow me. Obey me. You will be chosen. You will be blessed.

"Yes." Letta agreed, her voice soft and breathy. Inside, behind the whispered voice, her mind screamed a protest.

4

KIA PUT A soft hand on Letta's arm. "You wanna play in my room?"

The tingle and buzzing stopped. The whispers vanished as though they'd never been. Letta stared at Donna Ray. Her eyes were now a perfectly normal brown. She wore a kind, understanding smile as she patted Letta's arm. "You don't gotta be coy here, Letta. I can help you, if you let me. What are you doing with your life, child?"

Letta glanced at Kia, who smiled with the innocence and encouragement of youth. When she looked at Donna Ray again, she thought she caught a flash of irritation. But it was gone so fast it might have been a shadow or flicker or light from the storm outside. Nothing more than a surreal daydream.

"Just trying to find my place, Ms. Morgan." Letta popped a cracker in her mouth to avoid saying anything else. *What the hell is wrong with me?* She blinked and shook her head to clear it. The way Donna Ray studied her, she felt like a lab rat. *Religion. Always wanting to convert people. They ain't happy 'til you fall on your knees. Screw that.*

A knock at the door, followed by a shout, threw cold water

on the moment. Donna Ray stood, beer in hand. "You joining us, Letta?"

Kia tugged at Letta's hand. "Come on, Letta. Let's go to my room. They get boring."

Letta laughed, but it sounded a bit forced and awkward. She cleared her throat. "Thanks, Donna Ray, for dinner. I'll keep Kia company. You ladies don't need me underfoot."

Donna Ray tilted her chin as if to argue, but another loud knock stopped whatever she'd been going to say. "Go finish up in yo' room, child. Both of you stay upstairs tonight, less you feel like prayin'. You hear me? Don't be goin' out in the storm. Stay out the rain."

Donna Ray hurried to answer the door, leaving Kia to pull Letta upstairs.

Kia's room looked out over the street in front of the house. It barely held the twin bed, a small dresser, a tiny closet, and a few feet of floor space that sported a rug.

They listened to the women arrive with loud squawks. Kia pushed the remnants of her snack into a corner of her night stand, then pulled out a ruffled pink nightgown. Letta watched her change, keeping up innocent chit-chat while at the same time straining to hear what Donna Ray preached downstairs. *Nothing useful.*

She scooted closer to the door, but Kia pulled her away. "You read?"

"I can read this to you, if'n you want." Letta grinned as the child pulled out a book so worn it fell apart at the seams. *Alice in Wonderland.*

"Sure. I never read that one." Letta settled on the bed next to the girl and leaned her head back against the wall. She let the girl read aloud while she filtered sounds from the living room below.

"Jesus will take us through."

"Rook sure this is the next step? Seems sudden."

Donna Ray's voice rose, making it easier to hear. "All of life is give and take. Compromise. Negotiation. Rook's promised safety for our families, and in return we bring players for the game. If you want your own girls to be safe, that's the deal. No arguing. No backing out. This ain't a man you get a second chance with."

"But the storm…"

"The storm will bring strength and power to those who dance in it. We do as he says, we'll be there to get the blessings. And we protect our families. Keep yours inside tonight, but bring the others."

"If you say so, Donna Ray." The voice sounded uncertain.

A soft tingle started again at the back of Letta's head. This time, she rubbed at it. Nothing there, no reason for it. But Donna Ray started talking again.

"This is our time to shine, ladies. You bring the girls, and blessings will rain down upon us. The Lord's right hand has commanded it, and we will respond."

At the back of Letta's mind, a whisper. The same voice. *You will do as I say. Bring the girls. You want this blessing. You want to please.*

The tingling buzz increased. Letta felt the urge to get up, go to the park. The need so intense she tried to scoot off the bed.

"Are you worthy? Will you be a blessing to the Lord?" Donna Ray's voice rang out.

A cheer rose just as Alice saw a white rabbit run by.

Letta felt a strange desire to cheer along with them and an urgent need to stand in the rain. She rubbed at her head again. Kia looked up at her, a concerned look on her face. She placed her hand on Letta's. "You okay?"

The voice, the buzzing, the tingling, all stopped. It left her with a bit of a headache, like the beginning of a migraine. *What the hell? Must be getting the flu.* Though the flu usually didn't come with voices in her head telling her to stand in the rain. *Been working this case too hard. I'm tired. Overloaded on caffeine. That's it.*

Letta tried to smile, then pulled Kia back against her, encouraging the girl to continue reading while she listened to the raving downstairs.

"Rook will lead the way. The game has already started, and we will be crowned victorious."

Game. Again with games. I guess the name Rook isn't just a street label. It's a clue. Rook...chess. So what is Donna Ray, Rook? She a pawn?

Murmurs from the crowd caused Donna Ray's voice to turn sharper, colder. "This storm brings salvation to the worthy. Those touched by the rain who are not worthy shall be food for the devil."

"Amen!"

"The devil must be stomped out. And the Lord will give us the power to do it. I can feel righteous fury ready to burst over our heads. But the clear waters of Jesus will save us and protect us."

"Praise Jesus!"

"We must face the evil head on. Rook will lead the march, and we will beat the devil back to his hole. We will rise as the righteous few in the embrace of Jesus the Lord Almighty!"

The lecture turned extremely churchy, full of Lords and Amens but nothing more of value and no more real information. Letta played with one of Kia's braids as the girl continued to read, her lilting voice filling the room and mingling with the madness from downstairs.

At least she'd found out one thing. Donna Ray and Rook

not only knew each other, but Rook used Donna Ray to gather people in the park. *Just like I told them. I was right. But what's his game? Why's he need people at the park?*

If he were true to his business model, he wanted the girls to sell at The Exchange. *But how'd he convince Donna Ray to do the dirty work?* What mother would do something like this? Letta listened to the rhetoric downstairs. Donna Ray still spouted nonsense about evil and how they needed power to vanquish it. *Right. Even if that storm was magic and we all sprouted wands out our asses, it wouldn't be half as evil as someone like Rook, willing to kidnap, rape, sell young girls. Or church people on a vendetta.* She snorted, and Kia looked up at her with question in her eyes.

"Keep reading. I'm listening. What happened to Alice next?"

Kia narrowed her eyes, not fooled. She flipped a page, and her sweet voice continued. Alice fell down the rabbit hole to the sound of loud thunder. A chorus of screams and "Praise Jesus!" "Lord, protect us from evil" rose from below.

Lightning lit the room, followed by a loud crack of thunder that made Letta jump. A light *tip tap tip* at the window announced the arrival of the storm. Kia tossed the book to the floor, ran to push the curtains back, and tugged at the window. When she got it open, she put her hand out to catch a few drops.

"It's beautiful! Smell. Don't it smell nice?" Kia eyes widened with childish rapture as lightning flashed. Rain splashed on the window casing, and small flecks of wetness appeared on her nightgown.

From the living room, sounds of women praying drifted through the weak door.

Letta watched in silence, listening to the pit pat of raindrops mixed with female murmurs and the occasional "Yes, Lord." It made an odd sort of syncopated rhythm. She tried to ignore how it reminded her of a time, not so distant, when her own living room had sounded similar. When her Dad had died, the entire neighborhood filled the apartment they'd lived in for five years to "comfort" her. She didn't find their presence particularly soothing. Those who'd arrived that day were more interested in taking "mementos." She'd hidden all the valuable stuff but was still shocked at how little they had left when the Good Samaritans parted with promises of dinners and calls and condolences. Her mother had been so stunned, so grief-stricken, that she hadn't said a word that day, nor for many days after.

She snorted. *Church. Not good for anything. It brings out the very worst in people.*

Lightning flickered, followed by a loud crash, and the rain began in earnest. Letta took in the rapture on Kia's face. Each flash of lightning sent a different streak of color across it, lighting up her eyes like a pinwheel.

Letta joined her at the window, the first cool drops of rain tickling her arms. "You scared?"

Kia shook her head, and when she turned to face Letta, her eyes reflected lightning flashes and excitement. "It's the beginning. What's to be scared of?"

"Kia, you know you sound like you've lived five lifetimes. It ain't normal." Letta shook her head. "Most kids would be scared about now."

"I seen worse than this. And no matter what Mama says, this is a good thing. I feel it coming, don't you?"

Letta tilted her head. "What's coming?"

Kia grinned. "Change."

She really believes that. Letta reached to close the window. "All I feel is damp."

Kia grabbed Letta's hand and pulled her to the door. "Let's go outside. We don't get enough in here." She opened the door and rushed down the hall, to her mother's room. Letta hurried to keep up and found her unhooking iron bars which covered a window overlooking a balcony. They swung out with a crash against the side of the house.

"Kia! Your mama probably heard that. She don't want you going out in the storm." Letta crossed the room to put a hand on the girl's shoulder. "She thinks the devil is in that rain. She won't like it if you get wet. She'll want to beat the devil outta you."

Kia snorted and sat on the ledge to swing her legs over and out onto the small balcony. A drop-down ladder, rickety and unstable, provided access to a small courtyard filled with weeds. She climbed down , then looked back up at Letta. "Come on. You need this."

Letta watched as the girl spread her arms wide and turned her face to the sky, letting the rain soak into her face and hair. It only took seconds to slick her skin and make her shine with some sort of reflected inner light. Fascinated, Letta watched her turn and giggle.

"I ain't going out there. I didn't bring fresh clothes." The whispers tickled the back of her mind, a memory demanding attention. *Go to the park. Go in the rain. You want the blessings.* She hesitated, unwilling to do anything some odd whisper in her head told her to do. Instinct made her resist the urge to obey.

"Come on, Letta. It's wonderful. This is the best I ever felt, ever. It's like candy. It's Wonderland." Kia giggled and spun in circles. Her glee, obvious and contagious, tugged at Letta. *Why not? What's a little rain? I won't melt.*

Letta shrugged, sat on the ledge, then swung her legs over. She paused, glancing up at the sky. More lightning than she'd ever seen filled the spaces in between clouds, and a red hue tinged everything, including the rain. It fell hard and fast now, obliterating the houses down the block. The street glimmered with tiny street lamps reflected on every smooth surface and streaks of lightning.

Her legs, already soaked, tingled. Odd. Maybe her feet had gone to sleep, sitting cross-legged on the bed. She twitched them to get the feeling back. Her heart pounded, and her mouth ran dry.

Kia giggled. "You already wet now. Might as well come on out. It's fun!"

Kia held out a hand to her. Letta hesitated. Rain, driven by the wind, splashed on her face and mouth. She licked her lips, taking in the wetness. It tasted fresh, but had an after bite of something that tickled her mouth and crawled down her throat like a shot of cheap whiskey. The air around her pulsed with expectation. Her head suddenly throbbed, keeping time with it like some absurd orchestra. The pressure on her skull pushed against her eyes.

She hesitated on the ledge another second, unsure. Something about the rain... She shook her head, dismissing the thought. Rain couldn't do anything except get her wet. Her head hurt from the pressure of the storm, that's all. *Probably allergies or something. Or a cold.*

Throwing off the notion that somehow a "strange phenomena" might be responsible for it all, she climbed down the ladder into the rain.

5

LETTA STOOD IN the rain, uncertain. Now that the storm had arrived, her head whirled around all the news reports. If they were right, this wasn't exactly a smart thing to be doing. If they were right, she invited chaos into her own body. Her pulse pounded, anxiety setting in. *What if they're right?* Water puddled around her feet and soaked into every pore. It pelted her hair, face, lips, hands, breasts. Her shirt, soaked through, clung to her skin. Her jeans felt heavy, but her body lightened, buoyed by some unseen pressure which lifted her to the very tips of her toes. It was…

Magic.

Goosebumps marched along her arms. She thrust them out wide and turned her face up to the sky. Kia mimicked her. They stood there, letting the rain soak them, until Letta's head began to spin and her pulse raced as though she'd been running for miles. Euphoria swept her up in a tight embrace, and she laughed. Joy exploded in her heart and mind. It felt good. It felt right. It felt amazing.

It was every drug in the world wrapped up in the comfort of a cleansing salvation. The kind they sang about in church. The kind that was supposed to be the hand of God himself. Now

Letta knew what they meant. Now she knew why people rolled in the aisles and shouted. She laughed, unable to stop. Kia joined her, childish giggles spilling over into a happiness so contagious that Letta scooped her up into a hug and whirled around the tiny yard with her.

The two of them danced as though they hadn't a care in the world, high on an electrical charge that raced between them and around them. Kia giggled and twirled, eyes glittering each time lightning lit the sky. Her nightgown clung to her tiny body, but she didn't seem to care. She pranced barefoot in the weeds as though it were the most beautiful garden on earth. Letta laughed, delighted. She hadn't felt this kind of joy in her entire life. A life riddled by despair, disappointment, loss, heartache…somehow all whisked away in that moment.

Nothing mattered. Not the headache that built with each raindrop, not the fear of losing her job, not the hunt for an evil street thug, not her past, nothing. For this one moment, she existed, content to simply *be*. The rain brought music and poetry, sunshine and dark stormy nights. It was the universe, rolled into one delicious moment of ecstasy.

If heaven exists, surely it feels like this.

Letta clutched at her face. Her cheeks burned like she had a high fever. Her feet ached as though her shoes were too tight. She pulled them off, tossed the socks into the weeds, and let her toes dig into the sodden earth. A shudder ran up her spine as her toes connected with dirt. She'd found home at last, and it was a soaked patch of bare ground in the backyard of a religious zealot in Philadelphia.

Her pulse pounded against her throat and chest like someone on the other side of a locked door…loud, insistent, and a bit frantic. She opened her mouth in a gasp. Rain quickly filled it and spilled over, and she sputtered. Half of it she managed to spit out, the rest she swallowed. She tried to turn but found her feet rooted to the spot. Panic raced through her veins, cold and sharp. She wanted to dive back into the house, the moment of peace and joy followed quickly by mounting fear and panic. She wanted to cry. Laugh. Scream. Run. She wanted to rip off her clothes, the sodden fabric uncomfortable and confining. Her skin melted. Her head exploded in a shower of lights and colors, so bright it burned. She closed her eyes and screamed.

The sound went nowhere, muffled by another loud crack of thunder and the pounding rain. Letta dropped to her knees and fell forward onto her hands. When they made contact with the mud, her body convulsed. She tried to curl in on herself, but her body refused. A crackle of heat rushed from the ground into her hands and fingers and up her arms. The world turned sideways. Weeds, dirt, puddles fell away. Rocks rose up around her with a resounding *crack!* and swallowed, thrusting her into an abyss of darkness. Terrified, she closed her eyes, and a world appeared. One filled with boulders and crevices. She raced forward, though her feet didn't move and her body wouldn't listen. She'd boarded an insane roller coaster that took her for a ride. Letta cringed with the expectation of impact as she reached the wall of stone. But instead of meeting a solid object, she passed right through and continued on, dirt and rock speeding by too fast to really make out anything

"Letta?" Kia's voice followed behind her, muffled, indistinct, and curious.

Letta turned her head to look behind her, and the ground opened into an underground valley filled with pinpricks of light emanating from the rocks. Trees sprouted around her and grew above her head and out of sight in a blink. She dropped into the wide open space and fell toward the granite, hands in front of her to break the fall. Knowing she couldn't. Expecting to die. Waiting, again for impact.

"Letta!" Kia's voice, louder, frightened.

Letta felt a tug on one arm. She struggled against it. Against the fall. A scream ripped her throat as the ground raced to meet her. At the last second, she closed her eyes. Waited for impact.

"Letta! Wake up!" Kia shook her shoulders.

A loud crack, groan, and the cavern dissolved, leaving Letta on her hands and knees in the mud, breathless, with Kia's tiny arms embracing her body. She shook as adrenaline coursed through her veins.

"Holy....fuck."

"You back now?" Kia squeezed. A comforting warmth flowed from the girl.

Letta took a deep breath. Then another. Her heart continued to pound, but her arms and legs stopped shaking. She nodded, still trying to make her brain wrap around what she'd just experienced.

Kia sat back on her heels, taking the steadying warmth with her.

Letta struggled to breathe normally, rubbing at her temples in a futile attempt to calm down. She felt dizzy and slightly disoriented. The skin along her arms itched. She rubbed, but the itching wasn't on the outside. It was on the inside, deep down, like an internal tickle she couldn't reach. Letta stared at Kia. "What the hell was that?"

Kia grinned. "It's magic."

"Kia, this ain't normal. We gotta get inside." Letta struggled to move as fear pounded at her temples. She felt feverish and achy. It reminded her of the flu, but intensified a hundred times. With enormous effort she managed to scrambled to her feet, which seemed perfectly capable of moving now. She took a cautious step, then another, expecting the ground to give way at any second. She dragged Kia along with her toward the ladder. Kia tugged her hand out of Letta's grasp and crossed her arms, her feet planted wide and stubborn. "Kia, come on. I'm sick. We gotta get inside."

"I don't need to go inside. I need this, and so do you." Kia looked up, squinting her eyes against the rain. "We all need this. And those people who saved me, they good people. They had magic, and they were good and special, and I wanna be like them. If you're smart, you do too. What else we got?"

Something in Kia's voice...desperation, longing, hope... made Letta pause. *What else?*

"I feel like shit, Kia. It ain't normal. Rain shouldn't make anybody feel like this. And your mama thinks this is evil. She'll be real mad if she finds out."

"It ain't evil. Mama don't think that. She just don't want me to see it. She don't want me stronger. But this is *good*. And you ain't sick. It gets better."

Letta looked at the stubborn lips of the little girl and shook her head. "You don't know that. Kia, I..." She couldn't figure out how to phrase what she'd just experienced. *Was it real?* Obviously her body hadn't moved, since Kia had managed to pull her back from...wherever she'd gone. "It's just...my head is spinning. We need to get inside. What your mama believes matters. She's..."

"She don't like change is all." Kia stomped a foot. "She be okay when the rain stops."

This can't be real. Magic? It's just fantasy. A child's dream. Might as well be a story in a book. It's like she expects Alice will run by any minute, chasing that white rabbit. Stuff like that just don't happen in the real world. But drugs, acid rain…that shit happens too often. And this is…not normal.

A part of her, deep in the dark corners of her mind, leapt at the thought. What if it was? What if, somehow, this rain brought magic? What if it gave her something nobody else had, a special something? *What if…*

Hope and dangerous longing took root despite the wetness all around and the exhaustion that now settled into her body. It grew inside her, a tiny sapling which extended through the ground, her feet, up her spine, into her brain and heart.

Letta turned to Kia, who watched her carefully. Whatever Kia saw on her face made the girl break into a wide grin and dance a little jig. "I knew you'd feel it, I knew it. I could tell. You got the right color."

"What do you mean?" Letta looked down at her plain blue shirt and jeans. Her skin, a deep shade of chocolate.

"Nah, not that. Can't you see it? You have a glow around you now, ever since the rain touched you. I can see it. It's here." Kia put her hand just over Letta's arm and traced around her body. "It goes around you, and it's a pretty green color. You had it before, but now the rain touched you it glows strong. You got magic, and now it's part of you."

Letta shivered, though the rain was warm. *I glow green?* Kia didn't glow at all. Bewildered, Letta put her arms in front of her and examined them. Nope, same ol' brown.

She hesitated, uncertain. "What happens now, Kia?"

"Now we wait." Kia said the words so matter-of-fact, as though this were common knowledge.

"What for?"

"For the magic to take hold. I bet it's like learnin' to read. I bet you have to figure it out. You know, practice." Kia tapped her foot and tilted her head. "Wonder if they'll teach it in school."

Letta laughed. "I doubt it. Most likely they'll pretend it ain't happening. Your mama finds out about this, she'll have you living in church. She might do an exorcism."

Kia held out her hands, cupping them to catch the rain. She grinned and stuck out her tongue, licking the water from the air like a cat.

Letta turned her face to the clouds and closed her eyes. Water ran down her face and body, washing her with a tingling electrical energy she didn't understand.

6

THEY STOOD IN the darkened yard, pelted by rain, surrounded by thunder, and lit by jagged flashes of lightning, until they were both red-faced and exhausted. Kia giggled, a sound so infectious Letta had to join her. It transported her to a time when she and Jenna had danced and giggled in the snow, making silly little snowmen that marched down the sidewalk in front of their rundown apartment. *Before Daddy died. Before Mama took to the streets. Before Jenna was taken.* Letta stopped laughing. Kia reminded her so much of Jenna that her chest ached.

A shout from somewhere inside the house intruded on the euphoria. Letta glanced at the back door, still shut against the weather. Reality came crashing back with the next clap of thunder. *Donna Ray. Church ladies. Rook. The game.*

Shit. What the hell am I doing?

"Kia, we gotta get back inside, girl. Before your mama knows we out here. Something ain't right tonight, and I don't want you caught up in it." She reached for Kia's hand, relieved when the girl took it willingly. She'd thought she might have to drag her back in and didn't know if she had the strength. Everything felt heavy, even her eyelids.

Kia yawned. "I'm sleepy."

"Me too." Letta led the way back up the ladder, through Donna Ray's bedroom, and into Kia's tiny bedroom, the two of them leaving dark wet marks on the scuffed wood floor. As they sneaked past the narrow stairs, Letta glanced down at the living room and entry. The front door stood wide open. Rain pelted the front walk, porch, and the gaggle of women hovering there. Donna Ray commanded the top of the steps, framed by the doorway. As if she sensed someone staring, she turned, her gaze traveling up the stairs to meet Letta's.

For a moment they made eye contact, neither of them moving or speaking. Bright flashes lit the night, and crashes of thunder filled the silence. Letta pulled herself up straighter and held Donna Ray's angry look with defiance.

Behind Donna Ray, the group of church women hesitated, trying to shield their eyes from the rain as they turned back to their leader for guidance.

"Praise Jesus, you sure now's the time, Donna Ray? Lordy, that thunder." The woman who spoke held a large black purse over her head.

Donna Ray waved a hand as if to shoo the woman away. Her eyes narrowed as she studied Letta.

Letta raised an eyebrow, crossed her arms, and waited. *Go ahead. You just try it.*

"I need a towel!" Kia called out from the bedroom.

Donna Ray shifted her gaze to the bedroom door. The anger in them melted into concern that added years to her face.

"Just a sec, sweetie." Letta called back to Kia. She kept her eyes on Donna Ray.

Donna Ray glanced at the open front door and the women huddled just outside. When she turned back to Letta, she wore a defeated expression. Her shoulders slumped, and she raised her hands in a wide gesture that said "what else can I do?"

Letta raised both eyebrows then. *There's a lot you can do. Whatever's going on, you know it ain't right. You know it.*

Donna Ray pursed her lips. Her body shifted subtly from defeat to determination. Her eyes darkened to nearly black.

The buzzing tingle started up again in Letta's mind, so strong and fierce she slapped her hands over her ears.

Protect Kia. Watch over my baby.

"I ain't her mother. That's your job." Letta groaned against the pressure behind her ears. "Get outta my head!" She forced herself to remain instead of running to Kia immediately. The need to get to the girl was so strong, her feet shifted toward the bedroom without her meaning to.

"Sometimes, a mother can't do it all. Sometimes, she's gotta do things she wouldn't normally do. Sometimes she has to trust a stranger." Donna Ray whispered, the words nearly lost in the rain. She turned her back on Letta, and the buzz stopped abruptly.

Letta panted, trying to get her heart rate back under control, grateful to have control over her body again. *How the hell she do that? She spoke in my head. She made me… That's some sort of fucked up! She coulda forced me to…* Letta shuddered. Thinking back, she realized Donna Ray had already tried it on her once tonight, when they ate snacks at the table. *If she's doing it to me, she's doing it to them.* Letta watched the women as they stared intently at Donna Ray, hanging on her every word. *She's the one getting people to act. Why?* She'd seen no evidence of drugs or of large amounts of money providing for a more comfortable life. Donna Ray lived modestly, at best. *She's doing it for Rook, but why? What she get outta this?*

"That ain't right. You got no right to poke in people's heads." Letta told Donna Ray's back. "Kia deserves better."

Donna Ray stiffened. Her head half-turned, presenting an

angry profile with tight lips and lines around the eye, but she said nothing. Instead she held the Bible aloft over the heads of the other women like some sort of beacon.

"Our salvation is here. Ready yourselves. It's time to gather. You go on now, get your packages. Head to the park, just like we planned. Remember, two hours. And keep your own inside." The women dispersed into the dark night and the storm. Donna Ray stood in the doorway, watching them go. Her hair glistened from a fine sheen of mist.

Letta turned her back on the woman and continued down the hallway, lost in thought. *She wanted me to hear that. Two hours, at the park. I got two hours. What's Rook gonna do at the park? What packages? What the hell?* She hesitated at Kia's bedroom door, unsure which was the wiser move. Follow Donna Ray or one of those women in the hopes they'd lead her directly to Rook and maybe stop this thing? Stay with Kia, get word to Shelley, and wait for backup? Her skin still tingled from the dance in the rain, and her ears buzzed. She couldn't be sure if it came from the toxic rain or more of Donna Ray's manipulation. Just the thought of leaving the girl to investigate the park made her queasy. She suspected Donna Ray caused it with her little mind game. Her heart said stay with Kia, her head told her there was so much more at stake than one child.

Above all, she couldn't shake the euphoria, and the exhaustion that came with it.

Whatever happened in the rain to me, gotta be happening to others. Donna Ray, Rook, anybody standing in it.

She bit her lip. *Go, or stay? Leave Kia alone?* Her gut balked at the idea. She felt attached to this girl, above and beyond Donna Ray's odd mental command. She and Kia had shared something, out in the rain. They'd bonded in a way that defied explanation.

It's Jenna, all over again. I can't leave her alone. Whatever's going down, I want Kia far away from it. Letta frowned, analyzing the thought. *Was that my idea, or Donna Ray's?* Glaring at the woman's back, she realized it was probably both. *I didn't lie. I would watch out for her anyway.*

Letta shrugged, trying to ease the tension in her shoulders and neck. *I should report. Shelley's probably wondering what the hell happened to me. It's been hours. Damn, I'm tired.*

"I'm getting you a towel, Kia. I'll be right back." Letta peeked into the room and saw Kia doing a dance in the middle of the room, wet nightgown clinging to her.

"It's the next door." The girl offered and pointed.

Letta nodded and found the tiny bathroom tucked between Kia's bedroom and a small closet. Inside, she put the toilet lid down and sank onto it. She dug the cell phone out of her back pocket. The phone had a protective covering which had sheltered it from the worst of the rain. It still worked. She hit the number for Shelley. It only took two rings.

"Where the hell have you been, girl? I told you every hour. Dammit, I've been hiding in the bathroom for the last thirty minutes, waiting on your ass."

"Sorry, Shelley. Couldn't get away. Listen, I only have a second. This rain is seriously messed up. Have you been out in it?"

"Not yet. Why?"

Letta hesitated. "Just…try it. I can't explain it. And I've found out Donna Ray is definitely involved. She has that gaggle of church women bringing some sort of packages to the park in two hours. I think Rook will be there."

"Packages? What packages?"

"Don't know. Whatever this is, it's big. She had at least ten women heading out into the storm just now. And she's told them to keep their family inside, away from the park. She asked me to watch Kia." She didn't explain *how* Donna Ray had asked. Shelley would probably hang up on her.

"It don't sound good, I agree. But…"

"But nothing, Shelley! I need backup. I don't know what the packages are, but I get the feeling it ain't drugs."

"You haven't been watching the news. There's serious panic going on. Brass won't spare someone for what might amount to a group of people dancing in the rain."

Letta swore. "It's more than that."

"Do you know who Rook is? You got a name? Or something more specific, like the location of the Exchange?"

Letta huffed. "Shit."

Shelley shouted at someone behind her, then came back on the line. "I gotta go. I'm coordinating the Northwest."

"Wait. Rook is gonna *be* there. In person. It's our chance to nail him, in the act. I don't need his name, I'll have him. In person. It'll be the first time he's ever been out in public like that. Donna Ray is spreading the word, like a promise or a threat. They bring product, code for girls, and, their family's safe. It's happening at that sorry excuse for a park at the end of Peach and Strawberry. You know, the…"

"Drug triangle. Yeah, I know. You didn't get a time?"

"She said two hours from now, but no definite time. Best I can do is be ready. How long the storm supposed to last?"

"I'll have to check the weather reports. Shit. It's already a mess out there. No riots yet, but power is out in the Northeast, and the wind is starting to kick up. And the lightning. Have you seen it? It's been all different colors. Never seen anything like it. It's got people spooked, but so far most are staying off the streets."

Letta bit her lip. She'd seen it all right. She'd danced in it.

"Except here. Donna Ray just lead a group right out into it." Letta hesitated. When she thought of her initial conversation with Donna Ray, and the whispers in her mind, she knew what they were supposed to bring to the park. Her gut told her, even if she had no direct evidence. "It's girls, Shelley. They're bringing girls to the park. For Rook."

"She said that?" Shelley's voice was sharp.

Letta hit the sink with a fist. "That's what the word product means, Shel." She hesitated to explain the whispered voice in her head. The compulsion to be in the park Donna Ray tried to place on her. Nobody would believe it.

"You don't know that. And even if it does, hanging out in the park is not against the law."

"Come on, Shelley! If those women bring two or three girls each, that's as many as thirty girls. They'd be lost without a trace with so much going on. Nobody's gonna pay any attention except us. And that damn woman took off and left Kia here with me. If I go chase after Donna Ray, Kia'll be alone. I need backup."

The other end of the line fell silent except for the background noise of cops readying for something.

"Shel. How many times have I asked for backup?"

"Never."

"When the rain's gone, and the sun comes up, and those families start reporting their missing kids, what'll we do then? It'll be too late. What'll we tell them, Shelley? Bet anything they won't be street rats. They'll be from good neighborhoods. Nice homes. Important people who'll miss their kids, Shel. And they'll want answers. They'll wanna know how we didn't see this coming. We gonna admit we *did* see it coming but a little rain was more important?"

She heard her partner breathing and a pen tapping the desk,

something she did when she thought strategically. Once Shelley started tapping like that, she stopped listening. Letta waited.

Finally, Shelley sighed. "Look, I'll see what I can do. Might set up a border just outside the park. Provide a barrier. If he can't get them out of the neighborhood, then he'll probably slither away and it'll be no harm, no foul. This time." Shelley shouted at someone to put the map of the Mansion up on the board. "Can't make any promises, Letta, but I'll do my best. Containment is the word of the day. So far the neighborhoods are quiet, and yours is the only one hinting at anything. So I can probably convince them to focus manpower near there. Maybe. I'll play it up like a riot. Looting always seems to get more attention."

Letta stewed over that. "Don't feel like enough. And what about Kia?"

"It's the best we got right now. We gotta catch him *doing* something. Not just dancing in the rain." Muffled shouts in the background, followed by footsteps. "Hey, power just went out in the Northwest. You still got juice?"

Letta glanced at the small bathroom light. "Yeah. For now."

"Might not for long. I gotta go. Stay safe. Check back in an hour."

"Can you at least send someone to watch Kia?"

Shelley barked a laugh. "There's kids alone all over the city, Letta. No way I'll get someone to babysit one in the Mansion. You're on your own with that one. Sorry, girl."

"Fuck."

"Can't save the world, Letta."

"Not trying to. Just wanna save one small corner. And maybe a kid or two."

Shelley laughed. "You got big goals, I'll give you that. See what else you can dig up. Oh, and check your email. They sent a containment plan for after the storm. You're part of 9B, since you're already in that district."

"Fuck me."

"No, thanks, don't swing that way." Shelley laughed and hung up.

7

LETTA GLARED AT the phone, irritation at red tape and bureaucracy making her want to throw the thing. She resisted and instead pulled up her email. They were centering the bulk of security around government buildings and hospitals. She noticed a distinct lack of coverage in the Mansion and Northern districts. *Times like this, nobody cares about the 'hood. Nobody'll even miss these girls, with all the shit going on.*

Letta hit the off button and stowed the phone in her back pocket with an angry shove. She flushed the toilet to keep up appearances, grabbed a towel off a small shelf above it, then yanked the door open. She stumbled over the uneven edge between cracked linoleum and weathered wood floor, catching herself on the stair railing opposite. Every step felt labored, like walking through mud.

She glanced down at the living room and saw the front door waving in the wind, a muffled "thump" each time it hit the wall, as though swung by an invisible hand. *Bitch left without even shutting the door?* Letta frowned at it. *She wants her kid safe but she leaves the door wide open?* Growling, Letta stomped down the stairs.

Through the open door another streak of lightning lit the sky a rainbow of colors. Everything from red to purple to yellow and beyond. The light filled Letta's vision, temporarily blinding her. The crack made the hair on her arms stand straight up. The lights flickered and went out, plunging everything into darkness broken only by the lightning. Letta squeezed her eyes shut, waited for them to adjust, then opened again, still seeing an afterimage of colors. Holding tight to the stair rail, she made her way down the stairs to the front door and closed it. Her hand went to the lock, but paused. Donna Ray was out in the storm. Who knew when the woman would come home? *If* she would. Did she even take her keys with her?

Shit. She can knock. Letta turned the deadbolt, happier with the small bit of security. With the door closed and the dingy windows covered by curtains, it was difficult to see her way back up the stairs. She pulled her phone out, using it as a flashlight, holding it awkwardly in one hand with the towel tucked under her arm. The climb back up the stairs left her gasping for air, with sore legs and arms from the effort. She used the railing to practically haul her body up the stairs. *What the fuck is wrong with me?* Everything seemed a bit hazy, and colors seemed overly vivid, even in the dark. *I need to rest. I'm no good like this.* She hadn't wanted to admit to Shelley the real reason she needed backup was an overdose of toxic rain and a very real need for a nap. *Just need to close my eyes. Just for a minute.*

When she got back into Kia's bedroom, she shut the door and leaned against it. *How am I supposed to protect Kia, stop Donna Ray, and find Rook at the same time if I'm exhausted?*

She refused to admit the obvious, even to herself.

Kia sat in the middle of the floor with a tiny flashlight. She pointed it right at Letta's face when the door opened.

"Down, girl. That's bright!" Letta winced and shielded her

overly sensitive eyes with the towel.

"Sorry." Kia lowered the light and bounced to her feet. Her eyes were still bright from their trip outside, but she was obviously not nearly as fatigued as Letta felt. She'd made a puddle underneath her from all the water dripping off her nightgown.

Letta grinned at her. "Come on, girl, let's dry off. Where's some dry pj's?" Letta tossed the towel at Kia, who dropped the flashlight to catch it. The beam of light reached out and caressed their feet, but created eerie shadows of everything else.

"Bottom drawer."

Letta dug in the drawer, unable to see what she selected. She found what she thought was a nightgown and tossed it to Kia, then turned her back to give the girl some privacy.

While Kia dried and dressed, Letta did her best to do the same. She stripped out of the shirt and jeans, spreading them over the edge of the tiny dresser to air out. Wrapping the towel around herself, she sat down on the floor, trying to wring the worst of the moisture out of her hair. Relief at being off her feet turned the worn rug into a feather bed and the towel a luxurious blanket.

Kia twirled around the room, using the flashlight as a beacon. "The world's got magic, the world's got magic." She sing-singed as she danced. When she moved behind Letta, she stopped twirling. She turned the flashlight on Letta.

"Oh." Kia crept close. She stood still for a moment, her soft warm breath brushing Letta's bare back. She traced light fingers over a section of Letta's left shoulder. Letta knew every inch of it, though it wasn't something she looked at on a daily basis. She waited for the inevitable question.

"Why you got stars back here?"

"They remind me of people."

"Not very many. You only got three." Kia counted them off as she touched each one. "One. Two. Three."

"So far. I add to it."

"Why?"

"They remind me of people I…want to remember."

"Why's this one got a letter?" Kia's finger had stopped where Letta knew the largest, and oldest, star lay embedded in her flesh.

"That one's for my mom."

"Oh." Kia traced it a few more times before running over to her bed and jumping into it. "Why they on your back if you wanna 'member them?"

"I guess 'cause there's more room back there."

"You gonna get more?"

Letta pulled Kia around to stand in front of her. "Maybe. I got plenty of room, don't I?"

Kia nodded. "I'm gonna get stars too. I wanna 'member people like Mama, and the people who saved me from the bad magic man."

Letta frowned. Perhaps Kia's story held some truth because it never deviated. She'd seen the police reports, of course. She paid attention to everything happening in the Mansion, and three girls snatched out of a park did get a small nod of attention. But she hadn't connected the event with Kia. Did Rook have anything to do with this? "Kia. What were they like?"

"Who?" Kia stifled a yawn.

"Come on, girl, let's get you to bed." Letta pushed herself to her feet, not liking the effort such a simple movement took. She led Kia to the bed and waited for the girl to climb in between the sheets. Taking the flashlight from her, she set it on the tiny bedside table on end, so the light pointed up to the ceiling. Sitting on the edge of the bed, she tucked Kia in. "The people who saved you. You said they were nice?"

" 'Course they were nice. They saved me. Mean people don't save other people."

"Tell me more. What'd they look like?"

Kia picked at a loose thread on the blanket, a faraway look in her eyes.

Letta waited.

"They was special. Real special. He had green around him, and she had dark blue. I could tell they liked each other, though they didn't say so. He...I don't think he wanted me to remember what happened. But I do. I 'member everything."

"What was it like?"

Kia shuddered. "When I woke up, it was the scariest thing I ever saw." Her voice cracked. "There was blood on the walls and the floor, and two of the Sistas was there. Latesha and Casey. I 'member the man picking me up and holding me while I cried. I 'member the lady doing some sort of thing and then going through the magic hole in the air. And then we was here. I could tell they was important, and smart. He was nice 'cause his eyes twinkled when he spoke to me. They brung me back to Mama. Mama didn't believe me, though. She took me to church every day for weeks and weeks."

Letta nodded. "They sound real nice, Kia. They must be good people, to save girls like that."

"Wanna know a secret?" Kia looked up, a conspiratorial glint in her eyes.

Letta nodded again, curious.

"I think they'll come back for me. I think they thought I was special." Kia's face clouded. " 'Course now everybody's special. So maybe not."

"Oh Kia, I'm sure they'll always think you're special, no matter what."

Kia yawned, and her eyes blinked slowly once, then twice. "I hope so."

"Kia. You don't suppose...you don't suppose that mean guy, the one who snatched you, was Rook, do you?" Letta kept her voice light and let a troubled tone filter it. It was bold, to ask outright, but she had to know. She had to know if Kia knew Rook.

Kia yawned and kept her eyes closed. "Nah. The guy who snatched me was dirty and white, and he had scales."

Dirty, white, and scaly? What the hell? Was he in costume? She watched Kia as she drifted off to sleep, sad that someone so pure had endured something like that. This was a tough neighborhood, and somehow Kia was untouched by the depression that settled on most who lived here. Letta felt an intense desire to keep it that way. To protect Kia from all the evil in the world. Remembering the whisper in her head, and the compulsion, from Donna Ray made her mouth run dry. Donna Ray had pushed her to do this. Manipulated her. Used some sort of coercion she didn't understand. Her pulse quickened at the thought. Doing something against her own will, it was worse than...it was like... She licked her lips. *Don't matter. I'd have looked after Kia anyway. She didn't make me do it. She didn't.*

She thought about what Kia had said. *Dirty, white, and scales. Implying that Rook is the opposite. Not white, not dirty, no scales.* She'd always assumed that Rook was a black man, given the neighborhood he operated in. Kia obviously knew Rook by sight. Or at least had been told what he looked like. *I'll have to press her for details. If I can find out a better description before I get to the park, it'll help me find him faster.*

She pulled out the phone and checked the time. 11:30. Time slipped through her fingers like the pouring rain. *Two hours. I can*

rest for one. Just one. The park's a couple blocks away. Plenty of time.
She set the alarm app to go off in sixty minutes, then collapsed over
on the floor, eyes shut before her head hit the pile of wet clothes.

A blaring foghorn startled Letta out of the depths of a dream
filled with giant boulders and dark forests. She struggled to wake
up, cocooned in a sleep blanket that refused to let go. She smelled
fresh wet dirt as though she were rolling around in it outside, but
the hard floor beneath her body reminded her otherwise. Each
grain of earth that touched her skin lingered like a lover's caress.
The soft texture, the rich smell, the *welcome,* brought a smile to
her lips. The Earth comforted, soothed, and cushioned her body,
easing the ache she'd been feeling since she stood in the rain.

The foghorn blared again. Insistent. Demanding. Annoying.
She pried her eyes open, then cringed against the bright light
of the phone where it lay right by her head. She poked at it to
turn the alarm off, hoping it hadn't woken Kia. It made an odd
crackling noise. She listened but didn't hear anything else except
the sound of a storm that didn't seem to be lessening just yet.
How long is it gonna rain? This night has already lasted forever.

When the phone turned off, the room plunged into darkness
so complete she thought for a moment she'd gone blind. Then a
distant flash of lightning provided a dim relief.

Letta pushed herself upright and stretched, the coziness of
the dream lingered and soothed. Her head felt a lot better, though
groggy with sleep. She turned to check on Kia, clicking the phone
on for a little bit of light. The sleeping girl looked so peaceful Letta
didn't have the heart to disturb what must be a happy dream, if
the tiny smile was any indication. She let the girl sleep and instead
listened to her own body. Skin tingled all over, but she no longer
felt as heavy or feverish, and her muscles had stopped aching. Her
vision still seemed blurred, but it might just be the lack of light.

Letta turned the phone off to conserve the battery and sat in the darkness, collecting her thoughts. *What's the next move?* She glanced at Kia again. *What the hell am I gonna do with her?* She might be safe enough here in the house, but it felt wrong to leave her alone. And it felt wrong to take her along for a joyride in the park with a man determined to enslave young girls. *Protect my girl, my ass. Donna Ray shoulda been here. Then I wouldn't have to be in the damn park to catch her and Rook.*

Kia's not my responsibility. She's not my sister. Shelley's right, I can't make this personal.

Kia looked so innocent, tucked under the covers dreaming. Letta's heart tied itself around Kia's tiny fingers and formed a knot that bound her as tightly as it would have to her own sister.

I'm fucked.

8

LETTA PULLED ON her clothes as quietly as she could, trying to come up with some sort of plan. No way could she ask the neighbors to watch Kia. She didn't know this block. Didn't know who to trust. *Sistas definitely out. And the 5-0s. Shit, that's everybody.* Maybe she should take Kia to the station. *No way to get there and back in time. Shit, I shouldn't have slept. No time. Got no time.* Frustration built up inside and pushed into her head, turning the pounding back on with a vengeance. She rubbed her temples, trying to soothe it away, then stopped when she caught a flash of light. The stones in her bracelet *glowed*. Each one a different, soft color against the deep black of the room. Every time lightning flashed, she lost track of the glow, but it resurfaced when the room plunged back into darkness.

She took the bracelet off and held it up for inspection. One stone in the middle, light blue, sparked with tiny currents, like static electricity. *Ain't never seen static do this though.* She ran her finger over it. It wasn't anything special. Just a pebble she'd found during the one trip to the Jersey Shore she'd gone on with a friend's family when she was eight. No bigger than her thumbnail, it made a pretty bead for the bracelet and a nice reminder of a happy day. She narrowed her eyes and peered at it in the dim light. It sparked again. Like electricity or something ran off it and out. Like the lightning outside touched it, and it arched back.

Not possible.

Letta stared at the other stones. All of them gave off some sort of light, but none as bright as the blue one. As her fingers passed over each stone, it softened or dipped with the pressure of her hand. With just a tiny bit of effort, she could shape them into something new entirely. Or so it seemed.

She shook her head, disbelief coursing through her. *Things like this don't happen in Philly.* In the real world, a stone was a stone. Hard. Unmoving. Uncaring.

Somehow, the rock told her otherwise. It carried thoughts, emotions, and the need to be more. To be shaped. To be used.

Fascinated, she sat down on the floor and leaned against the bed, looking at the blue stone again and held it in between her thumb and forefinger. "And what would you like to be?" She winced at the sound of her voice.

The stone sparked again, a flash of light that made her thumb glow. An intense desire to create a shape consumed her. The stone wanted to be a heart.

She snorted. *Right. The stone wants to be something cheesy.* "And just how am I supposed to do that?" She said the words louder than she'd intended, and Kia muttered behind her. Letta turned to look at her, hoping she hadn't woken the girl. How would she explain this? She found Kia watching her with wide, eyes that reflected the glow from the stones.

"Do what, Letta? "

"It's nothing, Kia. You go back to sleep."

Kia crawled down to the end of the bed to sit next to Letta, her face lit by the occasional flash of lightning. "Why you staring at yo' bracelet?"

Letta cleared her throat. "No reason. I…well…can you see any light coming off this stone here?" Letta held out the blue one.

Kia shook her head, her eyes flashing with excitement. "It's yo' talent. Why was you talking to it?"

Letta stared back down at the bracelet, confused. It still glowed, each stone a slightly different sheen. Each one whispering words she didn't understand.

"This is ridiculous. It says it wants to be a heart. I was just asking how I was supposed to do that. I don't know how to carve. Never mind. I'm being stupid." *I'm wasting time. I gotta get out of here. I gotta figure out what to do with Kia.*

"Not stupid. You don't gotta know how. You just do." Kia reached out a forefinger and softly touched the stone.

Letta noticed the stone didn't seem to mind being touched. It certainly didn't react to Kia's prodding. She wondered what it would do if it did mind. "This is silly. We're just tired and still damp. You need sleep. And I…"

"You don't gotta believe it for it to be real." Kia pointed at the stone. "Maybe it's like making a wish."

"A wish?"

"Yeah, like when you want something so bad you close your eyes and wish real hard. Try it."

Kia stared at her expectantly. *If I don't at least pretend to try, she won't go back to sleep and I'll never get out of here.* Letta closed her eyes and closed her fist around the small stone. She pictured it in her head, round, a bit bumpy, a shade of turquoise, with black veins running through it. In her mental vision, she shaped the stone into a heart. When she had it firmly pictured, she opened her eyes and her hand. They both stared at the rock.

It hadn't changed.

Letta chuckled. "I'm not sure what I expected, but I got exactly what I deserved."

"You can't just wish. You gotta make it happen too. Mama says you gotta act if you want things to change."

"How am I supposed to act? I don't have any tools."

"You got fingers." Kia waited, staring at the rock.

Shrugging, Letta took the stone in her fingers and examined every angle. It was soft and malleable beneath her fingers, like putty, ready to be shaped. Some part of her wanted to mold the stone into something it desired to be. *What a world it would be, if magic were real.* Her pulse pounded in her throat when she realized the stone was no longer round. One side where she'd rubbed it was definitely straighter. Eager to see if it would work, she started rubbing the other side. She stared when she'd formed a point, like the bottom of the heart.

"Now make the top."

Letta went back to her focus on the stone. She felt so connected with it. So odd. An inanimate thing, yet in this moment it became everything that day on the beach had been. Happy. Carefree. She could almost hear the sound of the ocean.

She pushed at the rounded top until she had a reasonable heart shape, then caressed it a few more times for good measure. When she felt a happy sigh from the stone, she laughed softly and held it up. "Finished."

Kia took the bracelet, a look of pure awe and wonder in her wide eyes. "That's the prettiest thing I ever saw."

Watching Kia's face, so filled with joy, Letta had to agree.

"You wanna wear it?" Letta took the bracelet and held it out for Kia to slide her wrist into it. When she snapped the bracelet shut, it dangled like an anchor, forming a huge ring around the twelve-year-old wrist.

"Tomorrow I'll make it smaller for you so it don't fall off."

Kia stared at it, happily examining how it reflected the light from the street. Then her eyes fell. "What do you s'pose my talent is? Bet it's not that special."

"Kia." Letta pulled the girl into a hug. "I don't know how I just did that. I don't believe in all this. But I know one thing. Whatever your talent is, it's pretty damn special. Because it's yours."

" 'Spose so."

She squeezed Kia. "Now get back under the covers."

When she had Kia settled and tucked in, Letta sat on the edge of the bed. "Kia, I might have to go out. Do you have friends nearby to stay with?"

"Where's Mama?"

Letta hesitated. "She had to go out. She left me with you."

"I stay by myself most the time. No kids my age this block." Kia yawned. "Why'd you wanna know about Rook?"

Startled, Letta blinked at her. "I just…I need to know what he looks like. That's all."

"Why?" Kia blinked slowly, her eyes drifting closed.

"I just do."

"He ain't nice. His eyes are stormy, and he's creepy purple. You shouldn't know him." Kia yawned again, making a cute squeak noise at the end.

"Neither should you." Letta whispered the words. She patted the girl's shoulder. "Get some sleep."

"Mama say she wants to be his queen. But she ain't. He done took somebody white, made Mama mad. Mama got skills, but he didn't take 'em like he done the others. I want to be a knight. They get the horse." The last words were muttered into the pillow. By the rise and fall of her chest, Letta knew Kia had fallen asleep.

Letta stared at the stones now dangling from Kia's wrist.

Rook took someone to be queen. Someone white. That missing girl? Was there a chance that girl wasn't sold already? Had he really kept her for his own? *And if he did, what the fuck does that mean? What's the game, Rook?*

Something else Kia said troubled her. *Mama got skills. She certainly does. She can hypnotize people, talk in their heads. And Rook knows it. What's she mean by take the skills like he did the others?* She tried to wrap her mind around the ideas that stirred up. Between her rock carving and Donna Ray's mind talking, suddenly magic seemed like more than a fairy tale. It seemed very real. And something Rook already knew about. *Can he take skills from others with… Just say it, Letta. Stop being stupid. Can he take skills from people with magic?* She felt proud just being able to put the sentence together, though it still sounded so ridiculous she wouldn't say it out loud. Certainly not to anyone else.

Just how many people had this…ability…before the rain? How many have it now?

Suddenly the world seemed a lot bigger and more complex than it had before. Hiding right here in dirty ol' Philly were people like Donna Ray? Including, Letta realized with a start, Kia.

People had magic before the rain. She had to accept that or she'd never solve the puzzle. If it were true, it was a giant piece. A corner. All four corners, even. Everything suddenly made a lot more sense, even if she didn't have all the pieces. *Rook has magic. And he uses it on the girls he takes. He steals their power and then sells them. Makes perfect sense. They'd be no use after that. At least, not to him. Good enough for sex, not good enough for…whatever he's doing. If Donna Ray can mind-speak, then Rook must be able to do stuff too. That's how he avoids getting caught. That's how evidence disappears without a trace. He can magic it away, somehow. Shit, how we supposed to fight that?*

Her pulse pounded with the possibilities. She pictured stage magicians and how they cut people in half and made doves appear out of thin air. Could Rook do that? *Nah, nothing that stupid. But he can do something big. He can steal girls without a trace. No image on camera. No evidence left behind. He can traffic them and never leave a mark. Not one we've managed to rescue could ID him. Why? Can he erase their memories? What about Carl? Can he... Shit.* She shook her head. She didn't have enough information and nobody to call. No way to ask. Magic. Real magic. Nobody would believe her. Not even Shelley. The only people who might believe something this insane were the people Kia mentioned. The so-called good people, who'd rescued Kia from the lizard man. If what the girl said were true, those people definitely had magic. They'd used it to rescue three girls from...whatever or whoever. They'd believe, and they'd help.

How the hell am I supposed to contact them? They in the yellow pages? Just look under "Magic Spells Sold Here?" They got an 800 number? Letta snorted.

Outside, the rain continued, soft, relentless. Inside, Letta's mind continued to race around the information she'd gathered and her need to solve this puzzle fast. She didn't know a lot, but it was more than she'd started with. She turned on her phone to check the time. *Thirty minutes to get to the park and figure this shit out.* Before she clicked it off, she noticed she had no signal. No way to call Shelley or check in. *Probably a good thing. What the hell would I say? I know how Rook's doing it now. He's using magic to steal from others before he sells them, and Donna Ray uses magic to manipulate them into his arms.* They'd lock her up, or fire her ass. At least with the power out and her cell phone down, her boss couldn't fire her right this second. She had a tiny opportunity to prove herself and get Rook. The "how" wouldn't matter as much as the "what," once she caught him. Finding the girl he'd snatched would be good enough.

Another giant puzzle piece slept right in front of her.

Kia knows about magic. Kia can do it too. And Kia knows Rook.

9

LETTA WATCHED KIA sleep for a minute or two longer, unable to sort out her next move. Shelter in place, and protect the girl? Or leave Kia behind a locked door and hope it would keep her safe, so that she might save a lot more girls just like her?

Protect the many, or the few?

Even without Donna Ray's compulsion still pushing at her mind, Kia reminded Letta so much of her sister Jenna that it stabbed somewhere deep, somewhere forgotten. Jenna hadn't been much older than Kia when someone took her right off the street in broad daylight. Letta had been in school, and Jenna had been sick. She was supposed to be home in bed, but their mother needed to "work" and so had taken Jenna to hang on the block where she hunted for "dates." It took hours for her mother to even notice Jenna was missing, much less start to search.

Letta gulped the memory down. *Kia is not Jenna. She's in a locked house, and everybody will be busy with their own shit tonight.*

She thought about Donna Ray, luring other girls to the park, to a horror that couldn't even be described, just to protect Kia, and shook her head. *It ain't right. Wrong choice. Like Mama, dragging Jenna down to the street. Wrong. Wrong. Wrong. Fuck.*

She leaned over and kissed Kia on the forehead, tucking the light blanket tightly around the girl's shoulders. As if it would keep ward off evil or the future.

"Stay safe, Kia," she whispered.

Turning away from the sleeping child ripped another hole in Letta's heart. Tears poked at her eyes, but she glared, refusing to let them fall. Tiptoeing out of the room, she closed the door softly behind her. At the bottom of the stairs, she looked for a way to bolster the door from the inside. Settling on a chair wedged under the doorknob, she checked the windows to be sure they were locked, then quietly moved to the back door. A quick search of the kitchen drawers yielded a rusty screwdriver and other bits of unused junk. She took the screwdriver and exited, shutting the door softly behind her.

The tiny stoop provided no protection at all from the weather. Rain instantly soaked Letta from head to toe. Again. She pulled the hoodie up, but it did nothing to stop the deluge, and her hair hadn't even dried from her early excursion. She felt like a drowned rat, and probably looked like one too. Plus, the rain didn't burn exactly, but it made her skin tingle in an uncomfortable way, as though millions of ants crawled all over her body. At the same time, she felt again the euphoria, the lightheadedness, the pressure in her ears, and the thumping of her heart as it accelerated to match the pace of the rain.

She squeezed her eyes tight for a minute, willing the effects of the rain to ease up. It didn't. *Guess I gotta just put up with it. Damn rain.*

Jamming the screwdriver into the door lock, she twisted, trying to break the tumblers inside. They proved difficult to break, surprisingly sturdy given the condition of the house and neighborhood. She twisted hard, grunting with the effort. The screwdriver snapped in two, leaving the end stuck in the keyhole.

She tried the doorknob. It refused to turn. *Great. I've exited and broken, instead of breaking and entering. Good thing I'm a cop, not a thief.* She tugged at it one more time, satisfied with the result. The house was as secure as she could make it. Hopefully whatever happened tonight would be over before Kia even woke up. She'd deal with Donna Ray's ire over the broken lock and misplaced furniture later.

Protect my baby.

Guilt at leaving Kia alone on a night like this surged, but she pushed it away. *Protect ALL the babies, Donna Ray.*

She shook her head at the woman's misplaced ideals and moved into the shadows of the side of the house. She'd stick to the deepest shadows just in case the neighbors, most of whom had ties to the Sistas or the 5-0s, were watching. She'd grown up on the streets, but doing so left a strong sense of self-preservation. This neighborhood wasn't great in broad daylight. At night, it was suicidal to be out alone. Once hidden by the side of the house, she pulled out her gun and tucked it into the back of her pants for easier access, then zipped up her jacket. She felt cold and hot at the same time. *Is that even possible?*

After a few ragged breaths, her heart refused to calm down, and her body twitched. She gave it up as hopeless and moved around to the tiny gate allowing entry to the backyard and glanced up at the Donna Ray's bedroom window. Kia's small, dripping face peered out, lit by the glow of her tiny flashlight. Letta swore.

"You supposed to be sleeping, girl. Get on back to bed!"

"I had ta go pee." The girl stage whispered. "Where you going?"

Letta hesitated. "Got someplace I gotta be. But it ain't no place for you, so you stay here, got me? Go on to bed. I'll be back to check on you by the time you wake up."

Kia frowned. "What place you going in the middle of the night?"

Letta brushed water off her face. *Gotta convince her to stay.* "I gotta check on some people. Make sure they okay. I need you to stay here, wait for your mama. Can you do that? Don't let anybody in. Not nobody. Only me, or your mama. Got that? It's important, Kia. It's a secret mission. You gotta protect the house."

Kia glanced behind her, then looked back at Letta, doubt etched onto her forehead. "Ain't nobody coming by this time a night. What I got to protect from?"

Letta sighed. "Just stay put. You don't know how people will react to the magic. So you need to sit tight, and let it fall."

Kia nodded. "They might be feeling bad. Sleepy or tingly, like you."

"Right. And they'll need help tomorrow."

"Right." Kia smiled. "I'll help."

Letta cringed. "Not now, baby. Tomorrow. When the sun comes up. I'll be back after the rain stops. You stay here so I can find you."

"Okay." She yawned. "I'm sleepy."

"I know, sweet girl. Go on now."

The girl ducked inside, then stuck her head back out. "You come back, 'k? I get up early."

"I will."

" 'Night, Letta. Thanks for the bracelet." Kia shut the window and disappeared.

"Goodnight, Kia," Letta whispered. "Stay safe."

Letta moved into the shadows and watched another minute, just to be sure Kia didn't come back. She checked her phone, wincing against the bright light. *Still no signal. Great.* The screen crackled with static, or some sort of interference.

She tapped a short text anyway, on the off chance it'd send when she changed locations. *Still raining. Power's out. Checking park. Show time 15 minutes.* She clicked the phone off and tucked it in her back pocket. The last thing she needed was a beacon of light to point out her location to any onlookers. Her eyes adjusted to the darkness. A few candles in windows provided a dim glow here and there, and lightning flashes, jagged red and blue, ripped through the sky.

Her heart slowed down as she skulked toward the park, taking care to stay in shadows. For some reason, it felt as though she'd lost her only friend. Silly, really, that her only friend was a twelve-year-old girl she'd just met and barely knew. Letta rubbed her wrist. It felt like the bracelet still dangled there, a link to Kia. *Stupid. It's not a missing limb or anything. Just a trinket, nothing more. That thing with the stone…it was just soft. That's all. Imagination running wild. Focus on the job, Letta.*

She looked up at the sky, rain pelting her eyes, making it difficult to focus on anything. For now, it showed no signs of slowing. Her skin crawled. Pressure built in her head and behind her ears until she felt like both would explode.

It was past midnight, and the rain kept coming.

Letta pulled her jacket tighter and cinched the hood. It smelled of a mixture of musk and sweat. She wrinkled her nose against it and the rain. She thought about a plan of attack as she moved slowly from shadow to shadow, scanning her surroundings for any movement in the dark. The ground beneath her feet was barely visible, much less anything else, so she took advantage of every lightning strike to survey the area. So far, nobody ventured out in this mess but her. *At least, not on this street. They're probably already at the park.*

She kept moving, picking up the pace a bit. Even if she made it to the park before this...whatever it was...started, she'd no idea how to stop it. Like all street fights, it made sense to hit the leader. Without Rook, and maybe Donna Ray, everything would crumble. *Who else will be there? Carl, maybe. Donna Ray definitely. Rook. How am I gonna find him?* She remembered something Kia had mumbled. *Eyes like a storm? He's a black man with gray eyes. That should stand out, if I can see anything through this freaking rain. Shelley better have me some backup. One gun ain't gonna cut it tonight.*

Anxiety formed a ball of glop in her stomach and rotated. The headache that had kept her company all night stood up and demanded attention. She rubbed at her temples. The blasted rain put her teeth on edge, made her cranky. She winced at the pressure between her ears. Like popcorn, about ready to pop. An ache settled into her hands, arms, and chest, making the muscles stiff. Thigh muscles screamed at her as she walked. Every step seemed to take longer than the one before. It felt as though the asphalt had turned to thick, black sludge that threatened to grab and not let go.

She paused next to a beat-up Toyota, slightly winded. *What the hell is wrong with me? I've only gone one freaking block. I must be getting sick.* The park huddled at the next intersection. *One more to go. Just one.* The street leeched her energy right out through her shoes, which made no sense at all.

Get moving, Letta. She ordered her feet to move, to keep walking. She pushed one foot forward, then the other. It took all her strength to take even two steps. Panic surged, turning her mouth instantly dry despite all the water in the air. Her arms felt like they pushed through sludge. Her head barely turned, and her feet were heavy weights that anchored her to the ground.

What the hell?

She leaned against the car, panting with effort. When she touched the metal, electricity zipped from it through her hand and up her arm. For a moment it lit the night with an eerie green glow that lifted her off her feet. She tried to scream, but the sound caught in her throat. Lightning struck at the end of the block, illuminating the entire street for long seconds. Long enough for Letta to see the ground a good five feet below. Both she and the car were rising into the night sky as though lifted by a crane.

Jesus…oh sweet Jesus…

She wrenched her hand away from the car, severing the odd connection with the metal. They both plummeted to the ground. Letta's legs crumbled beneath her, and she rolled to the side awkwardly, hands trying to brace for the fall scraping against the asphalt. The car landed with a clatter and shriek of metal as it collapsed. Rotting metal, eaten by years of Philly winters, flaked off and flittered down like rusty glitter to color the puddles on the asphalt.

Letta gaped at it, then her hands. Her left hand and arm beamed like a green beacon in the night, casting light on the raindrops as they fell. The glow pulsed, in time with her racing heart, and slowly crawled up her arms. It shone through the fabric of her jacket. Pressure built on top of pressure, pushing in on her body until she couldn't breathe. Cold embraced her like a lover, freezing her down to the bones. Wind pushed at her, driving rain into her face, tossing debris at her like softballs at a game. The smell of wet dirt grew stronger. A trash can tumbled down the street next to her, followed by one of the plastic Jesus statues. In seconds the night spawned a tornado that swept the streets and gathered the rain into one hurricane of destruction that raced straight for her as though sent on a mission.

Letta struggled to move her feet, but ground clung to them, unwilling to let her go. She pulled on one leg with both hands. It refused to budge. Everything felt sluggish and slow. The tornado stormed down the street, tumbling cars, gathering anything loose up in its arms and pushing all of it straight for her. Letta dropped into a ball, huddled low to the ground, as the tornado slammed into her.

Wind slapped her with rain pellets and pummeled her with cans and bits of trash. Anything on the street was swept up by the tornado and used against her as a weapon. She trembled against the attack of nature, all thought gone but the need to survive. She screamed. The wind devoured the sound.

Loud grumbles filled the night. Letta screamed as the sidewalk cracked and buckled, rising around her to form a wall about waist high that blocked some of the wind. It left her crouched in a small zone of calm surrounded by madness. *This can't be happening. It can't be happening.*

Lightning crackled a slap of thunder that shook the ground and sent electricity racing up her body. Letta cringed and tried to get even lower. Another crack whipped the night, accompanied by hisses and the smell of burning grass. Even behind shut eyelids and shielding arms, she sensed the brightness that lit the night. Thunder roared and shook the ground with a giant's angry fist.

"Fuck!"

If she'd thought it rained before, she was wrong. That had been a light sprinkle compared to the unleashed fury of heaven and hell that pounded the world into submission. Pressure squeezed her skull and crushed her bones. Something crawled inside her, swelled, and pushed to escape. A rib snapped, and hot fire and icy needles forged a searing path through her body.

Letta writhed in pain, trying to get away. A rock the size of a soccer ball rolled down the sidewalk toward her. Sparks flew from it as if it'd been charged by the lightning. She barely registered the movement, but as it came nearer she thought she heard… something. Whispers. They circled her head, pressing in even as the energy inside searched for a way out through every pore.

The boulder continued to roll, joined by the creak of metal as a nearby railing unraveled itself from the house it was attached to. More rocks formed a bizarre rolling march down the street. They crushed anything in the way…cars, steps, plastic Jesus statues. A mailbox uncoiled from its post and walked toward her, the metal screeching in the night like an angry bird.

Letta raked fingernails down her arms and along her face, trying to claw away the sensation of a hundred thousand ants biting their way through her flesh. A bottle hit her shoulder and glanced off. She barely noticed. Another hit her leg. A greenish, vibrating glow reached out from her body into the night, casting an eerie glow on the macabre dance of debris. She groaned as a wave of nausea and muscle cramps rolled through.

I'm gonna die. I'm gonna die. Die. Die. Die.

I don't want to die. I don't want to. Don't. Don't.

The glow intensified. With the next crash of lightning, the glow expanded. It stretched from her body to form long tendrils that snaked down the street, caressing the pile of rocks, reaching into porches, lighting up dilapidated plants. As it went, it pulled something from inside her. Some essence. Her soul drained and expanded at the same time. She felt everything, from the cold metal to the soft grass, as though her own fingers touched them. Her awareness filled the street, and she *knew* what it was like to exist here, in this place. She knew how long the sidewalk had been here. How hard the last year had been on the grass. How sad the houses were. Everywhere the tendrils touched, she felt. They left a vibrating trail of green that continued to feed her with information she didn't understand, couldn't process, and didn't want.

Pain seized her brain and squeezed. She whimpered, collapsing into an awkward heap balanced on a raised asphalt bunker, legs at an odd angle since her feet still refused to budge.

Please. Stop. Please.

Her stomach roiled. She heaved, but nothing came up. Inside, something snapped. An internal string, stretched too tight, broke. A wave of cold that had nothing to do with the rain pounded her from the inside, forcing its way out through every pore.

Death had come to claim her with an icy hand, and there was nothing she could do about it.

Metal screeched and struck something, hard. The crash shook Letta where she lay attached to the asphalt. Shrapnel hit her head. Warm blood joined the rain on her face.

She heard the lightning, loud cracks that crashed through the night and set her hair on edge. She felt the rain, each drop dumping a gallon of water over her head. The ground that had been so hard before now seemed soft as a feather bed. It welcomed and embraced her. A long lost friend, who soothed and protected. Her cheek rested on upended asphalt and her ass on the ground, but she felt cradled in the arms of a lover.

The air smelled like fresh dirt, rich and fertile. It mixed with a hint of acrid metal, burning the inside of her nose.

The sensations assaulting her senses hurt, each one vivid and *alive*, each like a 3D movie on steroids. It *hurt* to see the colors, even in the darkness. She *tasted* them. Her tongue vibrated against dirt, ozone, and rust. Her teeth ached, the deep rooting pain of an infection.

Letta groaned. *Magic sucks.*

10

THE TORNADO LIFTED, gone as fast as it had arrived, sucked back up into the night sky, leaving nothing but softer rain and dancing debris in its wake. Pressure remained. Pain persisted. Stiffness in every muscle and an odd ache in her bones hampered every movement. Letta lifted her head to the clouds, tears mixing with the rain. Her skin burned and her mind raced. She wanted to beg whatever god would listen to release her from this. Let her die. Anything to stop this overload of…everything. But no god answered, and the storm raged on.

As her gaze shifted lower in defeat, something in the distance caught her eye. It was so far away that she shouldn't have been able to see it. With no power, the only light came from lightning, and it did more to blind her than anything. Yet she could make out details over a block away. The darkness had a life of its own, and she *saw* it. Or saw things in it. Hulking metal cars. Bricks of houses. Metal rails. Bulges in the asphalt. Mailboxes. Letta blinked. Squinted. Blinked again. Each metal thing glowed with a distinct shade. Railings and mailboxes emanated a red tinge, while cars glimmered bluish green. Each lit the ground around it. Every metal or brick thing danced before her eyes in an uninvited light show. *You got a nice color around you.* Kia's words held new meaning suddenly. *Is this how I look, to her?*

Letta studied the scene with wonder, squinting past the headache to study the movement in front of her. Though the sidewalk still jiggled and dust fell off houses, it wasn't an inanimate object she saw shifting around in the night. *People.* Gulping air, she struggled to sit up. Settled for lifting her head and part of her upper body, hands still attached to the ground. A block away the park broke up the dark asphalt, and shadows moved through it.

A thousand pinpoints of greenish blue light that floated in the air like fireflies brightened the park and backlit the shadows so they stood out as black shapes against it. She closed her eyes against the sudden intrusion, willing them to adjust. Finally, she managed to peek into the distance. Shadows resolved themselves into human shapes. Lots of them. So many, their shapes merged together to form bigger blobs that seemed to bubble as they shifted around. She focused on the nearest edge, hunting for details. As they moved, some came a little closer to her, enough to pick up facial features. Some of them grimaced as they rubbed their arms. Others danced in some sort of ecstasy, arms up with hands spread wide to catch the rain. Letta recognized their reactions, because she'd had them herself. But none of them were stuck to the ground or writhing with pain. None of them floated in the air, and none of them glowed. Not like the railings and cars.

She tried to get a quick fix on how many filled the park, gritting her teeth against the pounding in her head. *Hundred? Mostly female. Mostly young. Donna Ray. Bitch gotta be there.* Letta craned her neck to see, frustrated by her inability to move her feet. From this distance details were obscured, especially sitting on the ground. She thrashed. *Gotta move. Feet, move! Gotta get to them. Gotta stop this. Come on, move!*

As she struggled to unstick herself from the tar pit the street had suddenly become, her skin tried to crawl right off her body. She screamed with effort as she wrenched one foot off the ground only to have it sucked right back down again, as though the entire street were a magnet.

A loud grinding filled the air, drowning out the sound of raindrops and the screams. *Airplane?* The sound drummed her ears. Pounded. Hammered. Pummeled. Lightning shredded the night. Thunder pulverized it. Electricity squeezed her heart. Twisted her mind into a whirl of chaos. A wail rose, the sound raw against the raging storm.

"Letta!" A small voice. Innocent. Unsure. Weak against the night, but Letta heard it.

It was familiar. Important. She looked for the source. Kia stood on the steps of a row home, clinging to the railing and a small flashlight that formed a small shining beacon against the blackness.

Letta groaned. "Get…away…"

Kia jumped off the step and moved cautiously closer, crawling over a large mound of buckled asphalt. "I can help."

"No! Go. Home."

The ground shook, a violent shrug that forced more sidewalk up and toppled Kia down the other side of the mound. She squealed, scrambling to stop herself.

"Kia. Go."

"You need help. I can help." Kia's stubborn face screwed up with concentration. She bit her lip, examining the space between them. A large crack had formed in the street, looking too large for a small girl to jump over.

Letta screamed as the next lightning blast convulsed her body.

Electricity pushed through her feet to the ground below, which rumbled and tossed like a bucking horse in response. The crack near her feet widened. Sidewalk crumbled into the void it created. A bicycle bounced down the street, tossed by an unseen hand. It toppled in, followed by a plastic Jesus.

Kia screamed as she scrambled away from the widening gap.

Letta tried to move. Something bound her to the ground and refused to let her do anything but watch as the world fell apart. "Kia. Home. Now." She tried to make the words a command, but they came out laced with despair.

A frantic shout reached them through, slicing through the storm with fierce determination. "Kia! Kia! Get away!"

Letta turned to see a shadow moving toward them, a figure that became Donna Ray racing toward her daughter as fast as her feet would travel over the uneven ground. As she reached them, she screamed. "Kia. She's overloaded! Get away!"

"Mama, she needs help! We gotta help." Kia stomped her foot, her chin tilted at a stubborn angle.

Donna Ray reached Kia and grabbed her by the arm, hauling her away from Letta and the newly formed chasm. "She don't need our help." Donna Ray stared at Letta, hate filling her eyes. "She done this to herself. She can undo it. Done told her to stay in. Told her to look after you. She didn't listen. You'd both be safe, but she didn't listen."

Letta tried to open her mouth, but no words came out. *She's your baby, you bitch. You left her. This your fault.*

Donna Ray gasped. Her eyes fixed on Letta. They stared at each other, understanding passing between them. Astonished, Letta thought, *You heard me!*

I did what I had to do, to protect her. The words sounded loud and clear in Letta's head.

In the space between one word and the next, another

lightning bolt struck home in the heart of the chasm. The crackling electric jolt traveled along the gap, filling it with green and blue light that raced toward Letta. Donna Ray dragged Kia toward the park. Letta knew what it meant. Knew Kia would be one of the girls taken, and used. She'd never see her again. *Jenna.*

Letta squeezed her eyes shut as despair formed knots in her stomach. *Jenna. I. Failed. Kia.* The lightning bolt reached her, slamming into her feet and up into her body with a force that thrust her body upward into the night sky. Her arms flung wide, head tilted toward the storm. Her mouth opened in a gasp and quickly filled with rain. It ran down her throat, a river of power that demanded and took, destroyed and created.

It burned through her until she knew nothing but searing, relentless heat.

Screams reached her ears, but they made no sense to her. Daggers stabbed at her mind and eyes.

Lightning, followed by a crash of thunder, jolted Letta enough that her eyes flew open. Saw the shadows facing her. Felt the world as it shook and contorted, abused and full of rage.

She wanted to cry. To scream. To run. The universe ignored her, instead stretching her body even further like a rag to be twisted and abused.

Another shape emerged out of the dark, followed by another. Letta tried to focus, to see who or what it was, but film covered the world and all detail merged together. As the shapes moved closer, another lighting flash revealed Donna Ray, leading a black man. They paused a few steps away from the crack in the ground. A thought skittered through her mind. *I did that. No. Not possible.*

The man and Donna Ray spoke, the words stolen by the storm. The man gestured, and Donna Ray stalked away, leaving him standing alone on a shockingly even patch of asphalt. The crowd of shadows in the park swallowed her.

The man stepped toward Letta, edging close but stopping short of the never-ending hole. His suit clung, dark fabric on a skeleton. Death in a suit, arrogant and graceful and evil.

He tilted his head to study her, a calculating look on his face. A slow smile played on his face. She'd never seen anything so terrifying. She watched helplessly as he raised both hands, palms toward her. Something tugged at the core of her body, a rope pulled taut. It snapped, and she fell forward, flopping to the pavement. She rolled onto her back, needles shooting through her bones.

Through a haze, she saw Death smiling at her, a triumphant gleam in his gray eyes.

Rook.

Letta bellowed an incoherent sound of rage as a wave of heat rushed from her stomach and out through her chest, toward Rook. His eyes widened, and his expression shifted from triumphant to studious. As though he were studying an insect. She knew that look. He was a predator. She was the prey.

Letta pounded her fists against the pavement. Beneath her hands, cracks appeared and raced out into the night.

Rook sidestepped, then backed away, eyes wide. He looked from the cracks, to her hands, to her face. His hands formed tight fists.

One of the cracks reached his feet, a hole forming that filled instantly with rain from the unrelenting deluge. Another to the right, another to the left. Each one joined another. Rook danced out of reach, back toward the park.

Letta watched him go, the crack widening after him. Too late she realized what the crack indicated. *Sinkhole.* She grabbed for something, anything, to hold, but the ground crumbled as she crawled, each handhold dissolving down into the growing chasm.

She latched onto a large tree root, managing to get a good grip just as the earth disappeared beneath her feet. Fear surged along with the electricity coursing through her body. Below, a never-ending darkness yawned. Above, the relentless rain pounded.

From the darkness, Rook watched her struggle.

"Help me." Her plea died in the storm's fury. Her hand, slick with rain and sweat, slipped. Letta threw one hand over the other, trying to climb the thin root. The tree above leaned, dropping her several inches.

Her right hand slipped. Lost hold. Fell away. She gasped, thrusting it back up. It grabbed empty air.

She dangled by one hand for precarious seconds until she managed to swing her other hand back up and catch hold. Her arms ached, and her fingers were numb. She couldn't feel the root anymore.

"Help." She wasn't even sure the words were said out loud. Couldn't hear anything but clangs and groans and clashes as hard things fell on other hard things. For a bizarre moment, it seemed like someone played the drums. Then a rock struck her shoulder, and she knew music had no place, now.

Another rock, the size of a softball, hit her ear in a glancing blow and fell away into the dark. Then another. And another. Rocks fell out of the sky like rain. As if the angry red clouds had carried them across the country to deposit them on Philadelphia like some sort of prize.

The tree she dangled from slipped. A house nearby exploded into a shower of bricks that joined the rain of rocks. Another softball size stone struck the top of her head, and she saw black stars dance against the black void.

Please. Stop. She knew tears fell, because her eyes ached. They ached with an overload of emotion. But in the rain, nobody saw her cry.

Above, Rook leaned against the tree. She dangled helplessly below him, her fingers slick with rain. The rain of rocks fell harmlessly around him as though he were encased in a bubble that shielded him from everything.

"Help." She mouthed the words now. She'd no breath for speech. It was all she could do to hold on, but her fingers were numb and her grip slipped with each shake of the ground.

Rook shrugged, then backed away from the edge of the sinkhole. As his hands left the tree, it slowly tilted forward. The ground that held it in place crumbled around Letta, and the tree at last gave way. It tumbled into the endless black hole, taking her with it into the inky blackness.

Letta grappled with the tree as they both revolved in air. She clutched the tree trunk, the only solid thing within reach. Hugged it like she'd hug a friend.

Her breath caught as a hollow, mournful sound replaced the rush of wind in her ears. She raced toward something that boiled and bubbled, like an evil witch's cauldron of mud. She'd no time to even cry out. The tree struck, the ground ate it. Letta crashed into both mere seconds afterward, instantly swallowed by the gurgling, sifting dirt.

11

LETTA DRIFTED IN blackness for hours. Days? She had no way of knowing. She'd been cut off from sight and sound. The pressure inside her body diminished, and the headache dwindled to a dull roar rather than a full-on furnace of pain.

This is what dead feels like.

A chorus of voices filled her head, rough like stone scraping against stone. *Earth human has not perished. Earth human lives.* Thousands of voices all talked at once. Some said slightly different words. They blended together in a mishmash of discordant sounds that somehow soothed her raw nerves and surrounded her in a cushion of safety.

Inside, she cringed at the invasion of her mind. She felt possessed by something not human. Something old and alien. Letta tried to duck away, fear consuming her mind when she realized they'd encased her in a cocoon so tight it left no room to even wiggle a finger, like a full body straitjacket.

Earth human must relax. Must release. Earth human will destroy city. Earth human will die.

She tried to speak, but discovered a mouth full of dirt. The thought that she'd been buried alive made her blood turn to ice and her stomach churn. The urge to claw her way out overwhelmed her, and she spent several seconds pressing against the packed dirt in an effort to shift. Pain rolled through every muscle before lodging in her head as a reward for her efforts.

Earth human is safe. Earth human is embraced. Shielded. Earth human must relax. Earth human is not in danger. The voices soothed.

She stopped struggling, but it didn't slow her pounding heart. *I died. I'm going to die. I need to get out. I can't breathe. I can't breathe.*

Earth human is alive. Earth human breathes. Earth human must relax. The voices crooned, as a mother would to a child.

An image flashed through her mind of herself sitting in a meadow, warm sky overhead and cool breezes playing across her face. The contrast to her current situation startled her out of the deep panic that had paralyzed her thoughts. She stopped struggling.

Earth human can think the words. We will hear thoughts.

I...who...what... Even in her thoughts she managed only a word or two. Nothing coherent.

We are Caraigg. We are Earth. We shield city from Earth human. A picture emerged in her mind of a gargoyle-like creature. It was craggy and gray, like a statue carved from rough stone, with a squashed face, big monkey ears, and huge eyes that shone with the power of a flashlight. It blinked slowly. Next to it, an image of herself formed. In her mind, creatures surrounded her, all blinking. Around them, a rain of rocks began, though none of it struck her or them.

From...me? It made no sense. The damn rain was the problem. Not her. The rain, and Rook. The rocks... It had to be the storm.

Rain falls. Humans act. Earth human will destroy city. Earth human overloads. Must release.

I didn't... Who are you?

We are Caraigg. We are Earth.

The name meant nothing. Something thrummed inside her, squirming to get out. It made her tired. So very tired. Her thoughts drifted, the picture of the creatures in her head wavered.

Must release. The voices sounded more urgent.

Release. She repeated the word, but didn't understand it.

Earth human has absorbed magic. Earth human overloads. Earth human must release. Earth human will destroy city.

Overload. She remembered the word. Someone else had said it. Before. *Look, Craig.* She paused, her words and thoughts coming through thick molasses. *No idea. What.* She faded off, already forgetting what she wanted to say.

Caraigg. They corrected gently, their tone soft and soothing. Pebbles, rather than boulders.

Caraigg. Names. They were telling her a name. She responded automatically. *Letta.*

Letta absorbed too much. Letta must release. Letta will destroy city.

Magic. Ain't real.

Reality embraces, reality dictates. Letta must release.

How? Even in her mind, her mental tone sounded high-pitched and stretched tight. If she hadn't lost it already, she was about to.

Muttering erupted. The Caraigg spoke so quickly that it sounded more like trickling water than conversation. While the words were too fast to make out, the topic seemed plain enough. They worried what to do with her. When they finally spoke, one voice rose above the rest.

It is decided. Earth has chosen, earth will provide. Letta take gift, accept and disperse.

Gift?

Earth will provide. Take gift. Shape it. Letta must make it Letta. Letta must take it within, to control without. Letta must understand. Gift of power, to call power requires knowledge. Understanding. We will teach. We offer Agreement. We offer artifact in exchange for knowledge. We offer artifact if Letta will learn from Caraigg.

The way they said Agreement made it sound like *Let's Make a Deal*, but with millions involved instead of a car. In her dirt coffin, Letta tried to wiggle. Muffled rumbling in the distance twisted her stomach into knots. A quick rush of voices filled her head.

Letta must release. Artifact will allow release. Letta must learn Earth. We will teach. Letta will learn. Letta will use gift to assist Keeper.

Keeper? Confused, she tried to follow the words, but half of them didn't make sense. Artifact? All this talk of earth. Learning. Gifts. Keeper. So much swirled in her head that the headache blossomed behind her eyes again. Eyes coated in dirt. Mouth full of dirt. Body encased in… She tried to swallow, but no moisture reached her throat, and her tongue stuck. Her heart pounded with the effort, and the knowledge. *Buried. Dead.*

Letta safe. The voices took on the soothing tone again. *Letta cushioned. Earth provides life, Earth sustains. Earth buffers power so Letta does no harm. Letta not trapped. Letta not buried. Letta safe.*

She found herself relaxing to the singsong rhythm of the words and the soothing tones. Calm enveloped her, though it didn't really belong to her.

Letta must agree. We offer Earth Artifact. Object of power. Letta must use. Release so that Letta does not destroy. An image appeared in her mind so vivid she'd have cringed away if she'd been able to move. Philadelphia, a bird's eye view, with Letta in the center of it hovering in the air over Love Fountain. The entire city exploded and collapsed in on itself, swallowed by a giant black hole like the one she'd fallen into.

I...can. I... She couldn't even process what they were telling her. She lived in the real world, and in the real world, magic did not exist. *But...the hole. The glow. The rain...drugs. Donna Ray. Drugged me.*

Then she remembered how Donna Ray had spoken right inside her mind, just like Craig. And how Kia had already seemed to know about all of it. Even the people who had saved Kia...the girl clearly thought they had some sort of unnatural power.

I...can't... She paused. Collected her thoughts. Tried again. *How?*

Magic falls. Elements not balanced. Letta overloaded by pocket of storm. Letta embraced, absorbed, as Earth does. Must release. Letta will destroy.

Somewhere in her mind, a tiny kernel of acceptance bloomed. She stifled it. *This. Can't. Be.*

She remembered, before the hole formed. She'd been suspended in air. And Kia...

Oh...Kia! Donna Ray had dragged Kia into the crowd at the park. Suddenly the meaning of all those shadows became clear. The girls. So many of them. And Rook. He'd been there. He'd studied her. He'd done...something. Pulled on...something. He'd watched her suffer. She'd cried out for help, and he'd let her fall. Where were they now? Was Kia okay? What about the girls in the crowd? *He tried to kill me.*

But the sinkhole. She couldn't deny it, or the rain of rocks, the collapsed buildings, the trembling ground. The shaking ground might have been an earthquake. But no earthquake caused rocks to fall like rain or electricity to burn through her body. She knew, deep down in a place she didn't even acknowledge, that it had all happened because of her. She'd been angry. Panicked. And every time she'd felt overwhelmed, something horrible had happened.

Even when she was calm, she'd done something. She thought

of the bracelet and the stone she'd shaped with just a touch of her fingertips. The glow around it that had lit the night for her alone. The euphoria as she and Kia danced in the rain.

Kia was right. The rain was magic. It overloaded her with power she didn't understand. And if it'd happened to her, what had it done to others?

Kia stood in the rain too. Kia…Donna Ray. Those girls. They're all…I have to get to Kia. I have to stop Rook!

She tried again to move her hands. The need to get *out* and do *something* intensified. *Let me out. Let me out!*

Letta must agree. We offer the Earth Artifact. Letta must take, can use to control overload. Letta must learn Earth. Letta must aid Keeper. Letta must ally with Keeper. Caraigg are allies of Keeper. If Letta betrays Keeper or Xannon bloodline, then Caraigg will have betrayed Keeper. We will not betray Keeper. If Letta attempt to betray Keeper, Letta will be taken back to Earth. Caraigg's Agreement with Keeper will remain intact. To help her understand, they sent an image of herself being buried under an avalanche. She felt cold, watching it.

Keeper?

Keeper of the Water Artifact. Leader of the Human Society. Tarian Xannon, current Keeper. Now Leader of Human Court.

You want me to promise to be friends with someone I've never heard of? Some magical person who keeps water?

A rumble in the distance that shook her dirt cocoon sent a jolt of panic through her heart.

Letta must release. Letta will destroy city. Letta will die. Does Letta agree?

It seemed ridiculous to make a deal with something she didn't know, about something she didn't understand, with penalties that involved death and friendship with people who didn't seem real.

Even suspended in rock, the ground still shook. Explosions in the distance rumbled every time her pulse rate picked up.

But if she learned to control this power, she could stop Rook. She could save Kia and the rest of the girls. If others ended up with power like hers, they'd need more people with power to deal with it. Her mind swirled, thoughts going fuzzy again like she'd had too much to drink.

Power takes energy. Letta has little left. Death awaits. Letta is caught in power. We shield, dampen overload, but artifact will disperse. Caraigg offer artifact, but Letta must take. Letta must use. Caraigg may not use artifact. Only one with potential to bond may use. Does Letta agree?

Tired. So tired. Even resting in the tomb, pressure infiltrated her soul. It filled her past her capacity for…whatever it was. She needed release. They were right. And if it didn't happen soon, it wouldn't happen at all because she'd have nothing left.

Sure.

Letta must say words. Does Letta agree?

I. Agree.

A calm, deep voice intoned: *Agreement is reached.*

12

THE WORD "AGREEMENT" echoed in her mind, accompanied by a thousand rough Caraigg voices. They sounded relieved.

Gradually she became aware of movement. Though pressure remained, it seemed directed. Her body hummed with the sensation of passing through something solid.

A sinking sensation filled the pit of her stomach.

What... Why am I...

Letta patient. Accept. Earth arrives.

In her mind something appeared in the blackness. A small shape that at first seemed like a pinpoint of blue light. It throbbed and grew, or did it move? She couldn't be sure at first. Fascinated, she watched colors flash off it, though the surroundings were still dark and the light didn't seem to reveal anything at all except a round shape that rolled toward her, growing larger. Soon it resolved into a dark turquoise ball. It grew larger, quickly growing to basketball, then car-sized and more as it rushed toward her. It rumbled and bounced, filling her mind with the shape and sound of a pitted freight train that steamrolled through her mind and over her body.

The ball slammed into her, exploding into showers of blue-green filaments. The force took her breath, stopped her heart. She expected pain. Anything that large should have caused pain. But instead it took the pressure in her head and distributed it. Absorbed it. She sighed with relief at the sudden emptiness behind her ears. The momentum of the crash carried her down, down, down. Filaments of light carried her into a dark space.

After a moment of tightness, as if she were in a narrow tunnel, she felt space around her body. Enough to notice a breeze as she fell. *Where's the white rabbit?* The absurd thought rushed through her mind, replaced with a thousand questions she couldn't answer and a million beats of panic. The dark gave way in slow increments to a blue-green iridescent glow that filled her heart inexplicably with joy. Below, a small pond emerged, bordered by shelves of stone. The walls curved, with ragged bits of rock sticking out. All of them looked sharp enough to kill if she landed on one.

She windmilled her arms, trying to dictate her landing, but it did nothing. The glowing filaments attached to her arms and legs, covering her in warm soothing light that slowed her descent and guided her away from the objects of death, toward one of the shelves next to the pond. They placed her there and departed, a million iridescent butterflies, except instead of flapping away they raced toward the cavern walls and slammed into them in an explosion of color. The walls shook, rumbled, then stilled. Letta stood, panting, mind reeling from the trip down the rabbit hole. Her knees buckled, and she sat, confused. She took a quick survey of her body but found nothing broken. Even the bruises from being pummeled by rocks were gone. Her mind felt clear for the first time since she'd stood in the rain with Kia. Her body... relieved. That was the word for it. For a minute she just breathed.

No headache. No pain. Every muscle relaxed. *Release.*

Amazed, she took in her new surroundings. What she'd thought was a pond became glass. Stone so polished it reflected the scene back at itself. It created a haunting display of blue and green lights, jagged swords, looking more like teeth from this angle than rock. A musty damp filled the air, along with a vaguely fresh smell.

She glanced up. The room faded into blackness at the top. The glow gradually faded to infinite black, giving the impression of a space so large it defied reality. *Ain't getting out that way.* She licked her lips, trying not to freak out at the obvious. *Trapped.*

"Where am I?" Her voice sounded timid, even to herself, as it echoed around back to her.

Am I Am I I I I.

She cleared her throat and tried again. "Yo! Where is this?"

This this this this. The question repeated until the sound faded into a whisper and died away.

Scuffling on the right answered her. She twisted, trying to see what moved. She heard scrabbling behind her and whirled. Nothing. The wall behind her curved up out of sight, filled with pinpricks of light that created the glow. She moved closer, finding luminous glass beads or gems. She touched one, and it dipped beneath her fingers, then pulsed, as if breathing. She snatched her hand away, instinctively reaching for her gun. When she realized the gun had vanished, panic flittered through her stomach.

"Hello? Craig?"

Whispers filled the space. More rustling, behind her. She whirled, finding nothing.

"Shit." *No backup. No freaking clue where I am. No way out.* She gulped. Wiped hair out of her eyes. "How the hell do I get outta here? You can't keep me here."

Her voice rose to a squeak near the end. *Way to sound confident, Letta.*

A whisper tickled her ear. *Patience. Accept.*

A loud crack filled the air. Letta whirled, trying to locate the source. In the center of the mirror lake, a jagged blackness stretched across the surface, like ice about to break. The sound grew louder as shards jumped and popped, leaving a breach in the middle. Water bubbled out from beneath, iridescent blue and thick. It reached for Letta with thick, hungry fingers. She backed away, pushing back against the wall of the cavern.

A loud groan reverberated as a form emerged through the opening in the pond. It quickly overtook the space, spreading limbs that reached toward the walls and up. Tendrils of stone that formed branches, a trunk. Leaves unfurled and snaked outward, covering the floor and reaching up the walls. They spread quickly over the jagged rocks, the glowing gems, and around Letta, leaving her untouched.

When it finished, she stared in awe at what looked like a tree, grown from nothing in seconds, carved of stone. The thick trunk, etched with lines like bark, breathed. She blinked, studied it again. The trunk rose and fell exactly like it took in air and expelled it with a soft sigh.

Something about the way the lines formed a pattern caught her curiosity. She inched forward, nervous about stepping on any part of the tree but unable to avoid it. She stumbled over a large root, nearly toppling into the trunk. Forced to put her hands out, they landed on the trunk. It *breathed.*

What the…

She reached out to softly trace one of the deeper grooves. It was warm beneath her fingers. *Alive.* Yet obviously stone.

"Craig?" The voices remained stubbornly absent. She traced

the lines in the bark, marveling at the way they felt. Like flesh. Like a friend. The pattern formed into a face, with large eyes, high cheek bones, small nose, full lips. Even a mole near the side of the face. Startled, she snatched her hand away.

My face. It has my face!

Adrenaline rushed through, pushing her heart up into her throat. She studied the rest of the trunk. The face attached to a body that looked exactly like hers. Naked. She saw a tattoo of a sleeping sun and moon on the inner left arm and glanced down to check her own.

An exact match.

"Can't be. This ain't me. This ain't real." Her voice sounded harsh. The word "real" echoed around her, growing louder instead of softer, until she covered her ears to shut it out.

Finding herself embedded in effigy in the stone tree trunk struck a discord deep inside.

Letta must accept.

The thought drifted to her from a long way away. She knew the concept. Accept. *Grant me the serenity to accept the things I cannot change.* It was supposed to provide comfort.

It didn't.

She didn't accept that she couldn't bring her father back. That her sister was gone. That her mother...

She'd based every decision in her life on the fact that she refused to accept her place in the world. She would not be a street rat her entire life. She would not follow the same path as most of her family. She would not accept.

Her basic life principle: *never accept.*

And now? What, exactly, was she supposed to accept? That she couldn't change anything? She refused to believe that.

Letta stared at herself in the tree, and thought about all that happened in the past few hours. She'd started by simply trying to earn her place as detective. She'd ended up in the middle of the street, drenched with toxic rain, encased in rock and talking to creatures that didn't exist in a normal world, all while watching that world explode around her. They said it was because she didn't accept, didn't release...what?

She knew the answer. She didn't want to admit it, but Letta knew. She'd known since Kia first dragged her out to see the rain coming from angry red clouds.

"I don't know if I can."

Silence answered her.

She turned her back on the tree. "You're here. I know you are. Why are you hiding? Come out and face me."

Me Me Me Me.

"Show yourself!"

Both words circled around the space like a taunt.

"Fuck."

It joined the other two forming a chant until the words were unrecognizable. A tight knot formed somewhere deep inside. *Trapped.* She might never leave this place. At least, not until she'd done what they wanted. She turned back to the tree and stared at herself. *Accept. Accept what?*

She traced a finger around the mark on tree Letta's arm. It symbolized the one she couldn't save. The one she'd have given her life for, but never got the chance. The reason she'd become a cop. Her baby sister Jenna. Gone too soon. Taken from them, stolen and spirited away by some monster who remained faceless and nameless. A shadow that ripped the sun out of the sky and plunged the world into permanent night. The mark etched the pain into her flesh, made it real, and made sure she never, ever forgot why she fought. Why she wanted to be a cop. Why she wouldn't stop fighting. Ever.

Jenna had been Kia's age, with the same bright-eyed innocence and acceptance of the world. Her sister would have had no trouble with the idea of magic. She would have acted much like Kia, embracing magic with everything she had. She'd have loved it.

A slow tear trickled down her cheek. She didn't bother to brush it away.

Magic. I have to accept magic. It's real. This has all been real. Not a hallucination. Not a trick. I'm not dead. I'm...what's the word? Am I a witch now?

Tree Letta gave no answer. The voices in her head remained silent. The tree waited. For one long moment, time suspended.

I have to accept magic, in me. Truth. It felt right.

So how the hell I do that?

Letta placed her palm on the tree's tattoo. She could almost hear her sister giggle. That infectious sound that always brightened the day. She smiled, remembering for the first time in a long time her sister's face. She allowed herself to really see Jenna. *She's not gone. She's with me, always.*

What hurt the most was that she didn't know what happened to her sister. Not really. No body had ever been found. She just disappeared, like so many other girls. Gone, but not forgotten. Alive? Dead? Nobody had the answer. She might live on somewhere, tortured. She might be one of the girls Rook stole and sold into slavery. Letta searched every face she encountered, hoping that somehow, someday, Jenna would be there on the street. But the day never came. It'd been over fifteen years. If she were alive, she'd be forever changed. Letta didn't want that to happen to anyone else. Ever.

Right now, Kia is standing next to the man who does that to girls. Right now, Donna Ray is leading more into his arms. Right. Fucking. Now.

The only way to save them, the only way to ease the ache in her heart, was to get out of this cave and stop him. And the only way to do that…

"Dammit, I accept! I have magic. What do I do? What do you want from me?"

Letta must join. Letta must take Earth.

The voices in her head reverberated into a singsong. She glanced down, and found a gargoyle creature hunched next to her. It took her hand in its paw, then guided it to the tree.

Take.

She placed both palms on Tree Letta's heart and closed her eyes. *Take what?*

Reach. Letta shape stone. Take.

It clicked in her mind suddenly. They wanted her to dig into the tree. A giant stone tree.

Accept.

Kia's tinkling voice echoed in her mind. *Maybe it's like making a wish.*

Keeping her eyes closed, she pictured the tree and her own naked form and imagined what it might be like to dig within it. The idea of digging around in her chest, maybe touching the heart and lungs, sent shivers down her spine. Her mind refused to see it. Instead, she wanted to reach around the form and give herself a hug. In her mind, that's what she pictured. Stepping forward, reaching around, and drawing the body close to reveal a space behind it.

The stone beneath her hands softened, gave way. Her hands sank into it, reaching around behind the Tree Letta until she embraced the form. She hugged it, pulling it close, only slightly startled when the form hugged back. She didn't know how long she stood there in the silent embrace. Hours? Days? She might have stayed forever, except the form began to crumble, breaking into pieces that fell through her hands like dust. She scrambled to catch it, to save…what? A few seconds, and Tree Letta was gone, leaving nothing but a dust pile at her feet. A gaping hole in the trunk remained, and something green glimmered within. She reached for it, pulling out a stick about six inches long, tapering to a sharp point on one end and a round bulb on the other.

Letta stepped back with her prize, unsure what exactly she'd won. Rough stone formed the top, carved with an intricate symbol of twined vines and what looked like eyes. The vines draped down around the stick to a sharp point.

"A dagger?" It certainly looked like one, or maybe more like a stake. But stone, not wood. It warmed in her hand as she tightened her fist around it.

Earth.

13

THE CARAIGG RESTED his paw softly on the hand enclosing the dagger. Through the touch, Letta felt the connection of thousands of the creatures. She heard their thoughts, sensed their emotions, and even saw their surroundings. Some huddled near water, some in grass, others on rock. They spread over distances so great it defied comprehension. Some of them were moving at speeds that defied…everything. It wasn't until spots danced in front of her eyes that she realized she'd been holding her breath. She let it out, sucked in more air, and forced herself to breathe normally.

It is not enough to take Earth. Letta must bond.

"Bond?" *This can't be happening. This isn't real. They can't…* She gulped. One of them stood undeniably right next to her. *How are you doing this?*

Close eyes. See with mind. Hear with heart.

Letta closed her eyes. Once she'd blocked out the cave, she saw other things. Places she'd never been. They flipped by in rapid succession like a kaleidoscope. The voices fell over themselves as they tried to explain, a thousand of them.

Bond within. Send without. Power flows. Earth breathes. Earth provides stability, balance, a shield against chaos. Earth combines all elements. Earth opens all to Spirit. Earth swallows Fire. Earth smothers Air. Earth uses Water. Earth provides in return.

She winced at the cascade of sound in her head, staggered as though from a physical blow. The Caraigg tightened his grip on her hand, steadying her. Offering reassurance. It didn't do a thing to calm her racing heart.

"Provides what?"

Life. Balance. Shelter. Nourishment. Earth needs all, is all, covers all. Earth provides gate to Spirit. Spirit is balance. Connection is key. Letta must take Earth. Must connect. Must join. Must bond. Letta must be Earth.

"How? I can't just *be* earth. I'm not a rock. I'm human." She hesitated, remembering all that had happened in the last few hours. "Right?"

Letta is human. Letta is Earth. Letta must be Earth. Letta must accept Earth. Bond.

She gripped the dagger tighter. "You want me to… I don't understand."

Letta feel. Letta learn. This we teach. First lesson.

The Caraigg tightened his grip on her hand, and heat tumbled over it and up her arm, through her chest, quickly spreading through her body. As it went, pressure built again in her brain. The same pressure as before. Like a storm, something growing to some sort of climax she didn't understand. It wasn't sex. It was… She had no word for it.

Power.

"Power." She repeated in a whisper. *Magic power.*

Magic. Nature. Energy. Power. All is same. This Letta has. This Letta must learn. Release.

Suddenly the pressure started to drain away, releasing from

her body through the hand holding the dagger, into the dagger itself. She felt it heat up, but even as it did the energy, power, whatever it was dispersed.

Letta connect with Earth. Letta pull.

An image appeared behind her eyes, of her looking at the dagger held in one hand, while the other pulled a thin green line from it. She opened her eyes to examine the dagger, gently pulling her hand out from under the Caraigg's paw. It reached for her arm.

Letta maintain contact. Letta must have guidance.

"Okay." She stared at the dagger. "I don't see any green string."

Filament. Power.

A kernel of frustration nipped at her. All the fear, the outright panic, the overload of magic, had left her mentally and physically exhausted. But the thought of what happened, right now, to those girls. To Kia. She gulped. *Gotta try. It might save them.*

She glared at the dagger, willing it to respond. Nothing happened. She huffed. "I don't get it. How do I make it do anything?"

Not make. Take. Remember beginning. Magic falls, brings power. Power circles body. Power extends. He squeezed her arm, and the memory of her body suspended over the street flooded her mind.

"The electricity."

Power.

"Right. I remember."

Power calls to power. Letta pull power. Earth will answer.

Determined, she bit her lip and focused on the dagger. Still nothing. Staring at it wasn't going to do anything, she realized. She closed her eyes and, feeling ridiculous, thought, *I wish the dagger would give me power.*

No give. Take. Letta has power. Letta must use power to take power. Power is within.

She groaned. "I'm never gonna get this. This ain't me."

Is. The voices insisted. They fell silent, waiting. Expecting her to produce power.

Power is within. She thought at herself. *Fine.* Letta did a mental check of her body. Nothing ached anymore. Head, clear. Stomach…starving. She was hungry enough to eat the full buffet at Wong's China Palace. Somehow, she didn't think that was the power they were looking for. She thought back to her dance in the rain with Kia. *Maybe you gotta wish for it.*

She thought of the bracelet, which still dangled unseen around her own wrist, a constant reminder of Kia and the danger she faced. The glowing stones. The magical moment there in the center of Kia's room, with the rain pounding against the window. Her hair wet, the smell of damp clothes. The spark from the stones. The one that softened. Her hand against it, pushing where it seemed to want to be pushed. Almost like a massage.

As she pictured it, something deep inside tickled. Like butterflies in the stomach, except not in the stomach at all, but somewhere higher, near her chest. It wiggled and grew. A tiny speck of heat that tingled. She focused on it, wondering if it was the Earth they wanted her to take. Should she try to shape it, like stone? She put a hand to the spot on her stomach and felt something connect, like a jump of static electricity. It felt like a solid, living thing. A rope, or a thread that dangled from a sweater, itching to be yanked out. In her mind, she pictured that and tugged at it. The spark grew, stretched, and snapped. It raced outward from the spot inside her, traveling into her arms and legs, into her mind, stopping at her skin as though that were enough of a barrier between it and the outside world.

When it reached the hand holding the dagger, she felt the dagger heat up and respond with power of its own. She opened her eyes, unsurprised to find it glowing.

Good. Good. Good. The Caraigg sounded delighted. *Now release.*
The pressure built behind her ears again. Like being in a
plane, descending fast. "How?"

Letta called. Letta release. Push into Earth. Earth will absorb.

She shook her head. Buzzing in her ears grew louder, and a
headache blossomed.

Release. Now. The voices, frantic, concerned.

Letta tried to push, but it felt more like she needed to pee
than anything. The energy drowned out thought. Movement. Her
body lifted until she balanced on toes barely scraping the surface.
Rocks rumbled around them. A cascade of tiny pebbles hit the
floor, filling the air with dust.

The Caraigg shifted, placing both paws on her arm. She felt
the same electricity in him as it pushed through her fingers, into
her body. It joined with her own, an odd dance of something
foreign. At first, she felt nauseous, ready to throw up. Then she
felt it draining, water down a sink, into the hand, out through her
fingers, into the dagger, and dissipating. The pressure released, the
buzzing stopped. The headache stayed.

"Fuck me." She panted. Letta collapsed to the ground, unable
to keep her knees from buckling.

Letta must practice. Letta must learn.

"Just give me a minute." Letta lay the dagger in her lap and
leaned back, trying to catch her breath. If drawing power did
this every time, she wouldn't be catching Rook or saving anyone.
She could barely save herself. She hadn't been able to get rid of it
without help. The realization that obviously Donna Ray used her
abilities without all the side effects made Letta more frustrated.
And Rook. He'd been able to drag power out of her too. *How the
hell am I supposed to learn this? How does anyone?*

Most learn from birth. Knowledge gained over time.

"Yeah, well, that's one thing I ain't got."

Time is subjective. Letta must learn.

"So you keep sayin'." She took a deep breath and sat up straight. "But that little girl is depending on me. Those people… You just don't get it. You didn't see Rook."

We see what Letta sees. We see Earth used for evil. We see. In her mind, the scene replayed so vividly she winced. It was like watching herself in a movie, except in 3D…with a sense of smell too. She saw it all again, Rook, the smile on his face as he took something from her. Something essential. And she could do nothing to stop it. Not then.

"Can I stop him?" Her voice came out rough and raw.

His control is practiced. Experienced. Narrow. Letta has strength. Letta has Earth Artifact. Letta must learn control.

"I don't have time for this." She picked up a loose pebble and flung it at the tree. It bounced off the bark and tinkled out of site.

Time slows here.

She pondered that. It was too much to take in, on top of everything else, so she ignored it. "So teach me."

Practice. Again.

Letta sighed and picked up the dagger. This time, she connected to the spark within herself much faster. But release refused to come. She thought her head would explode before the Caraigg finally helped her channel it all into the dagger. When it all drained away, she collapsed on the rough stone. The dagger clattered to the ground.

14

"FUCK." THE WORD came out a hoarse squeak.

Voices whispered in her mind, taunting. Tantalizing. Encouraging. She tried to brush them away, but they persisted. *Practice.*

"No," she muttered. "I can't do it. This ain't me. I can't...do this."

Is. Concern rumbled through her mind. She heard herself being discussed. Words circled around themselves, playing tag. She tried to catch them, make sense of them. *Keeper. Human. Report. Help. Guidance.*

More muttering. *Danger. Storm. Others. Child.*

She caught a flash of a little girl that sent a surge of adrenaline through her system. "Kia? What about Kia?"

They continued their conversation without her. Letta pushed against the floor until she'd managed to sit up. She covered her ears against the onslaught of voices. "Stop it. Stop. I can't think with all this noise!" Her voice rose in pitch, bouncing off the walls. *Noise. Noise. Noise. Noise.*

The Caraigg conversation lessened, though snatches of images still rushed through her brain.

"What's wrong with Kia?"

The voice, when it came, sounded reluctant. *Child struggles. Storm enhanced. Action prohibited without Keeper. Keeper needs report. Others need assistance. Resources are...thin.*

It sounded so much like what Shelley had told her that for once she understood what they were saying. "You're saying others might be overloading, and Rook is there to steal it. Which makes him a lot more powerful."

And they, weak.

She nodded. "Got it. And some Keeper person somewhere doesn't have enough troops to send help."

Keeper will act. The voices sounded sure and certain. *Keeper has many calling, many reports.*

"We can't wait for her."

Letta can help. We can teach. Letta must practice. We send report to Keeper.

"Sounds like this Keeper needs an army."

Keeper has army. They sent her an image of a room filled with soldiers dressed all in white, wearing weapons on their belts. They lined up like any soldier preparing for battle would.

"Shit." She thought about it. Her body felt weak, beyond tired. But, in some strange way, she felt invigorated from the power she'd held.

"Okay. Again." She dusted her hands off on her jeans and picked up the dagger.

Energy flows. Letta blocks release. Letta absorbs. Letta must release.

She thought about the words. Absorb. "Like a sponge?" She pictured a sponge in her hand, dunked it in water, watched it swell with the added weight. Then she squeezed it, letting the water drain out. "Like that?"

Yes! The voices sounded triumphant.

"Okay. I'll try that."

Closing her eyes, she focused on her body, hunting for the spark deep within that meant energy and power and overload. She found it much faster, and it grew alarmingly fast. This time, as her ears popped and the buzzing started, she squeezed the dagger and pictured her body full of water that she let drain into the dagger. At first, it all seemed to pool in her hand, but then, a tiny trickle escaped. Once it started, she *pushed*, holding her breath as she *pushed* it out. Suddenly, whatever dammed up the flow collapsed, and it all rushed through her hand to the dagger. It glowed with the surge, green showers exploding around it as her energy drained away and dispersed.

Letta learns!

Letta leaned back against the rock. "Yes, she can be taught." She laughed. At least this time she didn't collapse from exhaustion. And the rocks didn't shake or rumble or crash around her.

She studied the dagger while she regained her breath. The glow had settled down, the stone now just mottled gray and green again. The symbol etched on it seemed more alive than before. As if the leaves waved in the wind and the vines grew as she watched. The chill of the blade seemed to leech the heat right out of her fingers.

"So does it work the other way too? If I wanted more power, would this thing give it to me?" She studied the sides, curious. It tapered into sharp edges that evolved down to a dangerous tip. A serious weapon, aside from the magic thing.

Earth moves as Earth wills. Earth absorbs.

"That don't answer the question."

Earth seeks balance. Always.

She grunted, still confused. "Well, at least I won't destroy the city now. Not with this thing next to me." She stood. "Time to go kick some ass."

Letta must practice. Letta not ready.

"I ain't got time to practice. I do best on the job. Kia needs me. Those girls need me. If Rook... I gotta get there. I gotta *do* something."

Mutters filled her head again. The Caraigg next to her gripped her arm so tight it made her fingers tingle.

Letta must be cautious. Power calls to power.

"There's a time for caution and a time for action. And right now, it's time to act." She looked down to where the Caraigg huddled. "You understand. Right?"

Remember agreement. Letta must learn.

She didn't miss the warning in the tone. "I know there's more to know. We can do more later, can't we? We can't let those girls...we can't leave them there. You go with me, you can teach on the way."

Their muttering filled her head again, too fast and furious for her to make out any words. She ignored it, instead looking around the space. "How the hell I get outta here?"

Letta must learn.

"I know enough. I can't leave Kia with that...I just can't. I need to warn people. I gotta get word to Shelley. Warn the girls in the park. Arrest his sorry ass."

More muttering. She got the sense they didn't agree. It might not be possible, but she wasn't going to let the impossible stop her from trying. She gripped the dagger, rubbing her thumb along the hilt like a worry stone.

"You don't gotta like it. I never agreed I'd do everything you said. I said I'd learn. I did that. I know there's more, but we didn't say I had to stop living to do it. I can learn as I go. You can come with me, or you can get out the way. That girl needs me. I can't let her down." *Not this time.*

She snatched her arm away from the Caraigg, breaking the connection with it. His round eyes blinked at her, but he didn't attempt to touch her again. She turned her back on him, determined to get back to Philly. Refusing to admit how ridiculous it seemed. She'd no clue where she was or how she got here, and no idea how to get back. But if they weren't going to help her, she'd figure out a way on her own.

She started pacing along the outer wall of the cavern, searching for any kind of opening. Though the rocks were craggy and deep crevices led to darkened corners, she found no tunnel or any other way out. The lake in the center didn't seem like an option, since the tree now completely filled it. *The tree.*

Letta marched over to the tree, studying the trunk and branches. The branches stair-stepped up and out of sight. Anything up had to be the right direction. *I can climb. Maybe it reaches all the way out.*

She tucked the dagger into her back pocket, then started to climb. It didn't take long for her to realize that looking down was a bad idea. Vertigo set in immediately, forcing her to stop and hug the tree. *I ain't afraid of heights. I been on roofs higher than this.* But standing on a roof overlooking the city was one thing, hanging off a stone tree branch with only her hands to keep her from plunging to an extremely painful death was another. She forced her gaze to focus on the trunk of the tree and the next limb and kept going.

The higher she climbed, the darker it became, until she couldn't see her hand in front of her face, much less the next tree branch. Letta leaned into the crook where a branch met the trunk and tried to relax. Tried to focus on breathing, on not falling, on anything but the darkness.

"Shit." Hugging the branch, she had to admit this was

probably the most stupid thing she'd ever done in her entire life. The way up, impossible. The way down… She couldn't even force herself to look. "Dammit."

Sweat dripped into her eyes. Letta tried to blink it away, but it blended with tears that came unbidden. Stuck, with no way up or down, no way to ask for help. "Some good magic does. Can't even get myself out of a tree."

It seemed like hours that she sat there, berating herself, the tree, the Caraigg, nature, rain, magic for putting her in the position she faced. "I'm a damned city girl. I ain't supposed to be in no tree." She hit the trunk with her fist, instantly regretting it when the solid surface didn't give. "I ain't supposed to have no magic. I ain't supposed to be here."

Get a grip, Letta.

Since it was too dark to see much, she closed her eyes. With them closed, somehow the situation seemed more manageable. She might be anywhere…like sitting on her bed at home, or on the porch step with Kia. She could be in PJs, sipping coffee. She smelled it, the scent rich and thick. The sounds of clinking dishes and registers forming calm background noise. People talking and laughing, discussing normal happenings on normal days. She pictured it in her mind, wishing like anything she could be there. The dagger pushed against her back pocket, a reminder of a strange new reality. She remembered the news reports of the storm blaring from the TV while she waited for Shelley to show up and the taste of the coffee. She licked her lips, relishing it.

The smell of roasted beans and the feel of a hard chair beneath her butt made her smile. *Damn, I have an active imagination.*

In her mind, she reached out to touch the worn table top. It felt solid. Real. Startled, she opened her eyes.

She sat exactly where she'd pictured herself to be, at the back table in a now dark and deserted PJs coffee shop. Through the front windows, she made out the familiar bar across the street.

"Well, I'll be damned." Maybe wishes were a kind of magic. Especially with a dagger at your back and a stone tree in your arms.

Letta rushed to the front of the shop and tried the door. Locked. "Of course it's locked, Letta. Curfew."

No movement on the street out front at all. No lights. No sirens. Nothing. The rain, however, appeared to have stopped. The sky held just a hint of light, a promise that dawn would break soon.

"Power's still out." She snorted at the irony. The dagger in her back pocket held more power than any plant fueling the city, she was sure of it. But it did mean one thing in her favor. *No alarms. No electronic locks.*

The doors had been locked with the deadbolt, but fire codes insisted on an easy way out for anyone already inside. Letta flicked the deadbolt, released the catch, and slipped into the silence of the early morning hour.

15

LETTA STARTED THE trip toward the Mansion district at a slow jog. She didn't want to sprint and tire herself out, but the need to get there pushed her feet faster and faster. She didn't bother hiding in the shadows, since the street was deserted and the map emailed to her earlier had shown where the beat cops were going to set up patrols around the edge of the city center. With any luck, she'd see someone she knew when she reached the patrols. *Hope Shelley's on the ground instead of behind that damn desk.* She patted her back pockets, but the cell phone was gone. Her jacket was gone, and with it, the gun. No power, so no point in stopping to ask for someone's phone. She broke into a half jog, her mind on the park, Kia, and Rook.

It didn't escape her notice that yet again she barged in without a plan. Without backup. She tried to form one as she jogged, running through the options in her mind, discarding most.

Can't take a squad, they won't spare one. Can't tell them Rook has magic, they won't believe it. Could say he's kidnapping girls, but right now don't think they'd care. They'll be more worried about riots, looting, keeping the violence and panic down. People gotta be freaking out. I can't be the only one who got hit with heavy dose of power. I got help. Others got nothing. Even the cops... Don't think anyone's immune to this. Don't know. Don't care. Gotta get help, gotta fight Rook. Save Kia.

Donna Ray's the key. She organized the group. She'd have 'em all hypnotized, like she tried to do me. If she did that, she can undo it. Get her to stop, get her to turn them against Rook. Good plan, Letta. Now how the hell I do that?

She kept up the internal dialogue, running through options as her feet pounded faster toward the edge of Center City. The edge of the Mansion District was eight blocks away.

Though darkness held the corners, a hint of dawn crept through the streets, painting everything with a peaceful glow. The city, after the storm, rested in stillness. The silence unnerved her. The city always made some sort of noise. But not today. Not here. The city held its breath, waiting.

Waiting for what? The worst is over, right? Storm's done. Sun's coming up. It's a new day.

Two blocks from the Mansion, buildings shifted from office and commercial to residential, gradually lowering in standards from rich to poor. She slowed to a walk, searching for movement or any indication of police activity. Sounds interrupted the silence, faint but noticeable. Talking from a few open windows or footsteps on wood stairs. Boots on pavement. The distinctive tinny voices on two-way radios. She'd reached one of the checkpoints. Another block, and she'd be on top of them.

Letta stopped, trying to think through the best strategy. *Bypass them? Or ask for help? Don't even have my badge. They won't believe me. If it's nobody I know, I'll get tied up in explanations. Rook will get away. He'll take Kia with him. Probably already has.*

I'll take a look, and if it's nobody I know, I go around. They can't cover every block. The map showed weakness to the east. I'll cross over that way and up Peach Street.

Letta moved slowly to avoid notice, keeping to the lingering shadows. One more block, and she discovered two squad cars. No lights. No sirens. A group of ten in uniform, talking, pointing. Old radios strapped to shoulders. *Surprised those still work. Nothing else seems to. No TVs blaring, no cars, no alarms.*

In the distance, she heard a motor start up. *Backup generators. Guess the magic didn't screw with everything.* Maybe it didn't affect anything not out in the rain. She shrugged. Didn't matter.

Letta searched the faces and didn't see anyone familiar. Not unusual, since she didn't hang out with the beat patrols on this side usually. She crept a bit closer, trying to hear their conversation to catch any new info she might need. Someone's radio crackled to life, and she heard a familiar voice order them to spread west and to send one unit to central staging area in the south.

Shelley.

She paused, uncertain. *Go south, try to find Shelley. Go east, and approach the park from the back, or try to use a radio to tell Shelley… Hell, it'd take too long to explain. Fuck.*

The pressure against her back reminded her of the weapon she now carried. Not a gun. Possibly something far more deadly.

She pulled the dagger out of her back pocket and gripped it tight. It heated slightly at her touch, and she felt a surge of tingles race through her fingers and palm, up her arm. Her body answered with a buzzing deep inside. The flow seemed a lot more natural now. She felt it, giving and taking, circulating through her veins. Not building pressure, simply there, waiting to be used.

Yeah, but how? Other than tearing down buildings and making sinkholes, what else can I do? Shoulda asked before I left. Bet Craig's pissed off at me now. The small creature hadn't followed her up the tree. Hadn't tried to stop her leaving, though she was surprised he wasn't next to her now. They obviously didn't want her running around, yet hadn't done much to hinder her movement. Maybe because she owed them. She'd promised to learn. The concern she'd felt from them when she voiced the fact that they hadn't set a time limit left her with a tiny triumphant grin. *They didn't count on me noticing, I don't think. They shoulda thought about the loopholes. I'm a street girl. There's always a loophole.*

Hole. She pictured Rook in the park, being swallowed by a deep hole. *It could work. Or maybe a rock prison, like they done for me. Wonder if it'd hold him. Wonder what kind of magic he does besides steal power from girls? He can't hypnotize, or he wouldn't need Donna Ray. He can't just snatch them from thin air, or he wouldn't need Carl. He's got weaknesses. All I gotta do is figure out what they are, before he figures out mine.*

She pressed her lips together. *I can do that.*

Letta crept away from the beat cops, heading east. Once the sun rose, Rook would probably vanish. He operated in shadows, he wouldn't want to stick around once the police started patrolling. He'd be finishing up whatever his plans were and running.

If he's even still there. Might be long gone. Lot can happen in an hour.

Letta ignored the despair that went along with the thought and broke into a run. Three blocks, then two. She used the next cross street to cut over to Peach Street. When she reached the corner, she paused long enough to check the situation. She stood on a small patch of ground next to the sinkhole, surrounded by collapsed houses.

I did this?

Astonishment drove every other thought out of her head. Slowly, she turned to survey the damage. A sinkhole yawned with a mouth so wide it stretched the entire block. The blackness of it swallowed all but a couple of houses at the far end of the street, a few teetering trees, and one lonely Jesus statue that rested dangerously close to the edge. The rising sun cast a glow that failed to reach even two feet inside the massive thing.

Letta shuddered, and turned to look at the park. Only a handful of people remained, and none of them young girls. Donna Ray stood on an old table, hands outstretched. Women hovered in front of her, chanting as though in church.

"Praise Jesus!"

"The Lord has delivered us!"

"Amen!"

Kia hovered underneath a tree near the bench, staring into the distance with wide eyes as though she saw a monster. Letta followed Kia's gaze to the other side of the park. The air shimmered, glistening with some sort of moisture as though the fog lingered only in one spot. She crept forward for a better look.

In the middle of the shimmer, she saw an image of a hallway. Letta blinked. Fog didn't project images. Fog didn't shimmer like that either. Something tickled the hair on her arms. She brushed at them and moved a bit forward. Nearby, a shadow stepped out from behind a tree, followed by several more shadows. As they got close to the shimmer, the morning light lit their faces and she saw four girls, all Sistas, and Rook. Letta gripped the dagger tighter.

In the shimmer, a shape appeared. She stared, shocked, as Carl stepped out.

"About outta room." His voice, though low, carried in the early morning air.

"Praise Jesus!" Someone shouted behind her. Their noise muffled his response. Letta huffed.

Carl took one of the girls by the arm, leading her to the

shimmer. All four girls followed him through and into the hallway. They took several steps, then disappeared from sight.

"What the…" Letta blinked again. *He's done snatched them all. That was the last. Dunno what that thing is, but they're all gone.* She looked back at the group of older women and Kia. *Why not them?*

With the dagger tight in one hand, Letta crept back toward the women. She didn't know what the shimmering thing did, but having watched it in action she could guess. *Some sort of travel thing. Like how I dropped out of the street into that cave. Only he's stepping through…air? A tunnel through air to some other place.* She didn't understand it, but she no longer bothered to deny it. She'd seen it with her own eyes. Magic, real as the ground she walked on, did amazing things. But she didn't know enough. *That thing could be sending them all straight to hell for all she knew.*

And Kia remained, the only young girl left in the park. Rook obviously didn't appreciate older women. Keeping her eyes on him, she circled around, getting closer to Kia. He stood motionless, as though listening for something. *No way he can hear me over their wailing.*

She reached Kia, who remained stationary, wide-eyed. Letta tried to grab her arm, but met some sort of invisible barrier. It felt spongy and slick.

"Kia!" Letta whispered. Kia stared at nothing, not hearing her. Not moving.

"Kia! Give me your hand." Letta searched the barrier with her fingertips, not wanting to get stuck herself.

"It's not your move." The deep voice behind her sounded amused. Arrogant. Completely in control.

16

LETTA SPUN TO face Rook, the dagger already poised for a fight. It heated in her hand and began to glow, the power within reacting to her stress.

Rook raised an eyebrow as he studied the object. She didn't see any fear. His arrogance remained firmly in place. The man clearly thought he had the upper hand.

Given the tingling now traveling over her skin, he might be right. It felt oily and foreign, like sludge on silk or grime that wormed into her pores. *Gotta be his.*

She tensed, ready to spring.

"Aren't you interesting. I thought, when the earth swallowed you, that you'd never return. I'm delighted to find you have recovered your energy, and that you carry such an unusual object." Rook licked his lips, his eyes glinting. "Welcome to the game."

"This ain't a game. What've you done to those girls?"

Rook smiled, a tiny thing that barely lifted the corners of his mouth. "Nothing. Yet. What you should be asking is what am I going to do with you." Rook flicked a hand, and she felt the dagger loosen in her grasp as though wriggling to get away. She gripped it harder, letting the energy flow through her fingertips.

"Let her go." Letta wrapped both hands around the dagger.

Rook shook his head. "No. A pawn doesn't dictate the next move. The next move is mine." He glanced at Kia. "She's fascinating. It makes for an interesting study of the board. Which to push forward. Which to hold back. On the one hand, a unique ability." He glanced down at the dagger in Letta's hands. "On the other, an unknown. An overloaded pawn bearing a hefty trinket."

"Fuck you." Power raced through her arms, urging her to lash out. But she only knew how to release it into the dagger. And right now, she didn't want to do that. Right now, she wanted to throw something sharp at his head. Her fingers itched to pull the trigger on the gun she no longer carried. As if a thing like that could have any effect at all on a man who commanded that much power. Beneath her feet, the ground rumbled.

Rook's lips twitched. He closed his eyes for a fraction as if savoring something, before giving her a level stare. "I look forward to it." He flicked a hand, and the table that supported Donna Ray flipped over, toppling the woman onto the group of onlookers. It melted into the ground, as if it had been made of liquid, instead of wood and metal. Stunned, Letta moved closer to Kia, testing the barrier around her. It squished, re-formed, but never dissipated.

Letta shifted the dagger to her right hand. She'd learned to fight with knives on the streets as a kid, and this thing was sharp enough to kill. She moved between Rook and Kia, blocking his access to the girl with her body, dagger ready.

Movement behind Rook caught her attention, and her gaze shifted. It only took a second to see Carl stepping back through the hole in the air and return her gaze to Rook, but a second was all it took for him to get the upper hand. She felt something hot and solid wrap around her legs. Startled, she tried to move, but remained rooted to the spot by liquid metal bands that quickly snaked up her legs.

Rook nodded to Carl, who brushed past Letta and reached through the invisible bubble to take Kia in his arms. A wave of power washed over Letta, making the hair on her arms tingle and filling her heart with dread. Kia's prison melted like vapor. Carl lifted a now kicking and screaming Kia and started carrying her back toward the air tunnel.

Donna Ray shrieked from where she lay on the ground. "No! You promised! We had an agreement!"

Metal continued to climb Letta's legs, securing her body in place. She couldn't fight Rook anchored to the ground like this. All she had was magic she didn't know how to use and the dagger.

Rook scowled at Donna Ray, his contempt obvious in the lines around his eyes and lips. "Our Agreement ended the instant you attempted to block my power. Do you think I couldn't feel that?"

"I didn't…" Donna Ray protested, struggling to get to her feet.

Rook flicked a hand at the women. The air *bent*, like a heat wave through mist, forming an opaque bubble around them.

Letta stifled a shout. The prison cut off all sound from the women. She wondered if it cut off their oxygen, too. It was a ruthless move that rushed ice through her arms and legs.

Rook turned to Carl. "Castle."

Carl hesitated, grunting as Kia landed a kick on a sensitive area. "You sure? I'm not sure exactly…"

Rook narrowed his eyes.

Carl gulped, held Kia out to Rook, who took her in one arm, seemingly unaffected by the squirming of the twelve-year-old girl. Carl turned to stand between Letta and Rook, who backed away toward the air tunnel. He licked his lips, tightened his grip on

Kia, and whispered something that made her go absolutely still.

Letta held the dagger away from the bands of metal that continued to travel up her body. *Gotta make a move. Fast.* They'd encircle her arms any second. "Let her go, Rook."

Rook laughed. "Oh, she's far too precious a piece for that. She is…unique. As are you. Your combined power will be…" He paused, as if he'd said more than he meant to. Then laughed again. "Oh, yes, this will be quite amusing." He squeezed Kia, who moaned in response.

"What are you doing to her, you bastard! Let her go. You hurt her…" Letta struggled against the bands of metal, to little effect.

Rook studied her with a calculating look, closing his eyes briefly as though savoring something. When he opened them, he looked from her to Kia and back as though there were an invisible string tying them together. He shook his head, his forehead wrinkled in confusion. He glanced at Carl. "Wait one minute, then bring her. And the dagger. Queen's pawn."

Carl nodded. Rook turned and carried the struggling girl toward the shimmering hole of air. Letta didn't think, didn't plan. She acted on automatic, the hand holding the dagger coming up, cocking back, and throwing before she really thought about it. The dagger missed Carl's head by fractions of an inch and sailed past him toward Rook's retreating back. She saw it strike home under his left shoulder blade just as he entered the air tunnel.

Carl snarled. "What the fuck?" He ran toward the tunnel, peering into it. Letta struggled to get her feet free. The tight bands loosened slightly, relenting to her pressure. She glanced at the scene suspended in the air tunnel while she tugged at the metal encasing her legs. Rook stumbled. Kia dropped from his arms, then crawled away from him as Rook fell to his knees.

One band came free. She tugged at the other. *Get it off get it off!* She had to follow. Seconds ticked by, agonizingly slow. Rook staggered, in obvious pain.

Carl looked ready to plunge through the window after the man. "You crazy fucking bitch!"

She had to get free before Carl turned his attention back to her. *Come on come on come on.*

Rook flapped his hands, trying to touch the dagger. His face contorted into a silent scream of rage and pain as he struggled to reach where it protruded from his back. It had sunk nearly to the hilt, the ball engraved with the cryptic symbol the only part showing. His face contorted with rage as he yanked the artifact out of torn flesh. Blood poured out of the wound, staining his shirt. Kia scuttled out of sight.

Run, girl, run. I'm coming for you, Kia! Part of the second band released.

Rook inspected the dagger, blood dripping from it to puddle on the floor. Letta gave one last tug, and the metal binding fell to the ground, freeing her foot at last. She shoved Carl out of her way. He stumbled back, twisting awkwardly in a futile attempt to stop her. She sprinted for the tunnel and Rook, who licked blood from the tip of the dagger as though savoring a tasty treat. When he glanced up, his eyes shone with a light that wasn't human. He smiled, mouthed words she couldn't make out. Five feet. She willed her feet to move faster. Three feet. Two feet.

Rook turned his back and walked down the hallway in the direction Kia had taken, the dagger in his hand.

One foot. Letta lunged, diving for the air tunnel. As she flew the last bit of distance, the tunnel in air shrank to a pinhole and vanished as though it'd never been.

Letta hit the ground, hard, and rolled to a painful stop just beyond where the tunnel had been.

"No!" The scream tore from her throat, primal and raw.

17

LETTA SLAMMED HER fists into the ground, rage at losing Kia providing fuel to the magical fire that leapt out of control within her. The ground shook and cracked underneath her hands. She roared out her frustration, and the nearby buildings echoed the sound, bricks flying out in all directions from buildings too old to fight the pressure. The asphalt nearby buckled up as though pushed by an invisible fist.

She heard screams, dim and far away. Shouts to the Lord. A male voice nearby commanded, "Chill." She ignored it all. If Rook created a hole in the air, then she could do the same. She had power now. What was the use of magic if she couldn't use it to save a child? What was the point? Why had it been forced on her if she couldn't wield it like the weapon she needed?

She continued to beat at the ground, letting anger and frustration pour through her hands until they glowed bright. The dirt jumped like a giant stepped through the area. Depressions formed as though the giant left deep footprints in his wake. It only took seconds, but the crash of a building behind her finally broke through where voices had not. Startled, she turned to see what caused the noise, then ducked as stones and bricks and bits of concrete sailed over her to pummel anything in the park. It rained destruction while she huddled on the ground, arms thrown over her head. Muffled cries of pain, screams, moans joined the tumult of stone and earth. Letta covered her ears. Tears poured out, a release of all the emotion she'd carried bottled up since her sister had been taken. *Shit shit shit shit. Stop. Stop! Dammit. I'm sorry. I'm so sorry.*

Release. Gotta release. Can't do it without the dagger. Gotta release.

Dust filled the air as bricks exploded on contact with the ground until the park looked swathed in a deep fog that swallowed everything. Coughing, Letta fought to regain control of her emotions and the magic pulsing through her, but it was like trying to stop a river after the dam broke. She held her fists tight to her chest, hoping if she didn't touch the ground, the chaos would stop. She whimpered the words, barely reaching her own ears with them. "Please stop please stop please stop."

"Chaos cannot be stopped." A deep melodic voice infiltrated her conscious, poured through her body, an odd calm in the middle of the storm. "It can be channeled. Redirected. Applied. But not stopped."

Letta looked up, her position on hands and knees making it impossible to see the man's face clearly. What she did see made the blood in her veins run cold. His eyes. *Holy fuck. Is that... It can't be.* She blinked and squinted, trying to really see. His eyes swirled, revolving through shades of red, orange, and blue, flickering like the flame of a candle. *Or a forest fire. Shit. His eyes are on fire!*

She scrambled to move away, but the ground heaved beneath her, sending her rolling onto her side and nearly into his feet.

The man knelt and placed a hand on her shoulder, a gentle

touch that sent shivers of heat. "If you wish to end destruction, then you must channel in another direction. Thus."

Where his hand rested, a vibration began, like the buzzing of a million caged bees fighting to get free. It raced down her arm and through her hand. A vivid green arc of electricity leapt from her fingers, cut through the dust, siphoned it in, and slammed it to the earth where it billowed out like a blanket.

The ground beneath her shuddered at the blow, then settled. Around her, grass sprouted, pushing up from the ground into tall spikes in the blink of an eye. Nearby, something pushed up through the new grass and stretched toward the sky. In seconds, it grew to a young tree, leaves popping out as though it were full summer.

Letta struggled to catch her breath. Emotions warred with each other for attention, and power still raced through her body, but the pressure had lessened.

"Only for a moment. You must channel what you create." The man's lips twitched. "I do not carry a mantle of stability. That is your task." He glanced up, looking beyond her into the park. His eyes widened, and flares licked his eyebrows.

Letta blinked, unable to believe her eyes. In the time it took her to blink, he vanished. *Fuck me. Was that...what was that?*

Ominous rumbling underneath her stole her attention. *Channel. Redirect. Without the dagger. Shit. I can't...do. This.* She groaned as the pressure built up force in her mind again, shoving all thoughts but panic and a fleeting sense of doom. Nearby, a haphazard pile of bricks began to boil, bouncing up and down like popcorn in a pot, ready to pop.

She heard voices then, distant, many voices, but ignored them. Focused so intently on what she needed to do, she tried to duplicate what the man...whatever he was...had just done. She imagined the spark from her hand to the ground. She pictured her hands as sponges and wrung them, willing the power overloading her system to release into the earth beneath her.

"It's not working!" she shouted. "Fuck. I can't. I can't." She felt weak and disoriented. So much energy coursed through her veins that it leaked out of her skin and eyeballs, blinding her with a headache, turning her stomach.

"Relax, girl. You gotta relax!" The shout, close to her ear, startled her so much she fell over, backing quickly away.

A Hispanic giant knelt next to her. He looked determined, concerned, and above all...kind. He held out his hand. "I can help. Let me show you."

"Don't touch me. Get back!" She struggled to get to unsteady feet, but the ground forced her back down on her knees. More stones fell, pelting her, the man. Behind him, she saw more people. A short, tanned woman with black hair. A tall white guy. Several more in white uniforms flanking around them, spreading out into the park.

The woman held her hands out, palms up, a determined look on her face. Something shimmered in the air around her, and the men and raced toward Letta. As the shimmering field reached her, she realized that flying debris bounced off it as though a shield had been erected. *She's protecting us. From me.*

The woman shouted something, but all Letta heard was "Kia." It was enough.

They're the ones who saved Kia. They gotta be. They got magic. They know. A dark lump near the woman's feet resolved into one of the gargoyle creatures she'd spent so much quality time with earlier. The ones who'd given her the dagger. *Craig.*

She glanced back at the man who still held out a hand to her. He hadn't advanced any further, but merely waited while bricks bounced off the barrier and the ground beneath them rumbled and tumbled. As she studied him, she realized that he remained steady while the rest of them stumbled. The ground did not shake, for him. She met his gaze.

"I got this. Let me show you." His voice provided the calm in the middle of a violent storm. It traveled through her anger, panic, and desperation and, somehow created trust. It didn't make sense. She shouldn't trust him. She didn't even know him. But something traveled along the ground and into her body, a whisper that spoke of friendship, truth, and help freely given. Letta put her hand in his and closed her eyes.

18

AS THE MAN'S hand closed firmly around hers, Letta felt a welcome sense of peace and the flow of something warm that raced into her veins and through her body. She sat in the grass on a hot summer day, not a care in the world. She sighed and relaxed, letting it take her away from the destruction around her for just a minute. The pressure behind her ears and in her mind lessened.

"Let it flow. It's like trying to catch a waterfall. Can't be done. Instead, you gotta ride it. It flows in, then back out. Sometimes it helps to touch with bare skin. You feel like metal and rock to me, so touch one of those." The man's voice calmed and soothed. "I'm sharing with you, and letting it funnel out through my feet. Can you feel it?"

Letta shook her head. "Shit. Don't feel nothing but…" She gulped.

"Panic. I know. Take a deep breath. You ain't alone anymore. We got your back. Here." He pulled her hand down toward the ground. "Feel this. Earth absorbs power. You can't keep it, you gotta give it back. Redirect it into the Cobain. It's like a river of Earth. It absorbs excess energy and moves it all over the world. It can take anything you give it. You gotta either give it back or channel it. You can't keep it."

"That's what he said. Still don't make no sense."

The man frowned. "Who?"

"The guy with fire eyes." Letta struggled to catch her breath. "Big. Flames. Chaos."

He looked into the distance as if expecting to see fire, then shrugged. "Here." He placed her palm down, then his own covered hers. She felt it then, like a stream that flowed over smooth rocks. Only instead of water, pebbles moved like the sand in an hourglass. Power trickled through his hands, her fingers, and into the ground below where it spread out. Now that she knew what to look for, she sensed a tingle coming back up through her feet.

"It's coming back."

"Nah. It's just the flow of the Cobain. You don't gotta take. It's always there, but it can just flow by 'til you need it. Now, let a bit more go."

She pictured the sponge again, but nothing happened. The trickle remained small, unsteady.

"Not like that. You gotta let it go. You try to hold back. It won't hurt, and it won't drain you. Trust it."

"I can't do it without the dagger."

He laughed. "You don't need no dagger. You just need you. And a bit of ground. Think of it like a lightning rod. You're the rod, and it's your job to shoot the energy down into the ground to disperse it. Here, I'll get you started."

Her fingers tingled, and suddenly she felt invaded by something that moved through her skin like molasses on a hot day. It was nothing like the fire man had done. It eased and comforted. Like a full body massage. It poured over her body, through her hand, and into the ground. The trickle became a stream, which turned into a roaring river. She opened her eyes and looked at her hand. It pulsed with the strange glow of before, but no arc to the ground. No lightning. And it didn't hurt. Her body felt like it did at the end of a long work out. Fatigued. Relaxed.

"Now, you take it." The man lifted his hand.

She started to protest, but as his power or energy left her, the river rushed in to fill the gaps. It took her anger and energy and fed the earth with it. The ground stopped shaking. No more bricks fell. As the last bit released through her fingertips, the earth sighed and stilled. Silence descended, deafening after so much noise. Only a distant moan, and a few sobs, broke the stillness.

She lifted her hand and stared at it. It looked just as it always had. She glanced around at the park. It looked more like the demolition site now. Dust still filled the air, sparkling in the early morning sun. Chunks of mortar, bricks, asphalt, and trash littered the ground. Mounds of stones, some crushed to pebbles, other still large pieces of what used to be building, lay scattered. Nothing had been spared. One of the abandoned warehouses had been reduced to a pile of rubbish. The church appeared mostly intact, though the steeple had toppled and the porch evaporated. The other warehouse remained remarkably untouched. The street... She gulped. *No more street.*

"Holy fuck." Letta sat back on her heels.

The man next to her stood and looked around. "Yeah." He held out his hand to help her up. "I'm Alex."

"Letta." Once on her feet, she looked behind her to see the entire row of houses destroyed. They all seemed to have relocated into giant piles in the park. "Shit."

I did this. Me. Oh sweet mother of... I'm a monster. She looked down at her hands, disbelief fighting with horror for the top spot in her mind.

"Hey, now, don't go getting all worked up again." Alex touched her arm. "I promise, it gets better. Got me? It gets better."

She stared at him. "How the hell am I gonna make this better?"

"With a little help from friends." The feminine voice called from across the park. Letta looked to see the woman kneeling next to Donna Ray, who lay on her side moaning. Blood dripped from a gash over one eye, and a large bruise already formed on her cheek. Her legs lay at odd angles, one of them bending mid-calf where no leg had any right to bend.

"Fuck me." Letta rubbed her face, trying to wash away the last few minutes, but unable to get the image of Kia and Rook out of her mind. She looked back where the air tunnel had been. Nothing. "Shit."

"Daric, can you bring Chloe and maybe Calliope? I think underneath all this most of them still live. Barely. If we can get help in time." The woman stood and glanced to a soldier standing nearby. "Try to locate the rest. I can't tell how many. Ten? Maybe fifteen? And someone try to clear that guy, though I think it's too late." She pointed at a foot extending out from under what looked like concrete steps. The man nodded, and began issuing orders to others. They spread out, their white uniforms creating bright spots in the dirty air.

Daric kissed the woman's cheek. "Just watch your back. She won't be the only unstable person in this area right now." He waved a hand. In the air next to him, a wiggling, shimmering hole appeared. Letta took a step toward it, confused. Inside, she saw some sort of hall, but it wasn't the one she'd seen before. Daric stepped into it and out the other side, the hole snapping shut behind him as though it'd never been.

Letta pointed. "How do I do that?"

The woman worked her way across some of the rubble to stand closer to Letta and Alex. "With practice. Lots of practice.

Though…" She frowned. "I'm not sure you'll be able to. Alex, what do you think? All Earth? I don't feel…" The woman tilted her head, as though listening.

Alex grinned reassuringly at Letta. "Definitely mostly Earth. Maybe a bit of something else. Hard to tell. She was so overloaded, and it's all kinds of whacked right now. It might take time for the minor one to show with all that."

"Maybe." The woman gave Letta an appraising look. "She doesn't look like she's been overloaded."

"Look, whoever you are, I need to make one of those tunnel things. I have to…"

"Explain what went on here. Besides the obvious." The woman smiled, but her eyes turned serious and commanding. Even standing on a pile of rubble in jeans and a tank top, Letta knew this woman was used to being in charge. "What made you panic, this last time?"

"That weren't no panic." Letta thrust out her chin. Even if deep inside she knew it had been sheer terror, she wasn't about to admit it. Not to strangers anyway. "And who the hell are you?"

The woman grunted, though Letta wasn't sure if it was amusement or irritation. "She's me. Great."

Beside her, Alex snorted. "Letta, Tarian. Tarian, Letta. Now maybe answer the question. Is whatever made you panic gonna come back?"

Letta rubbed her face. Exhaustion crept up and hugged her tight, now that the buildings had stopped exploding. "He ain't coming back. Though…" She trailed off. The impact of all that happened in the last few minutes slammed into her. *Kia's gone. All the girls he took. The park…the buildings…I did that.* She groaned, her knees threatening to buckle. *And he wants me too. Wait one minute, then bring her. What happens when Carl don't show? It's gotta be more than a minute, now.*

"Wish Calli would hurry up. Could use her right now," Tarian muttered. "Let's keep it simple. Who's he? And where did he go?"

Letta dropped her hands from her face and glared at the woman. "If I knew that, I'd be there, not here. He went through one of them tunnels in the air. It closed before I could follow."

Tarian glanced at Alex. "I don't feel it now, do you? Though I do feel..." Tarian looked around, peering into the dusty air. "It feels..."

"What?" Alex looked in the same direction.

Letta caught a flash of fire in the dust, then it vanished.

Tarian's eyes narrowed as she studied the area. Finally she shook her head. She mumbled something under her breath that sounded like an epithet regarding men. "Nothing. Never mind." Tarian turned back to Letta. "I can help, if you'll let me. Who is this guy, and why are you chasing him?"

Letta crossed her arms, exhaustion, hunger, and anger at war in her chest. This felt worse than talking to the brass. "He's my suspect. Rook. He traffics young girls, sells... He has to be stopped. He..." She gulped, willing the panic she felt at losing Kia to take a back seat. "I was supposed to bring back the intel."

"But instead you..." Tarian's lips twitched as if she suppressed a smile.

Letta kicked at a small stone near her foot. "He had it all planned out. Girls, gathered during the storm in the park. Had 'em stand in the rain, same as me, then when it was done he snatched them outta thin air through one of them tunnels. Last one he grabbed was Kia. Carl was..." Letta looked around and spotted Carl's body being dragged from under a pile of rubble. "I was supposed to be the last. I tried to stop him. Threw a dagger at him, but it didn't even slow him down. He has Kia. Hundreds of others. I gotta find them."

"Why during the storm?" Alex glanced at Tarian.

"He steals power." Letta rubbed her arms, remembering how it had felt. "He stole from me. But then Craig came, and I fell…"

"Craig?" Tarian glanced down at the gargoyle shadowing her. She put a hand out, and he grasped it.

Letta watched her face change expressions as they obviously communicated. When they were done, the look Tarian gave her was impossible to decipher. *Her body says she wants to fight, but her eyes say something else.*

"Alex, we have a serious problem."

"Worse than a bastard stealing young girls?"

Tarian pressed her lips together. "That's not an ordinary dagger she's talking about. It's the Earth Artifact. The Caraigg gave it to her to help her learn to channel. But they don't think she has bound it yet."

"What?" Letta glanced from one to the other.

"The bastard can use it, if he's got Earth. Which, if he's stealing power, he does." Alex clenched his fists.

"Maybe not. Fire returned to Macari every time she lost it, until she was able to bind it."

"Fire?" Letta looked from one to the other, trying to make sense of the conversation that refused to make sense. "You mean that guy with flames for eyes? He didn't do nothing. Well, he sorta helped me. But he didn't take the girls. He ain't with Rook."

The way Tarian and Alex stared at her, Letta was sure they were about to jump down her throat. But when Tarian spoke, her voice was calm, if not her body language.

"Lasair *was* here. I knew I smelled him." Tarian squinted into the distance as if she expected him to be standing there. "Great. Everything's falling to shit. We're all one plane now." She muttered the words.

"Look, can we focus? I gotta get to Kia. Every second…He could be…" Letta stomped a foot. "I can't just sit here and do nothing. And I can't call for backup now. No power. No phones. They got a mess to deal with. They won't spare boots for this. And they wouldn't believe me anyway. "

Tarian glanced around and began to walk a circle around the area. "Did Rook touch anything? A rock? Tree?"

Letta followed her, confused. "Don't think so. Just Kia. And he took her with him." She struggled to remember the exact sequence of events. Had he touched anything? *Weren't nothing to touch. It all happened…*

"He made the table melt, but he didn't touch it." She pointed at the puddle of hard metal barely visible now under all the rubble. "He just waved a hand at it. I don't think he touched anything. He told Carl to grab me and follow. But then…"

"You lost it." Alex supplied.

"Crap." Tarian muttered something unintelligible. When Tarian finally stopped scouting, her expression mirrored Letta's own frustration. "Nothing here to track. The portal is too long gone. Can't even tell where it was. You get anything, Alex? He's Earth. Maybe he left a mark?"

Alex shook his head. He scuffed at the ground with his foot. "Nada. Maybe the Caraigg?"

Tarian bit her lip. "They weren't here. They don't know. They have scouts out, but he could be anywhere. Without someone expending a ton of energy, it'll take them a while to find him."

19

LETTA THOUGHT OVER the recent events, looking for a clue. Some indication, however slight, of where Rook might be. "What's it mean, to castle? In chess, I mean."

Tarian frowned in confusion.

Alex gestured with his hands, demonstrating. "The king and the rook switch places. It's used to get the king out of check, sometimes. Other times to put the rook in play. Why?"

"That's what Rook did. He said 'castle' and Carl started to protest, then Carl handed Kia over to Rook, Rook went through the tunnel, and Carl stayed to deal with me. That's when I threw the dagger at Rook."

"Wait. You threw it?" Tarian's voice rose. "You threw an artifact, like a weapon?"

"It's a dagger, ain't it? I lost my gun, I had to do something."

Alex scrubbed at his hair. "Did you hit him?"

"Yeah, back left shoulder. Bled a lot. Hope it hurt like hell."

Alex looked at her with an almost admiring look. "Damn. Tari, what happens if an artifact stabs someone?"

Tarian looked thoughtful. When she answered, her voice was

low and controlled. "I have no idea. I hope it doesn't…Would it make it easier to bind? Damn, we need Calli." She looked around as if expecting someone to step out of the dust.

"What's this binding thing?" Letta said.

Tarian rubbed the back of her neck as if the words caused her physical pain. "When an artifact is given to someone, they must bind with it to invoke the full power. Once you've bound an artifact, it will be the best friend you've ever had. It'll respond to your needs, even anticipate them. It'll always act to protect you, and itself."

She tapped her chest. It seemed an unconscious move, as though she were used to grabbing something there so often she no longer thought about it. "A bound artifact will magnify your power to create something like synergy. You'd be able to accomplish all kinds of things you wouldn't normally be able to. Like having a super boosted engine in a car or a nuclear bomb at your disposal. And it'll remain yours until the bond is broken."

Letta swallowed. "What breaks the bond?"

Tarian flattened her palm against her chest. "Death."

"And if Rook's done this…binding…what then?"

"If he can steal power, and he has plenty of girls with overloads of new magic…" Tarian paused. "Let's hope he hasn't. Let's hope the artifact won't let him. They do have a mind of their own."

Letta thought of the consequences. Rook, with a nuclear bomb of energy at his disposal. "Let's get another one. Fight fire with fire."

Alex choked out a laugh. "They're not something you buy in the corner store. There's only four. And you don't wanna fight fire with fire. You wanna fight Earth with Water."

Four artifacts. Now Rook has one. He'll be unstoppable. "Make a tunnel. I'll go after this bastard." Letta pointed at the air. "Do it now. He has Kia and hundreds of others. The longer we wait…"

"I can't. I have to know where we're going." Tarian's eyes flashed. "If he didn't touch anything here, then there's no way for me to track him."

"Carl's the king in this game, right? We always thought he was the leader, 'til now. He's definitely been in that hallway where Rook took Kia and the others. Can't you use him? He touched something around here. Had to. Like them rocks." She pointed at the boulders that had crushed the man.

"The dead can't be tracked, Letta." Tarian stared at the body lying a few feet away. "Do you really think Carl is still the king? It seems to me that Rook has changed the game. I've faced this type before. Rook is after power, and now he doesn't think he needs to hide. Those girls he stole must leave him feeling pretty damn smug. He has the upper hand, and he knows it. Carl was just a pawn in king's clothing."

The words, so similar to what Carl had whispered to her in the bar, made Letta's heart sink. "There's gotta be something. He can't be that far."

"He could be a world away, Letta. Travel portals don't have limits." The patient, cold tone of the words set Letta's blood boiling.

Letta ground her teeth. "So you can't help. What the fuck is magic for if you can't use it when you need to?"

Tarian glared. "It's not perfect, that's for sure. But it's a hell of a lot better than the nothing you had before the magic fell. You just need to know how to use it."

"Yeah, look where that got you." Letta pointed at Tarian, anger building. "You mighta kept a few bricks from falling, but you didn't get here in time to stop anything else. You're just as bad as the brass. Day late, dollar short, full of shit. What good is your magic? Gimme a gun any day. If I'd had a gun, the bastard'd be dead and Kia would…she'd…"

Alex held out his hands in a "calm down" gesture, but Tarian stomped a foot, her eyes blazing. "What good is my magic? Got news for you, it's your magic too. It's landed on your head whether you want to accept it or not. And that is exactly why Rook has the dagger. Because you can't accept what you are." The last words seemed to drain Tarian's anger almost immediately. She paused, looking almost ashamed, then rubbed her face.

"This won't get us anywhere. We need a plan." Alex held out a hand to both of them, playing referee.

"Shame she can't track. She's held the artifact, she could use that," Tarian muttered. "Don't think she has any Air at all. So we can't travel my way either. She might be able to picture what she saw in the portal, but I'd never get a good enough fix to take us there."

"Not to mention you ain't going anywhere without backup." Alex raised his eyebrows, his voice stern.

Bet he says that a lot. In the brief time they'd been talking, Letta had noticed Tarian had that take-charge attitude. The kind that didn't like to sit back and wait. *Kinda like me. Shit.*

"I saw the tunnel. I saw where they went. How do I make one?" Letta stepped closer. "Show me."

Tarian shook her head. "Can't. I don't smell any Air in you at all. I get a metallic smell, like….iron, mixed with sea salt. Odd mix. No Air. You can't make a portal. You don't have the right elements for it. And I can't make it if I don't know where we're going. I can't track him because we haven't met and he didn't touch anything. Alex can't follow him because he didn't use Earth to travel. We can't track the portal because it's been closed too long." Tarian gave her a steady look. "I'm telling you all this because I know you won't just accept my word for it. I want you to understand why it's impossible for any of us to follow this guy. At least, right now."

Letta's pulse pounded harder with every sentence, every time she heard the word "can't." Once again, someone advocated she accept the inevitable. *Nothing you can do, Letta. Let it go. You're too young. Too inexperienced. Too weak.*

Fuck that.

She turned her back abruptly on the both of them, ignored the soldiers in white tending to the injured, and stomped over to where she'd seen the air tunnel.

It was a worm hole in the air, straight to the Exchange. I know that's where he is now. He'd take them to the place he sells them. She pictured it in her mind, the way the hall had looked. The way Kia looked as she scrambled away from Rook. The lights along the ceiling that looked more like those blue glowing balls than light bulbs. A long hallway with bars along one side and cages along the other. *It's a prison.* Shocked, she realized her brief glimpse had told her more than she knew. *Definitely a prison. Have to be an abandoned one.* But it could be anywhere.

"Letta, we'll find them. Come with us. We'll find a way to get them. I'll have Sentinels look for something connected to one of the girls he took, and the Caraigg are already looking for them." Tarian touched her arm softly. "They're Ancients. They'll find him."

Letta jerked her arm away, not wanting the sympathetic tone, the understanding, or the condescension she was sure was in there somewhere. A part of her recognized the stupid stubborn action, but the other part…the bigger part…just didn't care. She couldn't rely on strangers who couldn't seem to do a damn thing anyway. It was her job to see this through. More than that. It was her purpose. *I'm on my own. Like always.*

She closed her eyes and wished harder than she'd wished for anything that she could find a way to Kia. Figure a way to travel straight to her. Like she'd done to the coffee shop. Like Rook had done, with his air tunnel. *There has to be a way. There has to be. How the hell did I do it? Did the tree do it? The dagger?*

The river of power..the Cobain, Alex had called it…boiled just beneath the surface of the earth, waiting for her to grab it. Now that he'd had shown it to her, she realized it remained a constant torrent of energy and movement…a living thing that quested and provided. *Take me with you.* She pictured the hallway again. The stone floor. The curved stone walls. The red doors. And Kia. Letta's arms tingled as she focused on the girl, her wrist suddenly aching with longing for something that used to dangle from it. *The bracelet. She still has it.* The phantom remained on her wrist as a constant link to Kia. She sensed the girl, through it. Felt her panic and her desperation. *Oh god.* Fear stabbed into her heart and head, and knocked her to her knees. "He's got her, he's doing…he's hurting her. He's hurting her!" She cried out with the pain Kia felt as it ripped through her body.

"Letta!" Voices behind her. They meant nothing. They wanted to stop her. They wanted to plan.

"He's hurting her!" Letta pitched forward, thrusting her fingers into the ground. Hard, packed rock gave way beneath her fingers like quicksand. A sound filled her ears, rushing water and tumbling stones and a beat, like the heartbeat of the Earth itself. She grabbed at it, willing it to take her where she longed to go.

Her body sank into the ground even as hands tried to pull her away. They didn't stand a chance of stopping her as the power of Earth grabbed her body and thrust it into the river of power and down, into the blackness.

20

LETTA HELD HER breath as the blackness of Earth claimed her body and dragged her through a moving river of dirt, stone, roots, insects, creatures, and unidentifiable debris. It churned swiftly in what felt like a downward slope, tumbling as if it were water but with a rumbling grinding noise of thousands of stones rolling on top of each other. It reminded her of the buzz in her ears after a loud concert ended. Pinpricks of light danced in her eyes, like lanterns or fireflies. Then she realized she'd stopped breathing and gasped.

Instead of air, Letta drank in the stream of earth. She choked and thrashed, flailing arms and legs struggling against the stream, lungs struggling to breathe, trying desperately to stop moving, to get free. She pushed her hands out to the side, fingers reaching for anything that would stop her forward motion. The dirt tugged at her harder, faster. It pulled her deeper. She kicked, with no impact.

Chaos cannot be stopped. It can be channeled. She heard the words again as though the fire man stood right next to her. But he couldn't be. Nobody could be here. She'd sunk into the ground like a tiny raindrop in a giant sandbox. Gone so fast even the powerful people she'd left behind wouldn't be able to find her.

Frantic, she tried to move her arms and legs in a swimming motion. It didn't seem to help. Slowly, things changed around her, but it had nothing to do with her feeble actions. The dirt felt warmer. Squishier. It caressed her skin. Something flashed through her mind then. Images of trees and grass and plants growing. Of water seeping into the ground, to be drawn up by roots into the plants and then sent away into the atmosphere once again. A cycle that repeated and stretched for eternity. A whisper flitted through her ears.

Life.

The symbol on the dagger popped into her mind, a reminder of what she'd lost. It had represented that cycle, the intricate tree branches and roots swirling and pulsing around the stone as a representation of life itself. It seemed to be telling her something important. Something *vital.*

Let it flow. It's like trying to catch a waterfall. Can't be done. Instead, you gotta ride it. It flows in, then back out.

Remembering Alex's words, she did her best to relax. To go with the flow. The mere idea made her snort. *This ain't real. It can't be real.* She forced herself to breathe, even though every breath brought in a surge of Earth. It flowed into her lungs and rumbled through her body and somehow supplied what she needed. It sustained her body, and even the bruises she'd had felt healed. She took another deep breath of Earth and leaned back into it as though she floated on her back on a lazy river. Or rode the waves of the ocean. Once she stopped struggling, it felt peaceful. As though she'd finally found a place to simply *be.* She tilted her head back, arms wide, and let it flow around and through her.

As she sank into the comfort of Earth, colors began to whirl in her mind. At first, they flashed past, like a kaleidoscope. They began to take on shapes, human-like shapes. Finally, she felt herself plunge into a scene that felt like memory, but not one of her own. She found herself back in the park, dust still heavy in the air. She looked around, disoriented. *Is this real?* Nearby, she saw Tarian and Alex surrounded by a handful of the white soldiers. They looked like they were arguing, while two other women knelt by the injured, their hands hovering over the bodies and their faces intense. Tarian gestured toward Letta, and she jumped. "Hey, how'd I get back here?"

Tarian and Alex continued to argue, and nobody glanced in her direction. She moved closer to them and realized she heard nothing. They spoke, but no sound emerged.

Definitely not real. More like a hallucination.

She watched as the injured women were assisted to their feet and guards escorted Donna Ray like a prisoner. The look of defiance on her face told Letta what she needed to know. *She looks like she's under interrogation.* Tarian frowned, gestured to the guards, who stepped Donna Ray over to the air tunnel…*portal,* Letta corrected herself…and stepped through. Tarian gestured again, then she and Alex stepped through the portal as well.

The scene faded, replaced immediately by another. Letta took the entry far more gracefully and managed to keep her body relaxed. She found herself in the middle of a street lit by early dawn, surrounded by a squad of beat cops. Next to her, Shelley barked orders. The group split up, heading off in twos and threes with radios at the ready. Letta glanced toward the nearby street sign. They were two blocks away from the park. *They're probably looking into the mess I made. So much noise! It had to draw attention. But they won't find anything. Nothing left to find. Just babbling women and a dead guy.* Shelley pulled out her cell phone and glared at it, then shoved it back in her pocket and turned to give more instructions to someone. Letta shook her head. *She's still looking for me to check in, but there's no signal.* It made her smile that Shelley sent in the troops to check the park. Backup was coming. *Too little, too late.*

Letta turned away, and the scene faded. She stepped immediately into a scene that chilled her bones. Rook stood next to a stained mattress, staring down at Kia. He held a hand out, but other than Kia scrambling away from him nothing else happened. Letta's heart pounded as the scene continued. She knew what the bed meant. Knew what Rook did to the girls he took. Knew what he hand in mind for Kia. Her heart couldn't stand it.

Kia! She screamed, but no sound came out. By now she'd realized that the scenes showed life as it happened, right that moment. She'd witnessed people she knew. It was real, current, and maddening. It made her stomach turn and a hot pit of anger kindle deep inside. *Rook.* She wasn't gathering intel anymore. She focused on the bastard who'd done all those horrible things and let rage fill her with purpose.

Letta moved behind Rook and took a swing at him, but her fist sailed right through him. Rook held the dagger in one hand and ran his thumb over the edge of the blade. He touched Kia's arm, and she shrank away from him, terror in her eyes and tears pouring down her cheeks. Letta closed her eyes, wishing she were there. Not knowing how. When she opened them again, the scene had vanished.

No! Kia!

The Crebain thrust another scene at her before she had time to do more. Letta stumbled into a long hallway. Bar-covered windows extended down the left, while cage after cage lined the right. It looked like an old prison. She stepped forward, trying to see every detail. An exit sign glinted in the distance. On the wall behind her, a sign proclaimed visiting hours for Chochran Correctional Facility.

Her breath caught. She knew the place. It was an abandoned prison not two hours from Philly. The kind of place mothers used to frighten children away from dangerous things. Ghosts of violent criminals supposedly haunted the place, and the grounds remained a fortress keeping the outside world away. She'd driven past it several times, but had never seen the inside. It was just trees and a long stretch of wall that graffiti didn't touch. Her gut told her if she could see inside it, really *see*, she could travel there. She'd done it to get to PJs without realizing it. She scrutinized the scene, searing every detail in her mind to use as a focus for travel.

Letta ran her hand along the bars. Her fingers passed through them. She was a ghost in this place. Pitiful wails echoed in the air, coming from multiple sources down the long stretch of cells. She nearly gagged at the stench of human waste. She stepped close to the bars and peered in.

The first cell must have originally been intended for two. Small bunk beds hung from the wall on one side. A steel toilet hung off the back wall. Nothing else but girls of varying ages. She tried to count. *Four on top, five on bottom.* She did a quick scan of the floor. *Eight on the floor. 17. In one cell.* They barely had room to sit, some holding smaller girls in their laps. All looked straight ahead with blank stares.

She pressed her lips together and moved on.

The next cell held only five girls, all of whom looked under the age of ten. She paused, studying them, but didn't see any familiar faces. Some of the crying she'd heard issued from a small girl, about five years old, who huddled alone on the bottom bunk. Her eyes were large and stared at nothing. The other four clustered together on the opposite side as far away from the crying girl as they could get. They stared at her with wide-eyed terror. The smell of burnt flesh wafted through the bars. Letta frowned at that and tried to see further into the dim space. The mattress looked charred, with holes in it where there'd obviously been a fire. Next to the crying girl lay the black remains of another.

Letta stifled the scream building in her throat. Hurriedly she backed away and continued down the hall.

Cell after cell, group after group. By the time she reached the end of the hallway, she felt numb and exhausted. By her count, there were over two hundred girls, ranging in age from three years old to early twenties. Half seemed to be the new recruits, fresh from the park. They wore the cleanest clothes and still had fight in them, pounding on the bars and screaming occasionally. Of all the cells, only the one had a corpse. A door of bars at the end of the hallway showed her that the place continued. She stepped through and found another hallway that connected two more. It formed at least three rows of cells.

Letta hesitated, not wanting to see more. The Exchange was so much bigger than they'd thought. Than she'd planned. Bile rose in her throat as she thought about how many girls must be in this place. How long they'd been here. What they'd endured already. She forced herself to continue down the next row of cells. She realized this hallway must be the showroom, because the first two cells were decorated. Signs above them declared the merchandise within and the pricing. The cells here weren't as crowded, the first two holding only three each. As she studied them, she thought the other hallway would be preferable. It might be crowded over there, but here, hope had been abandoned.

In the first cell, the bunk beds and the toilets had been removed. Three girls, all around fourteen, were naked, each one chained to a wall, arms and legs spread wide. The sign on the cell proclaimed them experienced and available for S&M. Whips lay in one corner, along with other instruments of torture. Each girl looked bruised, with cuts and marks along portions of her body. Their breasts looked to have received the most attention. One of them appeared to be missing her nipples. Letta swallowed against the bile rising in her throat and shifted her eyes to the next cell.

In the next, three white girls about ten years old lay sleeping on a bed. They didn't show signs of abuse. Letta glanced up at the sign overhead and felt a chill run through her.

"Fresh, healthy organs." Underneath, a list of blood types and prices for various body parts. They were destined to be transplant donors for the wealthy. Letta rubbed her face, scrubbing at her eyes. She'd never feel clean again. Never. She moved on to the next cell.

Four girls, three white and one Hispanic, all about fourteen or fifteen, sat on the two bunk beds. All four looked about eight months pregnant. The sign above the cell proclaimed the price for each baby, including one who carried twins. Next to the price list, three were marked "sold."

Letta shuffled down the rest of the hallway, numb. Nothing she'd pictured even came close to the reality of The Exchange. Toward the end of the hallway, she stopped underneath signs that pointed the way to rooms for filming, for "recreation," and for "exploration." She wasn't sure she even wanted to know what that meant. *How many more are here? How many have been through and gone?*

She thought back to the cell with the burnt corpse and doubled over, heaving out bile onto the filthy metal floor.

Letta wiped her mouth and turned, intending to walk back down the hallway. As she took the first step, the scene dissolved, depositing her back in the flow of Earth. She relaxed into it with relief. Glad she couldn't smell the place anymore. Glad she didn't have to witness it. Angry that it existed at all. She traveled with the flow, speeding toward nothing, numb from the experience of what she'd seen. *So many.* Rook had made quite the haul in the park today. Including Kia. *He has her alone, in a room, not a cell. There's more to the place. More to the operation. He's…he has Kia. Oh.. Jesus…what's he doing to her?*

That he'd pulled her aside meant he intended something unique. Something he didn't do with just everyone. Something worse than the cells she'd seen. Hate bloomed inside her as she thought of what that might be. Her mind couldn't even picture it. *She's only twelve.*

Letta thrust her hands into the tumbling rock, trying to slow her progress. She felt like a worm, moving through it but not swallowed by it. No boat required, just sailing along on a dirt river. She had no other word for it. Though it felt more like she slithered through a tunnel of some sort.

Maybe it's like the tunnel in air. But how do I direct where I come out? Damn bitch didn't tell me how it works. Just said I couldn't. Well, I'm doing it now, ain't I? Doin' something. Don't know what, but it's something. She felt more connected to something bigger than herself than she ever had before. The enormous depth of it, the *life* that expanded around her, made her want to cry and sing at the same time. She'd never believed in religion. Never believed in God. He'd deserted her and her family a long, long time ago, if he'd ever existed. But this…this was *real.* Truth. A natural high she didn't want to come down from. It gave her courage and strength. *I can do this. I can save Kia. Save them all.*

More visions assaulted her, but she ignored them, letting them blur together into a stream of consciousness that just reaffirmed her determination. She focused instead on the bracelet and the stone she'd shaped. She remembered the moment she'd whispered to it, asked what it wanted, and then delivered it. *How do I get to you?* Letta's wrist burned where the bracelet should be. *I'm coming, Kia. Hold on, baby. I'm coming. Dammit, I'm coming!* She focused all her attention and soul on the location of the bracelet. *Show me.* She forced herself to picture Kia on that bed. Forced herself to really *see* it. Willed herself to be right there, in between Kia and Rook. To protect her. To save her. To save…everyone.

Take me! She commanded the earth around her.

The Crebain shifted, so subtle a movement she almost missed it. Instead of drifting down, her path diverged upward. The visions that assaulted the back of her mind fell away, and the dirt itself felt lighter, thinner. As if she were coming up for air after a long time under water. It wasn't until she broke through the ceiling that she realized just how fast she'd been moving. Her head hit the crust of Earth and shattered it. The ground around her erupted and spit her out into bright light and hard stone floor. She landed on her back, the wind thrust out of her. She coughed, rolled, and came up to her knees to find herself exactly where she'd wanted to be.

She stood slowly, bringing her body up to a fighting stance on instinct. Behind her, Kia whimpered. In front of her, Rook stood with the dagger drawn up, ready to strike, shock in his startling gray eyes.

21

LETTA STARED INTO Rook's eyes, absorbing the shock and consternation in them. She watched his expression slowly shift from surprise, to comprehension, to calculation in the space of a heartbeat. Her pulse slowed and relaxed, in direct odds with the situation. She saw his arms tense, the muscles contract as he prepared to attack. His mouth opened slightly. Everything felt slow, deliberate; each motion exaggerated as if a film had been slowed to quarter speed.

Something crackled, snapped, and crawled over and into her skin. She knew it, now. The sleazy feel of it. The invasive way it licked at her flesh. *Magic.* But before it did much of anything, it fizzled. Her own power, the steady hum of it that she'd come to expect in her chest, dimmed. Power swirled around them, then fell like so much dust.

Rook's look of confusion matched her own. His gaze flicked from her, to Kia, then to the dagger he still held aloft. When she'd arrived, the dagger had been glowing. But now it looked like nothing more than a fancy carved rock.

Rook took two slow steps back, until his back pressed against the wall opposite Kia. Letta slogged to the center of the room, slow and sluggish. She kept her body between him and Kia. She tensed and tried to find the Crebain beneath her feet, to reassure herself it still existed, but felt nothing. Her connection to magic had been severed. *No, not gone. Just wrapped in something.* It felt cocooned off, like something held it in a box. There, but unavailable. Not without opening the box. Time remained slowed.

What the…Is he doing this? One look at Rook's frustrated eyes told her he wasn't. That only left one other possibility. *Two. Either it's Kia doing this somehow. Or it's the dagger. Artifact. Whatever.*

"That's mine." Letta tilted her chin at the artifact, then pointed at Kia. "So's she."

Rook lowered his arm, holding the dagger just in front of his chest. His eyes crinkled with amusement.

"I seen The Exchange. I know what you've been doing. I can prove it. You're going down."

She used her best cop voice. Low, steady, commanding. *This would sell better if I had my damn gun.*

"Letta, go away." Kia whimpered behind her. "Don't get hurt. It's my fault. All my fault."

"No, baby. It ain't. It's his." Letta didn't take her eyes off Rook.

"I'm afraid you've overstepped, Letta. You're only allowed one square."

"I ain't no pawn."

"Aren't you?" Rook raised the dagger again, as if ready to throw it. "I'm the one holding a weapon. You seem to have arrived unprepared."

Letta tensed, shifting her feet into a wider stance. She'd had years of street fighting and years of martial arts. "I don't need a weapon. I *am* the damn weapon. Put the dagger down. Get on your knees."

Rook laughed. "Make me."

Letta tried not to think about Kia strapped to the bed behind her. Kia, the next victim in a long line of girls. Kia…so much like her sister it hurt. She swallowed hard. "You got two seconds."

"Right." Rook stood up straighter. He kept the dagger pointed at her. "Whatever you're doing, you can't keep it up. Power uses physical energy. I'm sure you didn't know. Right now, your body is starting to feel the effects, I would imagine. You'll drop your focus soon. And with this little toy on my side, even your overload of power won't be enough. You should run before I find a cell for you. I have one perfect for someone like you. They'll find you particularly tasty, I think, in the dungeon. I've never had a police officer on display before."

"One." Letta flexed her hands, warming up. The motion seemed faster. Reality stretched and tightened. Like an extended rubber band, it felt near the breaking point.

Rook grinned. "You didn't see the dungeon. It's here, on this floor. Reserved for very special clientele. Listen. You can hear the sounds of pleasure across the hallway."

Letta lunged forward. Time snapped back into place with a rush that thrust her forward at double speed. Her shoulder connected with his gut and pushed him backward. Off balance, they both slammed into the wall. Pieces of stone flaked off, crumbling to the floor. Caught by surprise, Rook took the full brunt of the hit, the wind whooshing out of him. He grunted, then brought a knee up.

Letta dodged to the left. His knee grazed her side. She shuffled back in front of him, hands up in front of her face. He might be taller, but his slender figure and soft hands weren't used to hand-to-hand combat. *Soft. Weak spots. More focused on the dagger than protecting his nads.*

Letta danced on the balls of her feet. She jabbed several times in rapid succession, then sent a kick. He moved to block, but he'd anticipated a face strike. Her foot connected with his manhood and doubled him over in a cry of pain and anger.

She jogged back a few paces, regained her balance, and kicked. Rook ducked and rolled out of the way. Momentum spun her body. She let the motion take her, swirling around to face him just in time to block the dagger from striking her face. He punched with the other hand, connecting with her cheek hard enough for her to see a few stars. She swore as she ducked the dagger, tripping over the edge of the bed where Kia screamed.

"Letta! Get out of here! Please!" Kia screeched. "You gotta go, Letta. Go!"

"I ain't leaving." Letta moved to the side, turning her back to the door so Rook turned away from Kia. She didn't want him getting any ideas. *Keep his attention on me. All on me.* "Give it up, Rook. You ain't a fighter."

Rook lips formed a slimy thing that slid across his face into his eyes, making them sparkle with sleazy delight. "Soon, you'll take her place on the bed."

Letta dodged, then kicked, connecting with his gut enough to knock him backward a few steps. "Dickhead. I ain't no pawn in your stupid game."

She rushed forward, throwing her shoulder into his hunched form and ramming him back into the wall with a loud crushing sound. Pebbles fell around them, creating a small cloud of dust that made her cough.

"I can turn anything into a queen, once I knock it off the board. You'd make an excellent one, I think, once trained."

"Your king is dead, you moron. Game over. You lose." She danced back out of the way of his fist and the swoosh of the dagger. "Ain't you ever been in a knife fight? You can't hold it like that." She kicked, hitting his wrist with a satisfying crunch. The dagger fell out of his hand and clattered to the stone floor.

They both lunged after it. Rook fell onto it first. Letta dove into him, shoving his body aside with her momentum. She realized her mistake a second before the pain shot through her stomach. For a second she couldn't breathe as it rushed through her, temporarily blinding her to anything but searing heat.

"Is this how I should use it?" Rook whispered, a triumphant gleam in his eyes. "Or this?" He twisted the dagger embedded in her stomach, rocketing her body into a spasm that buckled her knees. She collapsed on top of him, her body pressed into his fist and the dagger. She felt it inside her, a living thing that snaked into her insides and twisted them.

22

LETTA GASPED, UNABLE to stop the tears.

Kia.

"Now drop your guard. Let me have your power, before it leaves with your life." Rook held her close to him, one arm around her back, pushing her into the dagger.

"Mother. Fucker." She gasped. Life leaked out through the hole, and there was no way to stop it.

"Yes. I suppose I have." Rook chuckled, an evil sound that ground into her ears and pounded into her heart. "Though I prefer them younger, some have managed to procreate before I find them. Creating more for me. I don't mind." He twisted the dagger, sending another lightning flash of heat through her body.

Letta moaned, a sound that lit Rook's eyes more than anything else had.

"Drop the guard. I'll make you my queen." His lips teased hers, his breath hot and rancid on her cheeks.

She stared at him, her body twitching in response to the pain but her mind racing. *What guard? What the hell is he talking about? I'm not doing anything. And he's not doing it either. The dagger...*

With the dagger embedded in her stomach and sandwiched between their bodies, she couldn't look to see if it glowed. She felt the pain. Felt her life ebbing away. Felt the heat inside her. Felt…

Her mind drifted to the cave where she'd first taken the dagger. *Artifact.* It had been a living thing in her hands. The vines twined around it moved in response to an unseen force. The power filled her and drained her at the same time. It relieved the pressure in her head, the overload on her body. It had healed her wounds.

Healed.

It was a life force all its own. She pictured it, inside her. Vines reaching out into her body. Spreading. Connecting with her veins. Infiltrating the blood and growing. Reaching into places that scared her. Heart. Lungs.

Accept.

The word echoed around her mind.

Never. She wouldn't accept death. Not now. *Not now!*

Accept. The whisper insisted. Her stomach convulsed, and she heaved. Rook made a sound of disgust and threw her off him. Her body fell to the floor with a sickening thud and then rolled onto her side.

The dagger clinked against the stone floor. Her hand reached for it, closed around the round end that barely protruded from her body. He'd sunk it all the way in. It had to have penetrated vital organs. It was slick with blood, the carvings obscured by the sticky, warm liquid. She closed her fist around it and closed her eyes. Vines entwined around her vision and stole her away.

The jolt of pain in her shoulder brought her awareness back to the present. Rook dragged her by one arm, which felt as though it had dislocated. He tugged her through the door, into the hallway. She managed to raise her head enough to see Kia on the bed. *He took her. He's done it. He stole her power.* She had enough time to notice that Kia was still dressed. He hadn't done…other things. *Small comfort.* Her tiny body lay huddled on its side, eyes closed, one arm thrust out at an awkward angle, a bruise blooming on her cheek. *Bastard.*

Vines pushed through her arms and legs, wrapped around her muscles, burned into her flesh. As Rook dragged her down the hallway, she felt the dagger warm her insides. Heat raced through, everywhere the vines touched, little tiny jabs of a million needles. Ants crawled under her skin. The further they went, the more power surged through her body. Her own energy, lodged in her chest like a hard thing, broke free and raced toward her fingers, itching for release. She groaned as it pushed into her brain and pressurized her ears. *Not again.*

Accept.

The voice was louder now. No longer a whisper, it boomed in her ears as though shouted on the edge of a ravine that echoed the word over and over and over.

Accept.

The word reverberated and morphed into a new one. *Life.*

Inside her stomach, the dagger shifted. It wiggled, a live thing that writhed and infiltrated and demanded to be noticed. To be taken. She put her palm on it, a feeble thought that maybe, if she pushed it all the way in, it'd all be over. She'd accept it into her body. Her body recoiled at the idea. Accepting it meant death. Not life. *No.*

Rook dropped her onto the floor and kicked her legs out of his way. He stood above her, studying her as if she were an insect. She noticed his broken nose and the awkward way he held his arm. Satisfaction flared, then died as he raised a hand over her and his power began to swirl around her.

This time, Letta knew exactly what he planned to do. She saw an odd brown filament of light that extended from his hand to her body. It stretched around her like a net, and once it latched onto her, it began to pull and her own power drained into it. She saw it travel back up the brown beam, a green tone that blended with it and joined his until it reached his hand and lurched into his body. A green glow formed around him.

He's…taking…magic.

The dagger twitched inside her.

Accept.

The calm voice soothed. It promised resolution to her problems. Provided the solution, if only she'd reach for it. She squeezed the handle of the dagger and closed her eyes.

In her mind, she opened her arms. She stopped fighting. Even as her power drained away, she opened her body to be a conduit. To allow the energy from all around her, the very rocks, to take her body and use it. She couldn't fight magic. Didn't want to. She'd experienced more pain and joy in the last twenty-four hours than she'd witnessed in her entire life. The connection to the rock beneath her was a real, visceral, vibrant thing, and she didn't want to ignore it anymore. She embraced it. Welcomed it. *Take me.* She meant for the earth to swallow her. To end her pain. To let her die and join the soil.

Rook dropped to his knees, wide with excitement. "Shame. I'd like to keep you. But I see in your eyes that your time on the board is done. Such is the game." He put both hands on her face, caressing her cheeks almost like a lover. Through his fingers, she felt the last of her power drain, leaving her body for his. Taking any hope she had with it. Leaving her empty and hollow inside.

Too late.

"Checkmate." Rook's gloating smile raked her body, and she knew he was right.

He'd won.

23

LETTA BURBLED AT Rook, whose look of triumph filled her with a hate so deep it burned with the fire of a million suns. The pain of it shot through her skull, magnifying the odd light in the hallway until it blinded her. Searing heat traveled from her stomach through the rest of her body to join the blinding light until all she knew was pain.

Accept. Life.

The thought, warm and concerned, wasn't her own.

Death. She thought the word, since her lips refused to move. It beat at her brain until she cried out against it.

Earth. Life. Death.

The words chased each other around and around, forming nonsense sounds. They blended with the light in her mind. Dark spots mixed with light until they merged and formed shadows. They grew until they towered over her, shadows that looked human. That looked…like her. Letta stared up at them. They had her face. Three identical faces stared back at her. They looked expectant. They waited for her to do something. To decide…something.

Who are you? Her thoughts circled around them, getting lost in the shadows and then repeated back to her as a question she really couldn't answer. *I don't know who I am anymore.*

More. More. More. More.

As the shadows stared at Letta, she noticed movement around them. Vines snaked along their feet, traveled up their legs. Within the vines, eyes blinked at her. Bulges in the floor grew into small stones with eyes that also blinked. It reminded her of Craig, and of the moment she'd taken the dagger. *Artifact.* Beneath her body the Crebain moved, constantly seeking, forever churning beneath the surface. All of it, alive.

I. Am. She stopped, realizing she had no idea how to finish the sentence. *Witch? Cop? Black? Confused? All of it?*

The shadows waited patiently. They didn't move. Didn't judge. Just waited.

I'm still alive. She said it with a sense of wonder.

Alive. Alive. Alife. Life. Life. Life.

How?

The shadows gestured as one toward the floor. Letta noticed the dagger laying there, sparkling. She patted her stomach, startled to find it whole and unmarked. Slowly she pushed herself upright and took the dagger. It moved in her hand, the vines snaking off it onto her arm. She let them travel over her, reveling in the heat and contentment they brought.

The dagger healed her. Somehow, it hadn't killed her but instead gave her something she didn't understand. The game wasn't over, after all. She clutched the dagger and looked to the shadows. They waited for acceptance, for her to declare once and for all that magic existed, and she wouldn't fight it anymore. She knew they wanted her. Knew the artifact demanded her acceptance. She knew, yet she hesitated.

Letta built her life on the idea that she would *not* accept what life threw at her. She did not accept the life of a street rat. She did not accept the path her mother took. She did not accept that Jenna was dead. But standing in a hallway inside her mind filled with shadows of herself, she had to wonder…when did not accepting less become not accepting anything at all? When did she turn into someone so inflexible? She was far too young to be bitter and closed off. Life had barely begun, really. If she said no to this, to the obvious gift being given, when would she ever be able to say yes?

Her thoughts flashed to The Exchange hallways. To the girl who'd incinerated her cellmate. To the ones shackled to the walls. The pregnant ones. The beaten, abused ones. The ones who'd lost all hope, and the ones who still railed against their circumstances. She thought of Kia, bound to the bed by cruel metal straps. Words circled through her mind, demanding to be said and heard.

I am Earth. I take Earth, and Earth takes me. I'll be one with Earth. I'll take magic, and I'll use it to save those who can't save themselves. She bowed her head to study the weapon in her hand. *I. Am. Earth.*

Her feet sank into the ground, and light particles rose like dust, coating everything. In a flash, the shadows were gone. The vines were gone. The pain returned, more intense than before. Letta groaned as it rushed through her once more. She curled her fingers around the dagger, still embedded in her stomach. *It wasn't real.* Disbelief and disappointment washed through her. She'd meant the words. They'd been right. She was sure of it. Yet here she lay on the floor, Rook a few feet away. Kia in the next room, injured. Maybe dead.

The image of one little girl who represented so much that she'd gladly trade her life for the possibility of saving Kia. And she'd failed. All she wanted was to save Kia. *Failed.*

A sudden release of pressure made Letta's ears pop. The draining sensation on her magic ended abruptly, as if someone had cut the string. A second passed. Two. A loud, frustrated scream. A small voice. Something soft hitting something hard.

Letta blinked, trying to clear her vision, but everything blurred. The light that had blinded her now seemed more like a soft glow, but it obscured whatever happened beyond. As she focused on it, she saw small spheres of green and blue circling at high speeds. They grew and pulsed, creating large bubbles that zoomed in rotation. She took a deep breath, and they surged toward her. She let it out, and they moved away, growing even larger.

The burn in her stomach shifted into a tight shaft of fire that crawled along her flesh. Letta clutched at it, the dagger protruding like an alien ready to be birthed into the world. It wiggled and shifted, working its way out of her body. When enough emerged, she grasped it with both hands. The spheres of light circled faster with each pull on the dagger.

Blood flowed freely as the tip of the dagger popped free. She let out a primal scream of pain. Bubbles rushed away from her body and exploded into the walls. The dagger fell from her fingers, clattering to the ground next to her. It no longer glowed, and the etching on the top looked faded. No vines moved along the hilt. Confused, she touched it with one finger, tracing the instrument of her death.

She gradually became aware of movement nearby. Kia had wrapped her arms around one of Rook's legs. Rook kicked, trying to shake the girl off. His scream of rage brought a quiver to Letta's lips.

"Kia," she whispered. She couldn't get enough breath to do more. Her body felt heavy. So very heavy. But her mind was clearing as the fog of pain lifted. She tried again. "Kia. Run."

Rook drew back a fist and crashed it into Kia's skull. The girl crumpled to the floor.

"Kia!" Letta groaned. She pushed, trying to roll over, but her body wouldn't obey. Tears burned her eyes as Rook struck the girl again, then dragged her from the ground by her neck. Letta's need to save Kia lit the fire in her stomach again, but this time instead of pain she felt the unmistakable surge of power. Immense power. The small stream inside her had turned into a raging river. She wanted to direct it at Rook. Blast him with something that would make him stop. Make this end. *Save Kia.*

The ground rumbled, mumbling a response. Letta put her palm flat on the stone floor and whispered, "Stop. Him."

The ground answered her call. It shifted, and a shaft of bubbling earth launched from under her palm toward Rook with the speed of a bullet. It formed a worm that lurched up from the floor and struck Rook with the force of a bullet, throwing him back several feet, slamming him into the far wall. He fell, stunned. Kia rolled to the side and lay still.

Letta looked at Kia. "Is she dead?"

Nothing answered, but through the stone Letta sensed a beat, steady and strong. *Kia's heartbeat.*

Buoyed by the thought that Kia still lived, Letta managed to get to hands and knees. With her palms on the floor, she stared at Rook and thought *prison.* In her mind she pictured stone walls surrounding him. Closing him in. Shafts of rock shot up from the floor and surrounded Rook. He stared at her in amazement as the walls formed a tight seal with him inside. She heard him scream as a rock from the ceiling crashed down to complete the small tomb.

Letta licked a spot of blood off her lips and laughed, then winced as her stomach muscles protested. She had him. "I got you, fucker!" she shouted, ignoring the tightness in her belly.

Sore muscles everywhere screamed at her as she got to her feet.
Strength slowly returned to her limbs. The hole in her stomach
had disappeared. Dried blood covered her clothes and skin, but
her body seemed healed. Even the dizziness had evaporated.
Everything looked even brighter to her eyes than before. The dim
light beamed like a spotlight. She stumbled her way to the newly
created tomb and knocked on the outside. "You. Are. Mine," she
growled, then whispered, "Thank you," to the stones that trapped
her quarry in place.

"Kia?" Letta called out as she moved around to the edge of
Rook's prison. It'd left only a small gap between it and the wall for
her to squeeze through. She shoved her body through it. Though
it ripped at her clothes and took her breath away, she managed
to wiggle through. It was darker on the other side. Too dark. She
squinted, searching for a shadowy lump on the floor. Nothing.

Letta pushed forward, gently tapping with her foot before
each step. When she encountered nothing but the far wall, she
dropped to hands and knees to search for Kia.

Nothing.

Heart racing, she spun to examine the stone prison. Where it
should be solid, a gaping hole leered at her.

Rook and Kia were gone.

24

LETTA STARED AT the hole, and at the empty space at her feet. No Rook. No Kia. No sign of where they'd gone. He'd taken the girl and simply vanished. The roaring in her ears matched the roar that escaped her lips as the realization settled in. Kia had vanished, and there was no way to follow. She stomped a foot and screamed her anger, cursing the very air that provided Rook life. The ground rumbled a reply, as if shaking its disapproval.

She slammed her fist into the nearest wall, giving it an extra kick of power from within. The wall shook and crumbled. Chunks of rock fell from overhead, landing in heaps of dust. Letta coughed and backed away, instantly regretting her temper and loss of control. Power streamed unchecked through her body. With her back to a wall that bucked and swayed, she did her best to contain it. This time, instead of keeping it inside, she followed Alex's advice and let it flow down through her feet, into the ground below, where it rippled out in waves instead of dissipating. The sturdy bedrock accepted the power and spread it, magnified it, until the walls and ceiling collapsed. Letta dodged to the side, narrowly avoiding a falling chunk of rock big enough to squash her flat.

She did her best to focus and calm her breathing, but the power kept coming, generated from the ache deep inside. She almost didn't care. *Let it fall. Let it all fall.* Destroying this place was the least she could do. Then she remembered the others still trapped in the rest of the prison. Shame flooded her cheeks. *Fucking temper.*

Remembering the dagger, she pushed through the debris that used to be the tomb she'd created for Rook and tumbled down the other side. The dagger winked at her from beneath a large rock. She shoved the rock aside and took the dagger, clutching it tightly with both hands. She fed it all the power that continued to rage inside her. It took, but didn't diminish. Not like before. The stone began to glow, but the energy raced unabated.

"Damn it!" Letta placed the dagger against the floor and continued to push as walls fell around her. Faint screams reached her, and she knew walls were coming down in more places than the hallway. Those girls had no way out. *Well, they do now.* Sunlight streamed through holes in the ceiling, making the dust in the air dance. The wall to her left had fallen enough to leave gaping holes to the dilapidated courtyard beyond. The former captives would at least be able to escape into that, and from there surely they'd find their way home. Eventually.

Kia wouldn't. Kia might be a thousand miles away by now. Letta squeezed her eyes shut to stop the flow of tears. *Think, Letta, think. Relax. Stow your temper. Focus on the problem. You need a plan. Kia needs me to have a plan. Focus. Focus, damn it!*

Gradually the floor stopped shaking, and things settled into relative quiet as she concentrated on solving the problem instead of venting anger. Her options weren't great. *I could try to get back to the park, find Tarian and Alex. They'd help. Bet they ain't there no more though. No idea how to find them. Not like I can call. Do they even use phones? Shit.*

She thought of her current surroundings. It didn't help. The prison had been abandoned as long as she could remember. Nothing around it for miles. And with the havoc magic created across the rest of the country, nobody would be checking on this place.

Could wait for Craig. Maybe they'd help. She immediately rejected the idea. It might take them hours to find her, even with the temper tantrum shouting her location. She didn't have that long to wait. Kia didn't have the time. Right now, Rook… She swallowed hard and shoved the thought aside. It wouldn't help to get lost in the what-ifs.

How the hell did he get out? She explored the area where Kia had been, now a mountain of rubble obscuring any marks Rook might have made. *He didn't dig out.* She glanced back at the destroyed tomb. *Or did he? If he made a hole in that, he could make a hole anywhere, just like I did.*

If he traveled through the ground, she had no idea how to follow. Not unless it showed her where the man went. She didn't know enough about how it all worked and had no time to learn.

"Fuck me."

The words were barely out of her mouth when she felt tingling along her arms and legs. A thousand tiny legs crawled over her skin and bound her body in a tight web of invisible string. Her body lifted, held in air by some force field, even as she struggled against it. Slowly she rotated until she faced the rest of the hallway. In front of her, a tall woman dressed in white robes hovered a few feet above the rubble. If she'd been religious, she'd have labeled the woman an angel. White light blazed from her face, hair, skin to surround the woman in an aura that should have meant peace. Lines around her hard blue eyes and the tight line of her mouth suggested something far different from angelic grace. *Dangerous.*

More deadly than Rook even dreamed of being. Letta shuddered at the coldness of her eyes, without a spec of humanity in them.

The woman stared back, clearly performing some sort of assessment of her own. She didn't speak. She might have looked like an angel, but this was the furthest thing from heavenly that Letta had ever seen.

The woman finally held out a hand, and the dagger flew through the invisible bands around Letta to the woman's palm like steel to a magnet.

"Hey, that's mine!" Letta struggled against her bonds, but they held tight.

The woman raised an eyebrow. "Be careful, human, or the bonds will cover what's left of you. You have no kinship with Air. Best you stay subservient, as you're meant to be." She turned the dagger over, studying the markings with a gleam of triumph that made Letta's blood run cold. "This is far too important an artifact to be in the hands of such as you. You were never meant to have power. Humans have so little idea what to do with it. It can only come to disaster."

The woman glanced around at the ruined prison walls. "This is what comes when balance is not present. When a gift is bestowed where it ought not to be. Corrupt power. It won't stop until the world lies in ruins. This." She held the dagger up. "Is the first step toward righting the wrong."

"Give. It. Back. Bitch." Letta growled the words, gritting her teeth against the frustration of being unable to fight.

The woman studied her, calculating eyes raking over Letta's body, stopping near her stomach. When she returned her gaze to Letta's, her look contained disgust and revulsion. "Power belongs to power." The woman flicked her hand at Letta and vanished, leaving Letta to stare at empty air.

She'd have thought it a hallucination, except that she remained trapped in an invisible cocoon that grew as she struggled. It reached up over her face, covering her eyes and mouth, sucking out the air like a plastic bag. She choked, and the struggle to get free became a desperate search for air. Her lungs burned as she fought for even a drop of something to breathe.

As her vision dimmed, Letta realized her feet were still not touching the floor. She couldn't talk to the rocks. Couldn't ask for help. But she had to try. No other choice. The dagger was gone.

25

HER THOUGHTS TURNED fuzzy and mangled. The dagger... She hadn't realized. Hadn't protected it. *Think, Letta. Think. You have power. Use it.* Her first moments of learning about her newfound abilities came back to her. *Earth provides, they said.*

Earth swallows Fire. Earth smothers Air. Earth uses Water. Earth provides in return.

Earth smothers Air.

Air.

She didn't understand it, but she acted on it. Her chest burned from lack of oxygen. Before, encased in Earth, she'd been able to breathe. It was a chance. She focused on the stream inside of her and pushed it down to the dirt and rocks. Pictured them covering her.

Dust rose in answer and showed her, pushing her body down to the ground with enough force to knock the wind out of her, if she'd had any. Everything grew foggy. She stopped struggling. No strength. No hope. Nobody knew where she was except the rocks. She lay still as dirt covered her body, burying her alive.

The dirt felt warm and comforting. Through it, she felt

sunshine streaming in and a sense of renewal that didn't make sense, but she held onto it. Inside, she felt the vines that had traveled through her veins. They brought oxygen to her lungs and cleared her head. They grew into the dirt around her and brought back life and hope.

Letta took a deep breath, an act that should have filled her lungs with dirt but instead filled them with sweet relief. She shifted and discovered her arms were no longer trapped. The invisible net evaporated. Pulse pounding, lungs no longer aching, she pushed her hands into the soil and shifted it, digging her way out of the burial mound. Dirt stuck to her sweaty skin as she worked her way free.

Letta stood on top of the mound that had answered her call for help and let the sun warm her face. "Thank you," she whispered. The relative quiet was only disturbed by the chirping of birds and the sound of distant voices. *The girls are free.* She turned in their direction, but didn't move off the mound of dirt. *Plan, Letta. What's the best move? Who needs help the most?*

She thought it over. Rook's recent captives were now free, and most likely able to make their own way since he hadn't had time to do anything worse than lock them up. Yet. At least most of them were able to get out on their own two feet. Hopefully they'd help the others who were in worse shape. Worst case, they'd report the events and eventually people would come to investigate. Rook wouldn't return here. He preferred the shadows, so this hidey hole was no use to him anymore. She absorbed the implications. She'd dismantled The Exchange. Her mind spun with the thought. *He's out of business. He's done.* She felt giddy enough to laugh out loud. She relished the moment. All those girls, saved. Countless more, too, because he'd have no business to need more. She thought of his next move, and stopped laughing.

He'll have others. A rat like that always has a place to hide, and he'd be a fool to have only one outlet for his business. Whatever he is, he's no fool. He'll need to regroup. He's lost his harem. His base. With the confusion, even his regular contacts will be out of touch, at least for a while. All he has is Kia. And he knows I'm hunting.

She swallowed at the lump that refused to go down. *Where the fuck would he go?* Her heart sank. She just didn't know enough. He'd been too well-hidden. She could guess why he wanted Kia. He'd taken girls with magic, and he'd obviously used them to feed his own power. So he'd use Kia to rebuild himself. Except...

He couldn't steal her power. He was trying, but it wasn't working. Maybe the dagger stopped him?

She shook her head. *The dagger didn't stop Rook from stealing my power, so it shouldn't have blocked him from Kia's. So what was wrong? Half the time she was out cold. Maybe his ability doesn't work if the person ain't awake?*

And that bitch who stole the dagger, who the fuck was that? Why'd she take it? Letta pondered that, and the weight of what it meant. The dagger was incredibly powerful. It'd saved her from certain death. It had infused her blood with the ability to use even more energy. It still ran through her body, a raging river waiting to be used, despite all that Rook had already taken. Though exhaustion threatened to take her, and her stomach complained at the lack of food, power coursing through her veins sustained her. At least for now. *Wonder how long I can keep this up. Every drug wears off eventually.* Beneath her feet rose whispers from the stone, and she *knew* that if she called it would answer. She knew it the way she knew the sun would rise and the homeless would bathe in Love fountain. But knowing that wasn't helping. What, exactly, would she ask them to do?

The dagger had to be very important. And it'd been given

to her, by the Craig. *Caraigg, not Craig. Get it right, Letta.* How angry would they be to find it missing? Could they take back the benefits? Was she even now in violation of the Agreement they'd set? Her blood ran cold at the thought. She'd forgotten about that. What, exactly, had she promised? *To learn. To let them teach. What else? Support the…Keeper. Shit. Tarian. Support Tarian. So ditching her in the park was probably not what they had in mind.*

She shook her head. Nothing she could do about it. She couldn't undo the past. She'd left the park. The dagger was gone. Kia and Rook were gone. Those were facts, and couldn't be changed. Better to focus on what she could do, instead of what she couldn't. *No idea who that bitch was or where she took the dagger. She's gone. It's gone. Gone. Gone. Gone.* As she thought about it, her stomach burned where the dagger had sunk deep into her body. She rubbed the tender, raw patch of skin. Lifting her now tattered shirt, she discovered the mark from the top of the dagger etched on her skin, a raw pink symbol against her deep brown. It pulsed under her fingers. As she traced the pattern, vines spread out from the mark across her stomach, down her arms. The lines were faint, a darker brown barely noticeable unless she looked close. They entwined around the mark she'd had done on her arm, for her sister, creating one big tattoo.

The mark on her stomach beat out a steady rhythm, and she felt a slight tug to the left. She turned, and it aligned with something in the distance. She *knew* the dagger lay in that direction. *So I can follow it. Like I followed the bracelet.* At the thought of the bracelet, she focused on her wrist and felt the twinge of a pull to the right.

Dagger to the left, Kia to the right. Stolen girls right here. No backup. No way to call for help. Fuck. Wonder if there's a way to call someone with magic? She just didn't know enough. But she'd never been one to let a little thing like that stop her from her goal. The real issue remained, which way to go first? The dagger held power she needed. The ability to help her deal with an overload, and the ability to heal. She needed the thing to face Rook. She had power, but he did too and he was a lot more experienced in using it. *And he can steal from others, so probably stronger too. He can probably do things I can't even imagine. I need that dagger to stand a chance.* But the fact remained; the woman who stole it obviously outmatched all of them. Letta wouldn't get it back without a fight, if at all.

In her mind, she weighed the two opponents side by side, and felt herself shrink in comparison. Outmatched, on both counts. Rook was the lesser of two evils, because she at least knew him and a little of how he operated. He stole power, something he did routinely because… She thought it out. *Because it wears off. He can't keep what he steals. It doesn't last forever, so he keeps a stable of people to drain like a damn magical vampire.* Knowing a weakness, no matter how slight, was a definite advantage. She thought of the woman in white. *No fucking clue. She has a weakness. Everyone does. But no way for me to figure it out before she slaughters me with that invisible whatever it was.*

Her thoughts circled in on the choice laying in front of her.

Dagger. Or Kia. Get help for myself, or get Rook.

She knew almost before she finished laying it out what her answer had to be. Letta focused on the ground, reaching for the stream she'd used to travel before. She closed her eyes and let her body merge with the soil, this time connecting to the Earth with purpose and intent, a vision of Kia and the bracelet foremost on her mind. When the stream embraced her, she let her body flow with it, moving so fast the visions that assaulted her shot past in a blur.

Where's the bracelet? An image emerged from the stream. A

slight shadow lay in a pool of darkness, beyond a glimmer of light. Just a shaft in the dark, but it illuminated walls of concrete and brick. Giant walls, high windows, and large doors. *A warehouse.* She studied the area, hunting for any detail that might be helpful. Two long panes of glass framed the doors. They'd been boarded over, but the one on the left sported one board at a jaunty angle. Someone had pushed it aside to be able to peer out. Painted a once vibrant red, it now looked beaten, with the local 5-0 mark on it in fading black. She knew that board. She knew exactly where she'd seen it.

The warehouse, the one still standing, next to the park. Surely Rook wouldn't go back… She thought it out. It made a great hiding place. With the chaos in the city, nobody would even glance at the lone remaining building standing on that block. They might marvel at it later. But it always had the "go away" vibe. Nobody went near it. Ever. *Now I know why. Rook.*

It was familiar to him, and secure. Nobody would think to look there, because nobody ever willingly went near it. Now she knew exactly where he usually stashed the girls he stole, before he took them to the prison. No wonder nobody ever saw him in the neighborhood. He was there, watching from the shadows of a building he'd set up to deliberately hide his movements. He'd used it any number of times, most likely. The least of which was when Kia and her cousin were taken from the park just outside. *How easy it must have been. Just hang there and grab them as they walk by. Or go to church.*

The thought of the now destroyed white receptacle of lies reminded her of Donna Ray. The woman ruled there and obviously used her magic to influence those around her. *She's the spider, calling to the fly. Rook used her to bring new girls to the area, and he used Carl to grab them.* It all fit. The puzzle made sense, creating a whole picture. The records of recent abductions were nothing compared to what Rook actually did. So many missing girls went unreported. It wasn't until Rook branched out to richer neighborhoods that anyone really noticed the pattern at all. *Slick.* How many had he taken over the years? And now he was back to square one. He couldn't be happy about that. She'd totally disrupted his plans tonight. He'd be pissed off and lashing out.

No. Rook's not the act in anger type. He's a game player. Chess. Chess is about being calm. About strategy. He's gone to plan his next moves. This was just the loss of some pawns. What do you do when you lose your pawns? She thought about it. *Get new ones. And where would he go to do that? Somewhere he's comfortable. Somewhere he can call the shots. Somewhere he knows the board.*

So the rat has gone to ground in his own neighborhood. Satisfied she had it right, she felt again for the bracelet. The connection burned on her wrist, strong and steady. The small limp shadow in the warehouse didn't move, so Kia must still be out cold.

Her jaw set, Letta willed the Cobain to take her to the warehouse.

26

LETTA PLOWED THROUGH the surface with the force of a Baptist late to Sunday dinner. She rocketed out, leaving a cascade of stone and dirt in her wake, landing on unsteady feet and knees that buckled as soon as she touched down. She rolled with it, settling a few feet away from her entry point, head spinning from the sudden departure from the stream. It ebbed away, leaving her momentarily lost and empty. Shaking her head, she got to her feet, taking in the surroundings and listening for sounds in the silence, now that her own noisy entry was done.

Smooth, Letta, real smooth. Gotta work on that. Can't leave holes everywhere I travel. Shit. That entry coulda been heard from blocks away. He knows I'm here now. Fool. Angry at herself, she turned slowly to survey the area, ready to be attacked at any second. She stood inside the warehouse near the front doors, the 5-0 mark she'd focused on easy to see in the light streaming in through holes in the boards.

The high windows let in enough afternoon sun to make out some details. To the right, a broken chair lay on its side near a barrel of something smelly. To the left, the space stood empty even of that small amount of debris. She sensed no movement. Not even rats. She stepped slowly forward. A metal staircase clung to the far wall, the rust on it highlighted by the sun. She looked up to the second floor landing. It looked forlorn and empty.

She took another few steps, aware of the sound of her own breathing and the crunch of her steps in the grit. *Nothing here. But why'd the Cobain show me this place if…* She remembered the staircase from her vision and quickly glanced beneath it, into the shadows. A small form huddled there, dark and foreboding. She thought it wiggled slightly, as though a tiny figure breathed.

Letta moved cautiously toward the figure, checking the shadows as she went for any hidden surprises. Rook had to be here. He wouldn't just dump Kia and leave. *He knew I'd be chasing him.* She hesitated a few feet away, looking for signs of life. The bracelet lay just barely visible in the shadows. A soft blue light glowed around what had to be the heart stone she'd shaped and given to Kia. *Seems forever ago now.* But she couldn't make out any other features.

It felt wrong. Like a trap. But she couldn't, wouldn't, just leave Kia. If it was a trap, she'd just have to spring it. It'd be worth it, to get Kia out of here. Letta pushed forward, keeping down, sneaking into the shadows next to the stairs, creeping up on Kia from the side. The stone winked, but it seemed off. Her wrist didn't burn in recognition. She didn't sense the bracelet at all.

Odd. She'd come so quickly to expect that magical reassurance that it felt strange to have it vanish so suddenly. *Already used to magic. It ain't been a full day. Feels like a lifetime though.*

"Kia." She kept her voice to a bare whisper, but even that sound made her wince. The lump didn't move.

Letta inched forward, nearing what should be Kia's feet. *If it's her.* The doubt crept in unbidden and made a home in the pit of her stomach. She should leave. Duck back into the Earth and plan another way to attack. *This is stupid.*

She knew it. But she covered the last two feet anyway. If it was Kia, she had to help her. After a look around, and intensely listening for even the hint of a breath, she sprinted across and knelt to shake the lump. "Wake up, girl."

The leg gave way beneath her, crumbling into tiny pebbles that rolled from under the blanket to rest at Letta's feet. She sprang upward, thrusting her elbow back to connect with anyone standing behind her, but the lack of an opponent sent her off balance and she stumbled backward. Before she got her feet under her, she felt it, the first tingling crawling over her skin that signaled power. She managed to turn and face Rook before his siphoning ability embraced her.

Letta cursed as she realized what she should have done. She could have asked the ground if Kia lived. Could have felt for her heartbeat. *Fool. Don't you learn?* It was all so new she didn't even try to solve the problem with magic. Now it was too late. She stared at the glowing cord of magic pressing into her chest. It radiated heat and infiltrated something private, something vital. It violated her innermost self and ripped away a thing that she'd already come to think of as hers. To have a thief crash through her defenses and take the power she'd been given...

She glared at Rook. He stood not ten paces away, chin thrust out and chest puffed up like a peacock, gray eyes flashing. Self-satisfied. As though he'd just stepped out of a fancy restaurant, all put together and assured of his power and place in the world. His hands dangled casually at his side, though strands of light radiated from them, joining together in front of him to form the banded rope of energy that connected him to her.

Letta grabbed at the power stream, but her hands passed through it. Her feet refused to move. *Block it.* She pushed her will at the ground, but nothing happened. Envisioning a cascade of boulders on his head, she pleaded with the force inside her. *Do it. Please. Stop him.* Nothing. The glow from the power stream lit up Rook's face with an inhuman greenish hue and made his eyes glitter. She saw triumph there and excitement. He winked. Her stomach turned as the obvious sank in.

"Fuck you," Letta growled.

Rook grinned. "I intend to." He closed his eyes and pulled harder, his entire body lighting up with the surge.

Letta's knees buckled. The mark on her stomach burned as if angry at the intrusion. She gasped, clutching at it with both hands.

"You *do* taste familiar. I thought so before, but…" He kept his eyes closed but scrunched his forehead in concentration. The siphoning of her power dropped off to a low hum. "You are cinnamon, and honey, and…"

He opened his eyes to stare intensely at her face.

"What?"

Rook shook his head slightly. "Pepper." He said the word absently, an afterthought.

"What's that supposed to mean?"

"It reminds me of someone." Rook shrugged.

He raised his hands higher and intensified the hold on her magic. The mark on Letta's stomach stabbed her with a jolt of pain. The heat seared her palms and took her breath away. *Shoulda gone. For. The. Dagger. Can't fight. Without it.*

Energy drained like water down the sewer. It left her empty. A runner at the end of a marathon. A race she'd lost. She struggled to maintain focus. "Who?"

Rook licked his lips.

"Who. I. Remind you?" She fought to keep her tone neutral, but with searing needles running through her body, she couldn't stop the strained growl.

When Rook didn't answer, she tried another approach. "Where's...Kia?"

Rook's gazed flicked to the left, then back so fast she almost missed it. He circled her, surveying her body with an assessing look, taking in her pain, lack of power, and her empty hands. He raised an eyebrow. "Where's the dagger?"

"Where is...she?"

Rook kept his gaze locked on hers. It told her far more than his slip-up had done. *She's here. To the left. Can't see her, but she's there.*

Rook lowered his hands slightly, lessening the drain of her power again. Letta stumbled slightly, the force that had been holding her upright suddenly gone. Before she could take advantage of being free to fight, Rook waved a negligent hand, and her feet cemented themselves to the ground. She clenched her fists, grateful that at least he hadn't cut off that ability. She could punch too, if he got close enough.

"The dagger. Surely you didn't lose it?"

She glared at him. "Let. Kia. Go."

"Or..." Rook waited for her to fill in the blank.

"Hurt her, and I. Will. End. You."

His eyes danced with amusement. "You don't see more than one move ahead." He shook his head. "You'll never win the game that way."

"This ain't no game." She forced herself to breathe slowly. Sweat burned a path down the side of her face. The pain in her stomach continued, as though the dagger were still there, twisted up with her internal organs.

"Of course it is. All of life is a game." He gestured to the empty space around them. "This is but one of the boards. You've done nothing so far but remove a few pawns. And there are always more pawns." He hesitated, eyebrows furrowed in concentration. He muttered something she didn't catch.

Distract. "What did you do to her?"

"Do you feel the bond?" Rook waved a hand toward the vast empty space, diminishing the pull on her power to a trickle. "This place and I, we're connected. This place protects me. It serves me. It cannot be breached."

Letta tugged at her feet. They shifted, slightly. His hold on her slipped. *Not enough. Distract.* "That ain't true."

"I assure you, it is. It's bonded to me much like that bracelet is bonded to you." He licked his lips, a slow grin forming on his arrogant face. "An easy lure."

Being reminded of her own stupidity just kicked her anger into a higher gear. She pulled hard on her right foot. It slipped forward a fraction of an inch. Letta glanced toward the corner where she *knew* Kia must be. "Let her go, you dumb fuck."

Rook narrowed his eyes but didn't follow her gaze. "You're in no position to make demands. And you grow tiresome."

Letta gasped as hundreds of needles stabbed her from the inside. *The dagger. Something's wrong.* Another push with her right foot. Another fraction of an inch.

"Kia's been here before. Someone else took her out. And it weren't you. This place ain't all that. Didn't keep me out either, did it?" Her stomach seized. She held her breath, trying not to betray the weakness. Pressing her palms into the mark, she wished it would stop long enough to let her fight. And that he'd lose focus long enough for her to move her feet.

Rook stared at her. She watched him process the information.

"She was rescued from this place. By the Keeper," Letta taunted.

Rook's eyebrows shot up.

Letta forced a grin. "You didn't know. Thought you had a

bond." She shoved at her right foot, and it shifted an inch, maybe two. Triumph over that tiny victory gave her strength. "Didn't think I knew about the Keeper, did ya? She's on to you. She knows, Rook. You're done. Give me the girl."

He took a step toward her. "The Keeper is nothing."

"That why you hide here?" Her left foot edged over an inch. The bond felt weaker. *He's losing it.* Her heart pounded with the internal struggle and the effort of keeping her face neutral.

"*She* is irrelevant. Where's the dagger? You have it. I can sense it." He touched her arm lightly, sending ants crawling up her skin and a flicker of electricity through her stomach that flared around the Earth mark.

"Where. Is. Kia!" Letta screamed at him, spit flying, rage barely contained. The power in her stomach crawled, searching for an exit. Flecks of black danced in her eyes.

"It's here. It tastes…" Rook's voice was low, as if he spoke to himself. He circled around her, looking at her from every angle.

She tried to take a step away from him, but managed only a small shuffle. *How the hell is he doing that?* The words barely went through her thoughts before she had the answer. *Earth power.*

I can do what he can. If I got any juice left.

Rook pressed up behind her and tugged at her shirt.

Letta cringed away from him. Rook patted her down with clinical detachment, not even trying to feel her up. While he dug in one of her pockets, Letta sent her awareness to the ground. It pulsed in response. She pressed the small amount of energy she still controlled into the Earth, picturing it a fluid, living thing. Picturing a fluid connection. Just as Alex had shown her.

Something sighed with release as Letta's connection to Earth strengthened, and suddenly she broke free. She stumbled forward. Her shirt ripped in Rook's hands as she tore herself away.

Letta spun to face him, fists poised and ready. For a fraction of a second, her heart swelled with victory. Rook stared at the piece of her shirt in his hand as though it were an alien thing, incomprehensible and strange.

Her triumph was short-lived as he raised his hands, palms facing out, ready to steal her power once more.

27

"NOT THIS TIME." Letta moved, running to the side as she imagined a wall between them. Rocks rumbled in response, pushing up to create a barrier that grew quickly, extending outward toward the warehouse walls.

Before the wall completed, the center of it shattered. Stone raced through the air looking for targets, exploding against anything that couldn't dodge out of the way. The ground shook as the rest of it tumbled with a resounding crash. Letta ducked, arms over her head, shielding herself from the worst of the flying debris.

Rook flicked a hand toward her.

Letta dodged reflexively, expecting a knife throw, and ended up barely avoiding a large boulder streaking past her head and crashing into the wall behind her with the force of a bomb. Fragments flew through the air like missiles. She ducked and rolled, tucking her head under her arms until the worst had passed.

Scrambling to her feet, Letta found Rook facing her, doing the same. He hadn't escaped the blast either. Blood dripped from his nose and from several cuts on his face. She prepared herself to dodge whatever Rook sent flying, but he surprised her by turning toward the corner of the room where she'd thought Kia must be. His eyes narrowed, and power rushed from him, brushing past Letta, leaving tingles along her arms as the power fed something behind her.

A scream shattered the air. Letta chanced a quick glance toward the corner.

Kia, now visible, struggled against metal bands that extended from the high ceiling down to wrap around her wrists and neck. They retracted, lifting Kia off the ground like a puppet. Kia gagged against the pressure around her throat. Letta's heart stopped.

"Kia!" She ran toward the girl, hunting anything that might help her get the shackles off her. Anything to keep her safe. Kia rose swiftly out of reach. Letta stood under her, utterly helpless. Kia dangled precariously at least ten feet over her head. There was no way to climb up, no way to sever the bonds that held her.

"Kia! I'm coming. Just hold on." Letta tried to connect with the ground. She needed a mound of dirt or platform for Kia to stand on. The connection fizzled almost before it started. She'd been drained by the fight, and by Rook. *He took it all. I can't use magic.* Her stomach bubbled with frustration and the leftover ache of the dagger. *If I had the dagger, I could save her.* She fought against the despair that welled up. It felt too much like before. Too much like Jenna. *Couldn't save her. Can't save Kia.*

She gulped back a sob. *No, dammit. I do not accept this. I will save Kia.* She tried once again to connect and felt a small spark, but not enough to call for the help she'd received before. *Not gone, then. But weak.* She didn't have time for her power to regenerate. Kia didn't have time. The bond on the girl's wrists looked smaller, less substantial. It would dissolve any second.

"You bastard! Stop it!" Letta whirled to face Rook. "Put her down."

Rook's lips twitched. His eyes tightened as he looked up at Kia.

Horrified, Letta watched as one of the metal bands slowly dissolved, releasing one wrist and leaving Kia suspended by the other wrist and her too-thin throat. The increased pressure made Kia's eyes bulge. She gurgled and kicked.

Rook's icy voice cut through Letta's spine. "I have something you want. You have what I want. A simple Agreement, and we part ways. For now. The game continues."

His use of the word Agreement startled her. It sounded like something more, like the deal she'd made with the Caraigg, but more evil. *A deal with the devil.*

She tried to sift through recent memories for any use of her power that might help. "Not a chance."

"Perhaps the situation is not entirely clear. I've tasted someone like you before." Rook paused for a significant moment. "Exactly. Like. You."

Letta continued to stare at Kia, desperate for an idea. Any idea. The silver snake around Kia's wrist looked thinner already. "What the hell you talking about?"

Rook spread his hands. "If it wasn't you, then it was someone close to you. A sister, perhaps?"

Stunned, Letta slowly turned to face him. "You can't be..."

He smiled, eyes cold and calculating as he nodded. "I thought so. Such a fresh, young taste. I remember. It was... unusual. As are you." Rook licked his lips, as if savoring a meal. "She continues to delight."

Time stopped. The world hung suspended on the edge of a cliff as Letta grasped his meaning. *Jenna's alive. She's alive! She's... He has Jenna. He's always had her.* "Where is she?" She forced the words through gritted teeth.

A soft moan from above tore through Letta's heart.

"Tick tock." Rook glanced up. "Time is running out. Her bonds won't hold long. She seems to have a natural ability that negates such things. Will you deal? Her life, for the dagger. Your sister's freedom, for mine. It's a fair exchange, I think."

Heart pounding, Letta tried to connect to her power again. *Not strong enough. Think, Letta, think.* She didn't have the dagger to give. Even if she wanted to deal, she couldn't. *Jenna. He took Jenna.* It shook her to the core, to know that Jenna might be out there. That he'd touched her. That he'd... She tried to swallow the hard lump in her throat. It refused to budge.

Overhead, a strangled sound announced the end of the second wrist restraint. *She's dying!*

Tears blurring her vision, Letta choked out a strangled "no deal." She turned toward Kia, searching frantically for any sort of ladder, platform, stool, bucket...anything. Behind her, she sensed movement just in time to launch herself to the side, avoiding the boulder Rook launched at her by mere inches.

He wants to throw rocks? I can do that. Earth thrummed beneath her feet, eager and expectant. Letta sent her awareness into it and *reached*. It leapt to her call, cascading through her feet and up into her body where it mingled with the electricity racing through her. She bit her lip and focused on sending it out through her hands, as she'd seen Rook do, picturing it as a rock thrown with force.

A blast of small stones erupted with the force of a machine gun from her hands. The rocks were small, but the force was deadly. Her arms swayed with the backlash of it. Rocks rushed out in every direction, wild and out of control. Rook swore and dove. He dodged the steady stream but not the pummeling of stones that ricocheted off walls and pillars.

Startled, Letta lost concentration, and the barrage stopped

as abruptly as it started. She stared at her hands, new weapons filled with strange ammunition. Disbelief warred with triumph, distracting her long enough for Rook to seize the opportunity. The floor bucked and swayed. A wave of concrete and shards of bedrock boiled toward her. It slammed into her, knocking her off her feet. She fell back, hard, onto the wave of stone, sharp edges boring into her skin. She screamed as it lifted her high in the air, then slammed her back to the ground, ripping the breath from her lungs.

Letta gasped, clawing at the earth as it carried her up again. Pinpricks of lights danced in her eyes. She couldn't catch her breath. Her lungs refused to cooperate. Desperate, she clung to the stones that had been sent to kill her. Forced a ragged breath. *Pushed.*

The cascade altered course, bearing down on Rook like an angry wasp. He thrust his hands up to block, but an avalanche of stone buried him. Letta landed on top of the heap and rolled, out of control. She slammed into the wall and crumpled. Rocks settled with a loud grumble and ocean of dust.

Letta coughed, turning onto her side. Every muscle screamed with the slightest movement. Her lungs burned with every ragged breath. Dust obscured everything. Her body focused on surviving the next second. Then the next. The ground beneath her, docile now, felt alien and hostile. It was her friend, but could also be her enemy. *Lesson. Learned.*

Letta struggled to her knees. A groan reached her from somewhere to the left, followed by a string of curses. *Fuck. Not dead.* She turned toward it, trying to use the wall to drag herself onto unsteady feet. Mostly upright, she leaned against it, panting with the effort, coughing dust out of her lungs.

Across the warehouse, in deepening shadows, she noticed Rook doing the same. She sensed it would be seconds before he'd attack again. She readied herself, grasping at focus. Reaching for the earth beneath her feet, she tried to figure some way to block whatever he sent in her direction.

A shock wave pulsed through the air and slammed into Letta. It bound her arms to her sides in a tight hug and squeezed. Unseen hands lifted her into the air. She dangled, helpless, just below Kia, the girl's cries an echo of her own. The world danced as pressure intensified. She heard the snap as a bone broke somewhere in her left arm. Letta gasped from the shock, but no air entered her body. She forgot pain as she focused on the need for oxygen outweighed everything else. Her thoughts drifted as awareness flickered. Rook controlled more than Earth. He touched Air, too. *Like Tarian. Like that bitch who stole the dagger.*

She grasped at the memory of that encounter. It swam a lazy circle in her mind. She'd…done…something. *Earth smothers Air.*

She tried, but this time no rumble answered her call. She felt no life beneath her. Nothing came to her rescue. Rook chuckled. The sound circled around Letta, mocking her. Voices chased after themselves in a soft hiss.

Kia needs me. Inside, Letta crumbled.

The tingling on her skin told her Rook had started his siphon again. *Stupid. Got nothing left.* It felt different. Lighter. More gentle. Less an invasion and more an invitation. Letta tried to move her arms, to shift her weight, to lift her head. But it all felt like a dream, and her body floated without direction. *I'm dying.*

Even that thought failed to cause any concern. It drifted through her mind and back out, harmless.

The whispers grew insistent, even urgent.

She waits.

Yes, Letta agreed. Confused, she added, *Who? Who waits?*

Lights danced behind her eyes. Sparks flared, drifted down, down, down. They carried Letta with them until she stood on a dirt floor. Her bare toes curled in the soft earth. She was naked, but it wasn't cold and it didn't bother her. Rich darkness surrounded her, leaving only a small circle of light where she stood. Her body didn't hurt, anymore. Relieved, she turned slowly, scanning the area for movement.

She was alone. "Kia!" Her voice echoed through the empty space. Frantic, she searched for any sign of the girl. There was nothing.

She waits. Call. We will answer.

"Call?" Letta's voice sounded harsh and cold in this place. She cleared her throat. "Who are you?"

You You You You.

The word echoed as if she stood in the middle of a giant cavern. But there were no features here. Nothing but the soft dirt beneath her feet and the warm glow above her head. "Where am I?"

Am I Am I Am I Am I Am.

The words faded to silence. Kia had to be dead by now. But it seemed far away, an illusion of reality. This dark room with invisible walls felt more real. More inviting. She wanted to stay.

We will answer.

The words tumbled over themselves, louder now. A voice, rather than a whisper. Several voices, all sounding familiar, but not anyone she knew.

A distant searing heat prodded her in the stomach. She ignored it. Her body shook, and she ignored that too.

"Who are you?"

You You You You We Are.

Letta shook her head. This wasn't real. She was dying. This was her brain trying to tell her she was dying. Kia was dead. Rook would win. He'd go on, to take more girls. To hurt them.

Jenna. Sorrow welled up and grabbed Letta's throat in a vise grip. She sobbed, unable to stop it. Her sister was long gone, but hearing Rook mention her…saying he'd tasted her…she couldn't stand it. She was thirteen again, and it felt raw and new. Too young to cope. Too young to save Jenna. Too young to save herself.

Never accept.

She shrugged. What was left to fight? It was done. She was done. *No magic. No power. No help. No weapon. Nothing. I'm nothing. Jenna. I'm sorry.*

Her circle of self-pity wrapped around her and produced a memory of Tarian and Alex, standing in the park in the middle of all that destruction she'd wrought. Tarian clearly upset about the missing dagger.

"You have to bond with it or anyone can use it."

You have to bond.

She gripped her stomach, the raised mark embedded in the flesh rough against her palm. The vines still ran through her body. The essence of the dagger burned, separate but still a part of her. *I did bond with it. I accepted it. It accepted me. We are one.* The realization struck her, a flash against her calm, a catalyst that cut through panic and created strength and purpose.

Rook can't touch it. He knows. He knows it's here, but he can't take it. Because it's me. It's not a thing anymore. It's me.

She looked up, startled to find three dark shadowy figures standing in front of her, each with a puddle of light over them. Though they should have been well-lit, they remained shadows.

A darkness against the dark. It flashed through her mind that she should be afraid of them.

"I know you."

You You You You. The shadows repeated the word back to her. She studied each one and, as she did so, caught a brief glimpse of herself, from their point of view. Like looking in a mirror, but darker and more sinister. She commanded these shadows, somehow. But…

She waits. Call. We will answer.

They waited, tensed, their bodies stronger than hers. Ready for battle, even though they carried no weapons.

With them, she could win. With them, she could save Kia. She could save her sister too. Maybe.

Power costs. The voices whispered the promise and a warning.

Letta nodded. She had to make a choice. A bargain, like Rook tried to demand. *Kia, or Jenna. Not both. Right?*

The silence that stretched out in this dark corner of her mind was answer enough. If she destroyed Rook, she'd never know what happened to Jenna. He'd never be able to tell her. She closed her eyes, tears pushing against the lids and spilling down her cheeks. Her sister, who'd been missing so long. Or Kia, right before her, dying.

"It's not fair." She sounded like a petulant child, but she didn't care.

Fair Not Not Fair Fair Fair.

Rook might be lying. She knew it, even if her heart wanted to believe her sister was alive. He was a manipulative bastard. He'd lured her here with a lump of stone made to look like Kia. He'd lied about everything.

He probably doesn't even know Jenna. Or doesn't remember her. He doesn't track those girls once he's used them.

She brushed the tears aside and looked at her shadows. "Save Kia."

They held out their hands, pulling her to them to form a circle. *Call. We will answer. Accept. We will fight.*
She gripped the hands holding her own, and called.

28

THE SHADOWS PULLED Letta with them as they began to spin the circle, tugging on tightly clasped hands. They moved so fast, all sense of time and place were lost. They formed a bond, strong and steady, that could not be broken. It was a tangible, living thing that defied logic, because they were all shades of herself. She knew they were reflections of who she really was, underneath the face she presented to the world. The shadows pulled from within her, even as they represented something foreign. Through it all, a feeling of sisterhood that swelled, blotting out everything else.

Help me. Like she'd done with the tree, she drew the shadows in tight for a hug. They squeezed back. She felt them come, one at a time, adding their strength to hers. They released the power of the mark, and it rushed across her skin, a blinding flash of light and a clap of thunder as time sped up and thrust Letta back into the world, slapped with the pain she'd left behind, a pounding heart, the sounds of a girl strangling, and a scream of anger from Rook as his binding dissolved and she drifted to the ground.

Shadows poured from Letta's body, each one a filament of

smoke forming into a body that resembled Letta, but didn't. Letta felt each one as it emerged. If she focused on one, she suddenly saw through shadow eyes. The effect of shifting perspective disoriented and confused. Letta stopped immediately, afraid she'd lose track of who she really was if she spent too long in a shadow. She didn't have time to explore the implications or even figure out exactly what these shadows could do. She knew only a need so strong it couldn't be denied.

"Kia!" Letta pointed to the ceiling where Kia hung limp, her last bit of air obviously expended.

She expected the shadows to leap toward Kia. She thought they'd float up and release the girl from her bonds. Or perhaps bring a platform for her to stand on. They did none of it. Instead, they converged on Rook.

His eyes widened as they approached with slow purpose, an unstoppable force. He thrust a boulder at them. It sailed through the shades, landing with a loud crash against the far wall.

The shadows circled around Rook, creating a vacuum that stole air from his lungs and magic from his hands. His eyes bulged. Desperate hands scratched at his throat. Frantic eyes sought Letta's, the plea in them obvious. She watched him struggle, unsure whether to have mercy on Rook and stop the shadows, or somehow help them so that he didn't suffer. A part of herself, in the darkest parts of her soul, watched Rook writhe with satisfaction. A fitting end, for the evil he'd visited on others. Another part simply detached and observed, noting the process with interest. Still another part, a large part, wanted to look away, stunned and horrified.

It wasn't a normal death. No blood poured from a gunshot wound. No fresh bruises appeared. The shadows reached long, smoky filaments into Rook's body and pulled out ephemeral wisps of blues and greens. The power, or energy, or whatever it was sank into the blackness of the shades while Rook screamed the primal, guttural sound of a man condemned.

Each piece taken aged the man a decade. Lines formed on his face, racing up to a skull devoid of hair. His hands shriveled, and his eyeballs shrank in their sockets until they'd disappeared entirely. Rook deflated like a balloon, life leeching slowly into Letta's shadow selves. The bonds around Kia's throat dissolved as the last of his power drained and she plummeted to the ground, landing in a crumpled heap.

Screams filled the air as more magic collapsed. Along the walls of the warehouse, what had looked empty before now filled with cages and shackles, manacles and chains. Letta staggered against the released power. Forced to her knees, she crawled toward Kia. *She can't be dead. Please. Please don't let her die.* She didn't know who she pleaded with. Didn't care. If someone would help Kia, she would accept it, no matter who offered.

Letta reached Kia after what seemed like a century of crawling over rubble and dodging flying fragments of things she didn't bother to identify. Grabbing Kia with both hands, she willed it into the girl. Willed her to take a breath. To wake up. To respond. Anything.

"Kia! Please, baby. Wake up. Kia." Her voice came out as rough sobs. "Kia. Please."

Child of Earth must recall her weapon. Weapon will destroy all. Child of Earth must direct.

A rough hand on her arm shook her, but she ignored it.

"Kia. Please. Help her."

Child of Air and Water lives. She will not, if building collapses.

Thousands of Caraigg voices sounded urgent, but calm and reassuring. It took a second for Letta to register what they'd told her. She glanced up to see the walls crumbling around them and parts of the ceiling crashing to the ground. The deafening sound of collapse combined with screams from... She squinted into the dust-filled air. Girls. Everywhere she looked, girls stood in chains, in cages, shackled to stones and walls. None of it had been there before. She knew it hadn't. It was an empty warehouse.

He made it look empty. But it wasn't.

Terror filled her as the realization of overload struck. She'd let out a weapon of destruction, her shadow selves, and had no idea how to stop them or her own energy as it devoured the warehouse.

Power has a cost. She swallowed hard.

The cost would be far too high if she didn't get the shadows under control. She forced deep breaths. Tried to think calm thoughts.

"Come back. It's over. It's done." The shades ignored Letta, circling in a frenzy that wouldn't be denied.

"Stop! Come back!" She screamed as loud as she could, frantic with the need to make it all stop. The shadows continued to race, their movements a blur of black and gray smoke. The second floor of the warehouse buckled. The rickety stairs crumbled, crushing some of the cages below it. Terrified screams tore through the air.

Letta closed her eyes. Pictured the dark room with the glowing light. *Come home.* She envisioned each shadow figure there as it had been. Felt the bond connecting them, and willed it to tighten and contract. *Come home. Enough. You've done enough.*

The shadows slammed into her body, one after the other, so hard it threw her back across the entire expanse of the warehouse. She hit the wall on the other side full force, crashing through it to the street beyond. Her body broke on the rubble. A bone snapped with a loud crack, searing pain down her leg. It was nothing compared to the way her insides froze as each shadow joined her and poured everything it had taken from Rook into her. His essence joined hers, a sleazy snake-like thing that wormed its way into her body and burrowed there.

She screamed, clawing at her face. As she relived Rook's last moments, the terror in his eyes bore a hole in her soul. The memory of Rook's destruction scoured her insides raw, making a fresh wound rubbed clean with salt.

One by one, her shadows burrowed back into the core of her, dormant. It left her exhausted, spent, and miserable. She'd done it. She'd saved them. The girls he'd taken. The girls he had yet to corrupt. And Kia.

Kia was safe.

Jenna was lost.

Forever.

Grief engulfed her. Letta sobbed against it, unable to fight it anymore. She let it take her away, burrowing into the dark recesses of her mind where the shadows watched and waited.

29

LETTA DIDN'T KNOW how long she lay there, a broken heap on a mountain of misery. She didn't have the will to even care. What she'd released…what she'd become…terrified her. She couldn't wrap her mind around it. Didn't understand it. Didn't want to.

After a lifetime spent drifting in the darkness of her own mind, she felt herself jolted into awareness against her will by an unseen force that shook her body and demanded attention. She wanted nothing but to forget, but it refused to let her. She moaned. "Jenna. I'm. Sorry. Jenna." Grief tortured her. All that she'd felt as a child bubbled up to the surface. She'd never cried. Never admitted to herself that Jenna was truly gone. In her heart, Jenna was just missing and could be found, if Letta looked hard enough. But now she knew that wasn't true. "She's gone. She's gone. She's gone." She flailed against the knowledge, trying to brush it away, but it did no good. As her body shook, she realized what a bad thing that was. It meant a very bad thing. *Overloaded. Still.* She thought her energy was spent. How was the ground still shaking? She'd nothing left. Nothing.

"Letta? Wake up. Please wake up." Small hands gripped

Letta's arm and shook it.

Letta frowned. *Who was that? What?*

Soft voices soothed. The hands stopped their death grip, leaving her arm bruised. Or it might have been her fall on the rocks. Every inch of her body hurt. Even the inside of her nose and the back of her eyelids.

More hands, this time larger, touched her arms and forehead. They brought with them a wave of heat, and a sensation that all was right with the world, even though she knew it wasn't. She tried to open her eyes, but they refused. She tried to brush away the hands, but they remained firmly attached.

"Quiet, now. Just lie still. I know you're in pain. You had a bad fall, and… Just be still. I can help." The words softened into a hum that sounded suspiciously like a song she knew from childhood. A nursery rhyme? She knew, somehow, that this person meant her no harm. She tried to ask who it belonged to, but all that came out was a low moan.

"Calli, check her stomach. That's one hell of a bruise," the feminine voice commanded.

"I'm getting to it, Tari. Patience." The answer sounded amused. Soft hands caressed Letta's stomach, bringing a warmth to the area that activated the mark. It heated up in response.

Letta moaned at the stirring of power there. It hurt, like fingernails on a chalkboard, raw and bloody fingernails.

"Tari, I… This isn't a bruise. It's… Well, see for yourself."

Letta pried her eyes open a slit, enough to see Tarian bending over a younger woman with blonde hair. They both stared at her belly with an intensity that scared her. Something in the air tickled and crawled over her skin. She tried to brush it away, but her arms wouldn't obey.

"Skip that area, Calli. It didn't stop you before?"

The blonde shook her head. "No. Didn't react at all, actually. Odd."

"She wasn't conscious. That's probably part of it. See if you can help the rest."

A deep voice nearby interrupted their examination.

"*Chica*, I called in extra guys, but it's still gonna take a few hours to clean this. I can't clear the metal until the girls are gone."

Tarian turned away. "It's okay, Alex. Nobody is going to be wandering by here tonight. And the Caraigg have put up a shield to replace the one Rook had covering the place. It'll be fine. See to the girls first. The rest can wait."

Through the ache in her brain, Letta tried to place the voices. *Tarian. Alex.* It made her feel better to recognize them. She'd met them. She knew they were good people. At least, Kia believed they were. And if Kia believed it...

Kia.

Her pulse quickened. What had happened to... "Kia." She managed to say the word, through gritted teeth. She tried to sit up, but heavy weight on her shoulders made it impossible.

"Shhh. It's okay. Stop struggling. Really, you're worse than Tari." The voice once again sounded amused. Hands touched each bruise and sort spot, as the soft voice spoke. "I can't heal you if you won't be still. And I don't want to have to sedate you. You've had enough power for one day, I think. Please. Just a few more minutes. Kia is fine. She's right here. She's safe. You're safe. You have nothing to worry about. Relax. It'll all be okay."

Letta relaxed slightly, wanting to believe the words. Wanting more than anything to believe this kind voice meant no harm. She let herself drift, grateful for the inky void of nothing.

More voices. Murmurs. The warm hands went away, to be

replaced by tiny ones that gripped her own. "Letta. Are you okay?"

Letta smiled, then, recognizing the voice. "I'm. Okay. Just need to…catch…my breath. You?"

"I knew you'd come." Kia leaned in and whispered, "You got magic now, you can save the world."

"Happy…just you," Letta managed.

"Thank you, Letta," Kia whispered.

The warm hands returned. "Now, you know she's fine. It's all over. Sleep now." The soft voice carried a command Letta couldn't deny. She drifted off into the whirl of warmth and darkness, satisfied.

30

HOURS LATER, OR maybe a lifetime, Letta managed to pry her eyes open. She lay on a pallet of dirt in the warehouse, surrounded by piles of rubble that had been shifted to create paths. Around her, people spoke, worked, gave orders. She pushed herself up to a sitting position, surprised to find herself tired, but not broken. Arms and legs seemed whole. There wasn't even much bruising.

Her stomach growled, loud and insistent. Nearby a small voice giggled.

"You need food." Kia bounced into view, doing a little prance before handing Letta an energy bar. "They said you would."

Letta took the bar and tore into it. It landed in her empty stomach like a rock, but she kept chewing until it was all gone. Her stomach rumbled, far from satisfied, but she felt better. She got a good look at Kia. Except for holes in her jeans,a rip on her shirt and dirt smudges across tear-stained cheeks, she looked fine. More than fine. She looked like she'd just woken up from a long nap. No bruise on her neck or wrists. "You look good."

"Calli made me feel better." Kia pointed to a blonde woman kneeling by one of Rook's captive girls. The poor thing looked as though she'd been beaten, but even as Letta watched the bruises faded. "She helping that girl now. She got hit by the stairs."

Letta winced. *My fault.*

Next to Calli, Alex noticed Letta sitting up and called to someone. Tarian stalked toward Letta, stepping over and around any debris as if it didn't exist. She commanded the area with sheer force of will. As she got closer, energy came off the woman in waves, a pulse that alternated from soft to hard. Letta frowned, not understanding what it meant.

"Feeling better?" Tarian offered a hand.

Letta stared at it, unsure what would happen if they touched. She felt the mark stir at the surge of power from Tarian. Felt her own inner power react as well.

Tarian grinned. "I don't bite. Not unless you lose your temper." She shook her head. "You need to work on that."

Letta finally took the offered hand, letting Tarian help her stand, grateful for the steadying hand that kept her from falling back down. Her legs wobbled.

Electricity from Tarian snapped against Letta's power, but it seemed more like a dog sniffing new territory than an invasion or call to arms. She let it flow, and after a minute the incursion retreated and her mark rested once more. Tarian released her hand, and she stared at it, looking bemused.

"You'll need more food. Proper food. You can't spend power like that and not replace it, though we did try." Tarian smiled at Kia. "After we figured out to move Kia away from you, that is. She was so worried that her natural ability blocked any attempt to heal you."

"Blocked?" Letta stared at Kia, confused.

The little girl nodded, serious. "Like I do Mama."

Letta glanced around at the activity in the warehouse. She could tell night had fallen, because the windows were dark. But inside, light painted the walls with a soft shade of blue. *Glow balls. Like Rook's.* She turned her attention to the girls. There were a lot fewer than she'd noticed at first. Only a handful left now. "How many?" she finally managed.

"About seventy, give or take. That's the last count I got anyway. I'll get an update when they're all safely away." Tarian gestured to a corner where an air tunnel waited. "We're taking them all back to the healers. We can fix the physical wounds. The mental... Well, we'll try to make them forget, but that much trauma is tricky. Then if we can figure out where they belong, we'll take them home. If not...well, we'll figure it out."

Seventy. In the warehouse alone, he'd tortured seventy girls. Or more. Over how many years? Letta shuddered. That didn't count the ones at the prison. How many had been there? How many more remained chained up somewhere in some hidey hole they didn't know about? The thought made her angry. Inside, the dagger stirred. She stomped her foot, willing it to be quiet.

"Where's the dagger?" Tarian's voice was deceptively soft.

Letta turned to face her. "It's gone."

Tarian's anger flashed in her eyes. With clenched jaw, she asked, "You sure? Because I can feel power, you know. I can smell it. And I smell something on you."

"Yeah, well. I don't have the dagger."

"Why?"

"Some bitch with a pole up her ass stole it." Letta thought back to that moment. "She had a sour face, white hair, pale ass skin, and an attitude. And power. A lot of power. Damn near killed me."

Tarian swore, then looked apologetically at Kia, who grinned and bopped on her toes. "Kia, would you mind asking Alex to come here, please?"

Letta watched her go, knowing Tarian had sent her away on purpose. Probably didn't want the girl to witness a scene. *Let her.* She didn't care. The world had turned upside down. What else could the woman do?

When Tarian spoke, her voice was low and controlled. "We need that dagger."

"You sure about that?"

"Positive."

"Why?"

Tarian huffed, running a hand through her hair.

Letta raised an eyebrow. "I ain't the only one with anger issues."

Tarian stared back, the two squaring off as if they were about to fight. Letta watched the woman gain visible control, even as she kept her own body relaxed. She had no intention of fighting anymore today.

"We need all the artifacts. Including that one. Or the bitch wins."

Letta nodded. "You said it wouldn't work if it wasn't bonded, or some shit like that. But you never said what that meant. How do you bond with one of them things?"

"I can't explain it. It just needs doing. It's an acceptance, from both sides. The artifact chooses you, and in turn you choose it. But each of them acts differently. Each has their own...agenda. I hold the Water Artifact, because it belongs to my bloodline. The person who holds Fire had to fight for hers." Tarian frowned. "I have no idea what Earth might want. But I do know it chose you. So what happened to it?"

Letta hesitated. The vines of power that radiated out from the mark on her stomach wiggled, a living thing inside her that waited to be called. Was this something she should share with practically a stranger? Her instinct was to keep it a secret. Bury the knowledge deep inside, and ignore the shadows waiting there.

They were dangerous. Too hard to control once released. She thought of what happened to Rook and shuddered. *Too dangerous to call.*

Tarian raised an eyebrow, waiting for an answer. The Caraigg hopped next to her and squatted as if he, too, waited. *I promised to help the Keeper.* She sighed. *He's waiting for me to keep my promise.* She wondered what other consequences that simple promise had in store for her. She looked from the Caraigg to Tarian. The woman held her gaze with steady intensity. *I do trust her. I don't know why, but I do.* "I *am* the dagger. When I fought with Rook, I fell onto it. Instead of killing me, it healed me."

Letta lifted her abused T-shirt aside to reveal the mark on her stomach. "Left me this, and…other things. She got nothing but a fancy rock."

Tarian stared at the mark, her expression thoughtful. "The symbol for Earth." Letta felt the tingling of power again as it passed over her skin and the mark. The mark glowed slightly in response before settling back down.

Tarian's gaze met Letta's. She looked triumphant and eager. "Well, I'll be damned."

"How the hell is that possible?" Alex said as he joined them. "An artifact can't split like that. The power can't leave the vessel. Can it?"

Tarian tapped her chest. "I think it can do damn near anything it wants." She grinned, sharing a glance with Letta that felt conspiratorial and sent a shot of adrenaline through her system. "And it seems to me Earth is up for a few fun and games. Funny, I'd have thought it would be Fire."

"Fire?" A flash of memory reminded her of the man with fiery eyes in the park. "Why Fire?"

"Fire is chaos." Tarian smiled. "Odd things usually happen

when the Fire Artifact is active."

"Maybe this one is really Fire." Letta thought back to all the chaos. "It's sure been chaotic. And there was that guy with the fire eyes."

"Lasair." Tarian breathed the word. "I don't know why he was there, but he's nothing to do with the artifact you carry."

Alex shook his head. "She's right. That's definitely Earth. But I sure never heard of anything like this. How it split from the stone that formed it? Shouldn't be possible."

Letta rubbed the mark, thinking back to her shadows. "I think Earth can form more than one thing, if it wants to."

Tarian gave her a quick look, then glanced away before Letta could read her expression. The woman constantly moved, like water. Startled, Letta realized that was exactly what she was. Keeper of the Water Artifact.

If she moves like water, does that make me move like a rock? She hoped not. Hard to fight if you moved like a stone. *Though I'd be able to hit harder.* She grinned at the thought, ignoring the confused expressions around her.

Tarian motioned at Kia where she chatted with one of the captive girls remaining. "Kia needs a safe place to stay. I can set her up at my place, at least until things settle down. She'll be off the streets. She'll learn about her talent."

Letta frowned. "Why you asking me?"

Tarian snorted. "Because I get the feeling you'd come after her if she just disappeared. I'm not stealing her against her will, or yours, Letta. I'm offering her a home. I'm asking if you'd like me to keep her safe. You've earned the right to have some say in what happens to her."

Letta watched Kia, happy for the innocence on her face. She glanced at the destruction she'd caused. The girl couldn't stay here. She didn't have any family other than Donna Ray, as far as

Letta knew.

She considered what it might be like, to keep Kia with her. Raise her like... She swallowed. No. Kia could not replace Jenna. And Letta had work to do. She wasn't ready to be a mother, and Kia needed some place stable and safe. Some place that'd teach her about her magic. She nodded. Tears bubbled just below the surface, but she fought them back.

Letta searched for Kia, finding her next to the woman who'd done all the healing. Calli, she thought her name was. Kia watched intently as Calli worked on another injured young girl, one hand on Calli's arm as if to help. Letta swallowed, hard. Why did it feel like a part of her was being ripped away? She hadn't even known the girl that long. Barely any time at all. It was silly, to be this attached.

Impatiently, she brushed away the wetness on her cheeks.

Tarian gently touched Letta's shoulder. "She's not going away forever, Letta. You can see her anytime you want. Alex will teach you to control your travel. She'll be a thought away. Always. You're welcome at the House of Xannon, anytime."

"Does she...?" Letta's voice wobbled. "She know what her mother did? What *she* can do?"

"Well, none of us know exactly what Kia can do. Yet. And all she knows about her mother is that she's been naughty. For now. Kia's made of strong stuff. Have faith."

Letta smiled to herself. "I do." She left Tarian standing there, making her way over piles of rubble to Kia. The girl looked up with an excited smile.

"Letta, look! We healed her arm just by moving bits around. See?" Kia plucked at the formerly injured arm of a girl who looked not much older than Kia herself. The girl winced, but smiled.

Letta grinned. "I see it, but be careful. I don't think she's done healing yet. Gentle."

Calli looked up, a smile warming her yes. "She's doing fine. Though she does make it a bit more challenging."

Letta knelt beside the girl and flicked the bracelet that hung loose around her tiny wrist. "You keep that with you, okay? It'll help me find you, if you need me."

Concern filled Kia's eyes. "Where you going?"

"Not me, sweet baby. You." Letta glanced back at Tarian. "They wanna have you over to stay for a while."

Kia looked from Tarian, back to Letta. There was far too much wisdom in those young eyes to suit Letta. Wisdom and understanding. "They done come for me like they said they would."

Letta smiled. "They sure did. You *are* special, Kia. Never forget that, okay?" She tugged at one of Kia's many braids. "No matter what."

Kia studied her, head tilted to the side. "Don't worry. You'll find your way. When you coming to see me?"

Letta glanced at Calli, who smiled warmly. "She can come visit whenever she wants, Kia. Anytime."

Kia bobbed her head. "See you tonight?"

Letta laughed. "Maybe not tonight. There's things I gotta do, baby girl. But soon, okay? Real soon."

"K." Kia turned back to the now recovering patient, satisfied.

Calli winked at Letta and mouthed, "See you later."

When Letta returned to Tarian, she found both her and Alex waiting with thoughtful expressions. She stood in front of them, suddenly at a loss. Thoughts whirled from the mess here, to the girls who'd been at the prison, to Shelley and what she'd say, and to the brass. She ran a hand through tangled knots of hair and sighed. "What happens now?"

Tarian glanced at the warehouse. "Now I clean up your mess."

"My mess? I ain't the one dropped magic on the world." Letta gestured at the room. "I ain't the one unleashed this chaos."

Tarian clenched her fists, her eyes filled with pain and doubt. "No. I did."

"Then I'd say this mess belongs to you."

"It belongs to all of us now." Tarian hesitated. "You can stay with us too. It's a good place to learn. Alex can show you more about Earth, and we can figure out what other talents you have. We have tutors…"

"Tutors. Right." Letta thought about the girls at the prison. "There's others need savin'. I can't just leave 'em out there on their own. And I gotta check in with my partner. Make things right. She's probably pissed as hell by now." She hesitated. "I'll have to make a report about Rook. But there's no body. No idea how I'll explain this. Can't really tell them the truth."

"You don't have to explain it. Come with us. We'll figure it out. You don't need the job anymore."

Alex nodded encouragingly.

The job I spent my life trying to get? Letta glared. "It ain't just a job. I got responsibility here. People depending on me. I ain't gonna jump ship. Not that I don't appreciate the backup, but I left a lot of girls on their own at that prison. I gotta make sure they okay. And there's gotta be others. I need to find them." She paused, thinking of all she'd done with rocks and earth in the last hours. Thinking of what Rook said about Jenna. If her sister was still alive, she'd spend the rest of her life trying to find her. Starting with checking every girl who'd been in the prison. "I destroyed half the city."

Tarian snorted. "I wouldn't go that far."

"I gotta make it right. Somehow."

"You don't have to do it alone." Tarian tilted her head. "Trust me. Anything you're facing is easier with a friend or two by your side."

Letta glanced down at the Caraigg who waited patiently

by Tarian's side. "I promised to learn, and I will. I keep my promises." She looked back at Tarian. "I said I'd be your ally. But an ally and a friend are not the same thing. And I got stuff I gotta do. Someone I need to find."

"Jenna?" Tarian said the name softly, but it hit Letta as hard as a kick to the head.

"What the hell you know about her?" Letta gritted her teeth against her rising temper.

"Nothing. Yet." Tarian glanced down at Letta's stomach as if checking on something. "You kept saying her name. You said you were sorry. It was hard to miss. Who's Jenna?"

Letta felt her anger drain away, to be replaced by an ache that would never be soothed. "My sister."

Tarian glanced at Alex, then at the empty cages. "Was she here?"

"I...don't know."

"I can help you find her, Letta. I will, if you let me."

"She's gone. I gotta accept it." Tears burned Letta's eyes, but she refused to give in to it again. "She's gone. She ain't coming back. But those other girls, they got a life to live still. Families. They need help, putting things right."

Letta looked at the Caraigg. "I'll keep my promise, but I gotta do this first." She turned and started for the hole in the wall. She'd created it with her own body. It made as good an exit as any. The front doors were still, ironically, bolted shut.

"Letta," Tarian called after her. "We aren't done."

"Let her go, *chica*." Alex's voice trailed after her, a low rumble next to Tarian's frustration. "Let her go."

Letta didn't wait to hear anything else. She climbed over a pile of rubble and out into the afternoon sun.

31

A FEW WEEKS later, Letta stood outside a dingy building and flipped off the windows. Her boss was probably watching, the prick. She'd never liked him anyway. She briefly considered letting her anger show by blowing out the bricks around his window. She could do it. She'd done nothing but practice since the rain fell. She'd learned a bit of control.

With the artifact, I could bust your shit up. She bit her lip and resisted the temptation. *You're just lucky I'm still learning.* Practice on her own hadn't been all she thought it would be. She'd tried to travel, but ended up somewhere in Florida before she'd managed to work her way out of the Cobain. The plane ride home had cost money, and pride.

She glared at the blank window. *Dammit, I did my job. I tracked down Rook. I took him out. I saved those girls.*

"Fuck you." She told the building.

"No, thanks, I've already been laid today." The amused voice behind her made her spin, already crouching in an attempt to shield from a blow that never came. She stared in astonishment at the short black-haired woman who'd ruined everything.

"What the hell you want?"

"You're like a bull, you know that? Wanna go for coffee? I know a great place not far from here." Tarian turned, then looked back at Letta. "Unless you have something else to do today? Pretty sure you just lost your job."

"Fuck you."

"As I said, no, thanks. Damn, you remind me of me." Tarian laughed. "Let me buy you a coffee. I assume PJs is still open? God, I hope so. You do drink coffee, don't you? Or are you one of those chai people?"

Letta glowered. Chai reminded her of Shelley, which reminded her how much her partner had let her down. "Tea is for kids and grandmas."

Tarian's lips twitched. "I need a favor. And I don't ask favors without coffee; it's just rude. Come on." Tarian turned and descended the steps into the street.

Letta followed. She couldn't shake the bad mood. It pissed her off that she had nowhere to go. No job. No future. She'd been blaming Tarian for it, because she'd caused the stupid storm that had rained chaos down and screwed up everything. It didn't help that she knew, underneath the anger and hurt, that it wasn't really Tarian's fault, and that she wouldn't trade her newfound power for anything. Her connection to Earth brought her alive in a way nothing ever had before. But it didn't ease the frustration of dealing with stubborn people who refused to see her as valuable. She watched Tarian's back and fought against the urge to scream. *What the hell could she possibly need from someone like me?*

Curiosity overrode anger. She picked up her pace to catch up to Tarian, and the two of them walked in silence to PJs.

When they entered, one of the baristas waved and grinned. "Usual?"

"Definitely." Tarian turned to Letta. "You?"

"Straight. Hot. Large."

They collected their coffee and sat at a table in the back. Today, only a few other small groups had braved the streets to get their caffeine fix. Most businesses operated on abbreviated schedules for the time being, which meant workers were staying home and out of Center City. The National Guard patrolled along with the police, making the streets more like a war zone than a city. The city was basically on lockdown, dealing with all the fallout from the storm. But most people were gradually starting to venture outside, to try to resume some sense of normal after weeks of chaos.

The table they chose was the same one Letta and Shelley used, only a few weeks before the storm. Her partner now remained behind her desk, happily employed and studiously avoiding anything to do with magic. Shelley wouldn't divulge if the rain had affected her, or if she'd even gone out in it. Most of the uniforms refused to say, like it was a disease to be ashamed of. Letta was one of the few who wore it proudly.

Hell, Kia was right. It is something special. Something to celebrate.

"In case you're wondering, Kia's fine. She's being tutored in magic and regular school subjects, plus she's helping me out with babysitting."

Letta nodded acknowledgement of the information. She rubbed the side of her cup, trying to ignore the stab of guilt. She'd been so busy the past few weeks that she hadn't even tried to visit Kia. Hadn't checked on her. She knew Kia was safe. But that was no excuse. Fact was, she'd spent the time trying, in vain, to find a clue to Jenna's fate. That, and learn to control magic enough to travel without an overload. With very little success.

"She sent me to you. She said her bracelet didn't feel happy." Tarian sipped at her coffee and looked over the rim at her as though expecting something.

Letta rubbed the wrist where the phantom bracelet dangled, connecting her to Kia. "Yeah, well."

"Wanna talk about it?"

"No." Letta glared at her.

Tarian nodded, as if she'd expected that answer. "What happened to those girls at the prison? What was he doing with them? I got some of the story from Kia, but she didn't see everything. Seems like she was knocked out for a while. I've been there. The place is…I've never felt anything like it. It collapsed, by the way. It's really just a pile of rubble now, so although we managed to figure out some of what was going on, there's giant gaps. Fill me in?"

Letta stared at her. "Fill you in? What am I, your grunt? I ain't on your payroll."

"Yet." Tarian stirred her coffee. "I take it you told your boss what happened. What'd he say?"

Letta snorted. "Said I was full of shit."

"Figured." Tarian took a sip. "So tell me."

Letta picked up her coffee and scowled at it. "Don't know what good it'll do."

"Try me." Tarian paused. "It's my job to protect people from abuse of magic. If I'd known it was happening, that asshole would have been locked up years ago. Decades even. Rook was careful. It wasn't until Kia that there was even a clue that magic was being used anywhere near the city. And trust me, I looked for it. He was damn good."

Tarian shifted in her seat, shoulders hunched. "I can't be everywhere."

She muttered under her breath, but Letta heard it. She studied the woman curiously. *She takes it personally. Thinks it's her fault. How could it be? Hell, we didn't even know the full operation, and we live here.* Her anger dissipated a bit. Mistakes were made on all sides. If Letta had known about magic from the start, maybe it would have all played out differently. *Maybe. The Caraigg said ally with Keeper. Shit. What the hell's that supposed to mean anyway?* It might mean she had to share information, like this. It wouldn't hurt to tell her.

"Rook ran a place called The Exchange. If you hunt online in the dark corners, you can find it. It was a shopping mall, of sorts, for deviants. He trafficked girls, all kinds, for all reasons. I saw the setup, before I...before it collapsed. Each cell had a different... product. And prices." Letta's blood ran cold just thinking of it, and her stomach churned. She set the coffee down.

"I saw one of the signs. Kidneys are going for quite the bargain." Tarian's voice remained calm, business-like. It helped to restore equilibrium. "Kia told me you fought with Rook there. She said a stone box appeared but that he stepped right through it and took her."

"Yeah."

"When did the bitch steal the dagger?"

Letta put a hand on her stomach. She'd been doing that a lot lately. It was irritating, but she couldn't seem to stop herself. "Right after he left. I was upset. The building fell, then she showed up."

"Power calls to power," Tarian muttered. "That's how she found you. Shit."

"Yeah. You gonna tell me who she is?"

Tarian set her coffee down and leaned on the table. "She's the First Mother of the Benata. An Air daemon with a hell of a lot of power and attitude."

Letta tried to process that, but it meant nothing to her. *Benata? First Mother?*

Tarian's lips twitched. "Think about how much power you

have or think you have. And mine. Multiply them by ten, and you might get close to her level. She's a daemon. They look human, but they aren't. They control pure Air to an insane degree, and their body chemistry aids them in a way ours never will. It makes them incredibly strong in their element. But they're limited to that one element. Humans aren't limited that way. They usually connect to two, with one being dominant. You have Earth, and a bit of Water, I think. With the artifact, you'll be a force to be reckoned with, eventually. Still not her level."

Letta shook her head. "I don't get it. I understand that I connect to Earth but not why. I don't get how this all happened. How does something like a daemon even exist?"

Tarian spread her hands. "How do *we* exist? Life is life. There's no explanation for it. There's a ton of history you were never taught in school, but all you really need to know right now is that First Mother is extremely dangerous. She's older than you can imagine, she's powerful beyond even normal daemon, and she's afraid, which makes her incredibly volatile. I don't understand why she took the dagger. She has no affinity for Earth, and it's not likely the artifact would bond with her even if you hadn't already done it. And I really don't get why she left you alive. If you *had* bonded with it, her best move was to kill you so that it freed the artifact to bond again."

Letta thought about how she'd been wrapped in something that stole her breath. It'd nearly strangled her to death. She shuddered as goosebumps traveled up her arms. "Not sure she intended to. She left me trapped in some sort of cocoon without air. She probably thinks I suffocated."

"How'd you get out of that?" Tarian stared at her with curiosity.

Letta shrugged. "I buried myself."

Tarian laughed. "You have no idea how smart that was. Earth

smothers Air. Was probably the only move you had, and you played it perfectly. You're right, she probably thinks you died there. She'd never think that a lowly human could command something that would trump her." Tarian glanced down at the table. "So what happened with your boss? Besides getting fired, I mean."

"They don't believe me. They think I let Rook get away. I couldn't tell them what really happened."

"What did happen?" Tarian glanced around at the coffee shop. Only a few other people in the place, and they were engrossed in their own conversations.

That's why she's here. She wants to know how I did it. Letta thought about that, and about how she should respond. She hadn't even wanted to admit to herself what had happened because the truth was, it frightened her. To have something hiding inside her, waiting, made her blood run cold. She'd never killed someone before. As a cop, she'd never even had to fire her weapon beyond the practice range. But that day in the warehouse, she'd watched a man's soul sucked out of his body and then his body dissolve like dust. She'd taken his energy. His... She still couldn't process it had been her doing. Shadows of her, anyway. Shadows fed by an object she still didn't understand, though she was bonded with it for life it seemed.

The fact that she had homicidal maniacs inside her wasn't something Letta wanted to spread around.

Tarian seemed to understand the internal war going on in Letta's mind, because she leaned forward, keeping her gaze locked on Letta's as she whispered, "You had no choice. Anyone would have done the same. I would have." Tarian's eyes took on a faraway look. "I *have* done that. It doesn't make you a monster. He was the monster, and he had to be put down. Think about those girls any time you start to feel guilty. Think about Kia. She'd have died, or worse, without you."

Letta nodded. She opened her mouth to speak but couldn't think of what to say and closed it again.

"Was it the artifact?"

"I...think so." Letta hesitated. "It was me, too. It was..." She didn't even have words for what it was.

Tarian leaned back, easing the pressure. "I've done some research into Rook and The Exchange. Turns out, he wasn't even a big fish in the pond. Maybe a medium-sized fish. Rook had associates all over the country, and a thriving export operation besides. Most of it will continue without him. You put a dent in the operation, for sure. But it's not gone. Someone will step up to fill the gap."

Letta wasn't surprised to hear this. Her boss had said as much just before he fired her. She'd won the battle, and that was all fine and good, but she hadn't won the war. As far as he was concerned, Rook remained a threat, his operation intact. She couldn't tell him otherwise without admitting she'd vaporized a human being with shadowy versions of herself.

It was an impossible situation really. "You gonna get to the point?"

Tarian's lips twitched, but she continued in a serious tone. "Here's the thing. Donna Ray was doing something we jail people for. Manipulating others like that isn't allowed. And someone like Rook? If I'd caught him, he'd have been stowed so deep he'd never see light again. Though your way works too." Tarian's expression looked grim. "But they aren't the only ones out there doing bad things with magic. And no normal prison or jail can hold someone like that. It takes a special setup to keep someone from using their own power to escape. Think about it. No regular prison could ever hold *you*. Not anymore."

Letta nodded, listening. She'd thought of those things, in the weeks with nothing to do. If her shadows hadn't killed Rook, how would they have locked him up? What other skills did people have that would get them out of a spot like that? Too many to contemplate. Law enforcement had just become a whole lot harder. And it was harder still because the powers that be weren't accepting the change. They thought the world would return to normal, and that the odd things happening were just a phase or something.

She knew different. How many people would die while they figured out what to do?

"What choice we got?" She took a sip of coffee, needing the distraction from the dark thoughts.

"The jail I have, called the Cellar, is great for the worst offenders. We can set up a system to transport them there, expand our current operation so that the very worst are contained. But now the whole country has magic where only a few had it before. There's too many potential criminals for me to handle it in one place. Our little Society has expanded, and the justice system needs to expand with it. That's where the favor comes in."

32

TWO GROUPS OF people left, the door chiming a cheery goodbye as they left. It was now Letta, Tarian, and the two baristas. One of the TVs played the news quietly in the background.

Letta swirled the coffee around in the cup. "I'm no good for favors right now."

"Yes, you are." Tarian took a sip of her coffee, closing her eyes as she savored it. "You're not weak."

Letta glanced up at her, then back down at her own coffee. "People died, because rocks fell on them or buildings collapsed. My fault. That Caraigg was right. I need to learn. But whenever the Caraigg tries to teach me, all I get is a headache. And I can't practice unless I go out to a field 'cause something always explodes."

"They've told me they can't seem to connect with you well enough to teach. I doubt it's your fault. They're Ancients, and I think they just don't get the way humans think. Not really."

"I shouldn't even be in the city. I shouldn't be near people."

"Bullshit," Tarian barked. "This is exactly where you should be. Stop feeling sorry for yourself."

Letta glared at Tarian. Through her anger she felt the first stirrings of her power. "Fuck you."

"No, thanks." Tarian glared back.

They stared at each other for long minutes, animosity and anger ripening the air. The tension broke when Tarian laughed. "You *are* a Philly girl, through and through. Abrasive and a pain in the ass."

"So my boss says." Letta scowled.

"Your boss is a fool."

The announcement caught Letta by surprise.

"If he can't see your potential, then screw him. You don't need him, Letta. You don't need that job or his permission to keep doing what you want to do. What you *need* to do."

"What the hell you know 'bout what I *need*?"

"Tell me about the stars on your back." Tarian's eyes gleamed over the cup as she took another sip of coffee.

Letta crossed her arms and sat back. *Kia must have told her.* Her reasons for the tattoos were private, and nobody's business but her own. "Anybody tell you how nosy you are?"

"Not usually to my face."

Letta tried to get her anger under control. "I don't need your help."

"Maybe." Tarian tapped the table. "But I need yours."

Ally with the Keeper. The words of her Agreement reverberated in Letta's head, a stark reminder of what she'd promised. She grimaced. "I gotta get out of that deal."

"Agreements can't be voided. Well, not without a lot of work." Tarian drained the last of her coffee and stood up to throw away the cup. "Besides, I have a deal with the Caraigg too. I promised them I'd teach you."

Letta absorbed the true impact of the Agreement she'd made.

She was stuck with this woman. Well, she couldn't act against her, but she didn't have to be her friend.

But wouldn't it be nice to have a friend? Something whispered in her mind. She shoved the voice aside. She watched Tarian tidy up the condiment bar, trying to figure out the right move. The confidence she'd seen from Tarian in the park and in the warehouse was gone, though the woman still held an easy command of the space around her. She appeared more vulnerable somehow. There was tightness around her eyes and mouth, and her shoulders seemed to hold the tension of the world.

Curiosity pricked at her. When Tarian returned, Letta stared at her thoughtfully. "What do you want, Tarian? Why'd you come here?" She watched the release of tension from Tarian's face with interest. *She played me. She thinks she has me cornered now.*

"Until the magic fell, there was no need for anyone to know about people like us. They wouldn't have believed it anyway. Now that it's here, it's we need some sort of structure to deal with the fallout, and we need it as fast as possible." Tarian perched on the edge of her chair and leaned forward, eyes burning a hole right through Letta. "There's a lot of people out there like you, Letta. Well, not exactly like you. Your signature is beyond strong for someone so new to magic. We've been assessing as much as we can, and you're off the charts. So far. Between the artifact and the rain, it's like you got hit with a triple dose or something. I'm shocked you… Well, the destruction I saw should have drained you so dry you'd never recover. But you did. Kinda curious how that happened. Calli couldn't explain it."

Tarian shifted back in the chair. "Anyway, there's a lot of people who gained power in a short amount of time, and they have no idea what to do with it. We've actually come off fairly lucky. Not too many died in the initial fallout. But that doesn't mean they won't, in the future, if we don't get a grip."

Letta shrugged, acknowledging the discomfort of the other woman but not wanting, yet, to alleviate it. "So? Go on the news. Tell 'em what's up. People will come around. Eventually."

Tarian snorted. "Everything's still in chaos. Chunks of magic clumped together, and no way of spreading them out. Some received power they can't control. Others are taking advantage of what little control they have to manipulate, steal, or other bad things. It's a freaking mess. Any announcement from me is bound to make things worse." She drummed her fingers on the table, obviously following a train of thought that she didn't much like. "They aren't ready to know there's always been people with magic, or that there are things far worse than earthquakes and hair on fire. There are daemon in their world now, far stronger than anything they can imagine. You know how people, in general, react to change. And to things they don't understand. They're not ready."

Letta shuddered. *Not sure I'm ready for it either.*

Tarian tapped the table with her index finger. "You're one of the strongest in this area, so far, and the Caraigg tell me you have a very strong affinity for both stone and metal. I'd guess once you train a bit your strength will be close to my own, at least in Earth."

Letta rubbed her stomach. She still wasn't used to the artifact, or the power within her. She found herself wanting to confide in someone, anyone, who would understand. "It don't feel powerful to me. It feels like a fucking nightmare. Every pissed off thought I have translates to bricks flying through the air or crumbled pavement or…anything, really. The last few weeks I've had to sleep with classical music playing. I *hate* that shit."

Tarian laughed. "With training, it won't be like that. I can teach you. I have people who can show you how to control it, and yourself. Come to the House of Xannon. Learn, so you can use this skill for something besides taking out a street riot. I'm offering you a job, Letta. I'm offering you a chance to use this talent to do what you always wanted."

Letta shook her head. "What do you know about what I want? You don't know me."

"I know you went out of your way to save one child. I know you went even further to save hundreds. And I know you'll go to the end of the Earth to find your sister. You want to stop bad things from happening to innocents. So do I." Tarian sighed. "I used to think I could do it all by myself. Not anymore. I need help. I want to recruit you to be on the first team of city-based magical law enforcers. Alex calls it a task force. We'll have to recruit others for the team. You can help with that, maybe lead it. If you're willing."

Letta stared at her, stomach lurching with the possibility of a future she'd never imagined. Leading her own task force, fighting to protect people. It *was* what she'd wanted. What she'd spent most of her life trying to accomplish. "You for real?"

Tarian smiled. "Yeah. It's a real job. You'll have help and resources. A hell of a lot more responsibility than your idiot boss was willing to give you. You can master your talent and lead the way. That's what I'm offering. Whether you take me up on it or not, I'll help you find your sister. I told you I would, and I keep my promises. You get me something that belonged to her, something she touched or thought of as hers, and I'll find her."

Letta's mind whirled around the possibility. In the last few weeks, she hadn't managed to find one shred of proof that Rook had told the truth. There simply weren't any records of anything related to Jenna Roberts. She'd vanished, without a trace. She'd even tried to catch a vision of Jenna in the river of Earth, but come up empty-handed. "She's gone. She can't be found. I tried."

Tarian patted her chest. "Not my way, you didn't. I have skills too, you know. Trust me. I will know if she's alive, and if she is, I'll find her." Tarian spoke with such conviction that Letta found herself beginning to hope. A spark of real hope, not the false promise from Rook but the chance to finally know, for sure, what happened to her sister. She wanted that, more than anything.

Letta wasn't about to tell Tarian that though. She'd lose any bargaining power she had. She tried to harden her expression. "What makes you think I wanna help people in this city? They don't give a shit about me. They proved that."

Tarian's eyes danced with victory. "Because underneath that tough Philly exterior is a girl who puts a star on her back for every person she saves. That's why. I'm curious, Letta. Did you get new ink recently?"

Letta felt her face heat up, but refused to answer.

"You did good, Letta. Real good. Probably better than I would have." Tarian stood up. "Look, you don't have to take the job. Just thought you'd want to. Was I wrong?"

Letta looked up at her, then down at the empty coffee cup. She crumpled it and threw it into the trash. She grabbed a napkin to wipe up the inevitable spills on the table, then stopped when she realized there weren't any. *So much has changed.*

Tarian watched, her eyes triumphant. "Damn, won't Calli be proud of me. Nobody thinks of me as a negotiator."

"Well, I ain't said I'll stay. But I'll see what ya got."

Tarian nodded at her. "Fair enough."

They left the shop, and Tarian led the way to the alley next to it. Letta watched, dumbfounded as Tarian stared at the air behind a garbage bin and it bubbled, wiggled, melted right in front of them. Through the disturbed space, Letta spotted an entrance hall of some sort. She saw the alley behind it. The whole thing created an odd mixture of dirt, Philly grime, and something else entirely. Some other place, some other time.

"All you have to do is walk through. But make sure I'm touching you. I don't want to lose you on your first trip. When you get control of your power, you'll travel your way instead of mine. But this will do for now."

Letta stared at it the portal. The hallway within looked dark. She couldn't make out any details at all. She'd be stepping into the unknown with nothing but Tarian's assurance that things would turn out okay on the other side. She took a step toward it, then paused. "What's in there?"

Tarian rolled her eyes. "Not quick to trust, are ya? It's the entry to my house, Letta. Probably Kia's waiting just inside, since I told her I was coming to get you. She was sitting on the floor by the alcove when I left."

Letta squinted at it but didn't see Kia within the image. *A leap of faith then.* She glanced at Tarian, then held out her hand. *Hang on, Jenna. I'm coming.*

Letta stepped into the portal with Tarian, hope driving her forward.

###

I hope *Taking Earth* took you away, if only for a short while, from the day to day stuff life heaps on us.

If you'd like to be part of the inner circle, and find out inside information about my magical little world, be sure to sign up at **melindavan.com.**

The best way to tell an author you appreciate their work is to leave a review. Just a few words of review at your vendor of choice boosts sales, and sends little fuzzies that warm the author's heart at the end of a long day of fussing over letters and words, sentences and paragraphs, fueled by far too much caffeine.

If you're so inclined, you can find me here:

Website: *http://melindavan.com*

Facebook: *https://www.facebook.com/MelindaVanLone*

Twitter: *MelindaVan*

Instagram: *http://instagram.com/mvanlone*

Email: *melinda.van@gmail.com*

More in The House of Xannon

STRONGER THAN MAGIC
Tarian Xannon fights demons like the rest of us.
This time, the demon just happens to be real.

FINDING FLAME
All that has been is written on the wind. But
will the past save the future or destroy it?

PROMISE OF MAGIC
Some promises are deadly to keep.

TAKING EARTH
The whole world can change in 24 hours.

ELEMENTS OF MAGIC
Balance is hard, and sometimes deadly.